TALES OF THE END TIMES
BOOK TWO

THE DEER STALKER

MARY TREPANIER

Published by Cwtch Press, Redmond, WA 98052

Cover design by Mariah Sinclair

E-book ISBN: 978-1-947234-26-0

Print ISBN: 978-1-947234-27-7

10 9 8 7 6 5 4 3 2 1

Trigger Warning: Graphically violent scenes in this book might be disturbing to some. The material is not appropriate for people under age 18.

Praise for The Deer Stalker

Like Arachne's web, the intricate weaving of Trepanier's Deer Stalker lures you into a tale that builds slowly with disturbing revelations. Her characters are completely three-dimensional, and could be your neighbors or your friends. An excellent delving into the dark and light sides of modern paganism, age-old destiny, racism, and the lure of the human heart.

Colleen Anderson, author of the collection *A Body of Work* and more than 200 other works in print.

THE DEER STALKER

MARY TREPANIER

Smoke from the two torches flanking the throne floated in nonair, in the vastness of space. Jeweled stars sparked. Nearby, Sirius flared blue-white.

On the throne sat a goddess, toying with the key around her neck—Hekate Soteira, Hekate Savior, ruler of spirits from demons to angels. By her sandal-shod feet, red flames flickered. Their murmur was the only sound in the silence.

By the goddess's feet knelt Puabi-Ekur, an incubus-succubus in Hekate's service. They'd come to Hekate's call.

"My lady, you have a mission for me?"

The Lady shifted on her throne, and the red flames bowed.

"You will know it when it comes to you," she said. "Hold out your hand."

Into Puabi-Ekur's palm, the Lady dropped a charm, a tiny deer skull carved of bone.

"You have lived many human lives—as Puabi, the

dancer of Inanna; as Ekur, the general, sworn to fight Inanna's wars. But the life this object speaks to is far from these, in the northern woods."

When Puabi-Ekur looked up toward the Lady to question her, she was gone.

Chapter 2

Joanie yanked off the coffee machine's filter, added ground coffee, and tamped it down. Another order came in; she listened to it with half an ear. She preferred making coffee to running the cash register, but she knew she'd be cashier in a few minutes, when the current girl went on break. Customers loved Joanie—she had the whore smile.

The rush passed, and she went out to bus tables, her mind only half on the work.

She was grateful for the work, though. She was broke.

At least she wasn't dead.

She never missed her sugar daddy as a lover, though they'd had a few hot nights. But over time it had become clear he was a psychopath. He'd tortured her, in the end nearly killed her.

Still, what she made at the coffee shop didn't touch her former income as a sugar baby and escort. With her friends, she put on temples to Inanna, the Sumerian goddess, a patroness of whores. But it was harder than it had been to get the word out on the web. To make money now, you had to go on the street, or go total pro, set up a site on an offshore ISP, and seriously go into business.

Did she want to do that while finishing her hardest classes? This fall, she'd started the last year of her economics degree. But she didn't want most of the jobs she could find with an econ B.S., which were in finance and accounting. A couple years ago, she'd been sure she wanted a master's. She'd hoped to help map out the way to a new, fairer economy.

But now she didn't feel the same way. The future was so uncertain. She didn't want crazy student loans. And tugging at her always was the realization that she was a servant of Inanna. The world of the temple, the world of divine sexuality—that was her world.

But how did that square with this world, now?

It was nearing the end of her shift. Alyssa was in next, from two to six p.m., closing. Alyssa had also done whore time, on the street; she was glad to be done with it. Now the young blonde girl ran in, all in a flurry, heading for the back to put her jacket away.

As Joanie collected cups and plates and wiped down the espresso machine, Alyssa sidled up, tying her apron. "What do you think of that guy?"

"What guy?"

Alyssa pointed with her shoulder.

A quiet guy, a regular customer—Joanie had smiled at him and sold him coffee, then hadn't given him a second thought. He was dressed all in black: black t-shirt, black jeans. He was quiet, studious-looking, skinny, with long, sandy-blond hair.

"He's hot, isn't he?"

To Joanie, he just looked young. She'd almost always dated older. But Alyssa was barely eighteen.

"I guess? He's not really my type."

"You think I should say something to him?"

Joanie shrugged one shoulder. "If you like him, sure."

She and Alyssa locked eyes.

"I don't really know how to talk to guys," Alyssa said. "Talking to a client doesn't count."

Joanie shot a glance at the guy, working at his laptop.

She didn't see what Alyssa saw. To Joanie, he was a blank. Something about the blankness tripped a wire for her, but she couldn't name her concern.

He was a blank—what kind of criticism was that? She was being too harsh.

"Just say hi and let the conversation be natural. Don't worry about it too much."

"Can you stay, just a little bit, while I talk to him?"

Inwardly, Joanie rolled her eyes.

"Sure. I have to leave by two-thirty, is all. Why don't you sweep up? It'll give you an excuse to go over there."

Alyssa grabbed the broom. Joanie took an order with half an eye on her, then got caught up in making coffee.

Alyssa appeared by her elbow, flushed and smiling. "We're going to have a date!"

"Wow, that was quick. How'd you do it?"

Alyssa went redder. "I just asked."

Chapter 3

*I*n the woods before dawn at midsummer, dark-blue, smelling of flowers, the trees loomed as silhouettes. A breath of fog lay along the stream.

The boy had gone alone, without his foster-brothers, taking his bow. He'd tramped these woods most of his life, and last time out he'd seen a stag. He knew the glade this stag haunted.

There was danger; there was always danger.

Deer were wild and shy—some said they were fairy cattle, milked by the glaistig, a spirit of ill omen. But if you caught a white buck, it could grant you a wish. If you had a fairy lover, she might put on her deerskin and leave you, but only if you crossed her. He was fourteen, and he thought about fairy lovers at night.

He was a younger son, his family part of the Angle tribe. He'd been fostered with a Briton family across the border in Celtic Rheged.

Little Daegal, they called him. But he'd begun to get taller. His fair boy's hair had darkened to sandy blond.

If he killed this stag and brought it back, no one would tease him anymore.

The light had changed, grey with approaching sun, still dark-blue shadow under the oaks. The birds shouted, covering his movements.

If he picked the right spot, downwind or crosswind, he could wait for the stag to pass. He'd only have one shot.

As the sun rose, he followed a game trail across uneven land, passing crooked old oaks up to their knees in ferns. Scent drifted from lilies of the valley, pale in the hollows. A light breeze whispered. He chose a blackthorn bramble for a blind.

He sat still, breathing from his mouth for quiet. A thrush whistled. A large movement shook the green understory.

Then, magnificent and huge, from the brush emerged the forequarters and head of a stag. Antlers branched, six-tined. The stag huffed in surprise. The great dark-brown eyes caught his.

A moment passed. Another life, different, wild, unknowable, gazed into his.

He nocked and loosed his best arrow in one motion. It hit the buck full in the chest.

The buck jumped left, then right for one step, then his face and antlers crashed to the ground. He slid down a slight slope till he came to rest in a blackthorn.

Daegal prepared another arrow just in case, but the

deer's eyes had gone glassy. Blood leaked from the wound, puddling on the ground, staining the noble face.

He sent a silent prayer to his patron god, Woden—a hunter, who led the Wild Hunt over wintertime.

All-Father, thank you for sharing life with life. Bless this flesh for me and mine. Give fair travels to this spirit.

He felt again that moment of wild life staring into him.

A pang crossed his heart. Almost he wished he hadn't killed him.

What must it be like, to live in the woods with your harem, to fight the other bucks, to feel rut?

But his household needed the meat.

He spent all afternoon draining the carcass. The green scent of the woods, the scent of flowers interleaved with the iron smell of blood. Then he field-dressed the deer, leaving the offal and taking only the best cuts. To carry the meat out of the woods, he cut a sapling and lashed the quarters to it, then padding himself carried the meat home with the pole across his shoulders.

It proved a long walk with a heavy burden. He paused often.

Part of him sang in triumph.

Part of him still saw the great dark eyes.

Spirits can dream too. This dream took Puabi-Ekur by surprise.

They—he—was male in this life.

In the dream, two men fought to the death, locked in combat for days. First, the men fought with throwing spears, later with swords. He had two. He wore mail and a helmet. Sweat fell in his eyes. Cuts burned, adrenaline coursed in his veins. He had a dogged insistence on winning.

But why were they fighting?

They got no information from probing their former mind, only sorrow and the immediacy of the fight: moving constantly, dancing, striking.

Their opponent was heavily clad, and they took him in mostly as a physical form. Tags of sandy-blond hair from below the helmet, arms and legs dirty and bloody but well-muscled. A fine man's body, for which he felt—lust?

Sorrow, love, and lust made the undertone of this fight.

Was it to the death?

A shadow passed, and the dream ended.

Chapter 4

It was evening when Gus let himself think about it. He'd propped his window open and, sitting on his bed, carefully smoked a joint into the breeze. The last vermillion of sunset died to burnt sienna, to a pale noncolor, to cobalt. The breeze made a branch by his window creak.

At the coffee shop, she'd come out of the blue. He went there because it was on the way from campus to his house. He found the decor silly, retro-hippie, mushrooms and lady-bugs on chocolate-brown walls. But it was sunny on good days, and not too fast-paced. The baristas mostly left the students alone.

All Gus had registered was that she was pretty, slender, pale, with dark-blonde hair bleached blonder. And she didn't seem stupid. She'd asked to meet for tea at a shop a few blocks west. Of course she didn't want to meet where she worked—too many eyes on her, it'd be embarrassing.

Despite himself, anticipation drummed inside him.

He was in his third year at the university, working toward a biology degree. He wasn't sure what he wanted to do with it. He'd considered research and med school (everyone needed doctors; it helped the planet; his mom was a nurse so he understood that world). But mostly it was a good general-purpose degree for someone who liked science. He enjoyed lab work. Maybe he'd end up teaching. He didn't know what he wanted.

Or he wanted things that opposed each other, canceled each other out, were impossible. Like Brett. Brett and Shailagh both.

Lots of people were gay, were bi even. Were pansexual. Were witches and heathens and magicians. But lots of people didn't come from his Utah Mormon family.

You wouldn't think a nurse would be fragile, but his mom was—solid at work, at home she disappeared into her room, reading one romance novel after another. She was gone, a cipher, an automaton.

That left everything to his father, the paterfamilias—solid, square, like a block of concrete. Dad was a police chief, a hunter, a good old boy, as different from Gus as chalk from cheese. He showed up in Gus's coloring, and Gus was named for his father's father. But Gus's frame was his mother's. Since high school he'd gotten taller, but when he was younger it was always "little Gus." The little guy, the watered-down copy.

He was always proving himself. Apparently, he always would be. Maybe at some point he'd give up.

Like his mom, a point he despised about himself—she'd

abandoned her kids—he ran away into fantasy: tales of the Vikings, Norse sagas, Conan the Barbarian. He went to the gym and took karate classes. He might be only five foot ten, but he was quick, and he had muscle. He'd seen a few people look at him out of the corners of their eyes. Guys and girls.

Brett had wanted him, too.

If he let it, it would haunt him, that camping trip in the hills, a fire under the stars. The shadowy interior of the tent.

A mouth on his, a mouth on him, hands milking him. Brett in him, his hand on himself.

"Oh my god, that was amazing," Brett had whispered. "I've wanted that for years."

Gus had too. Just once, out of years of longing, wasn't enough. But now Brett was far away, at the University of Wyoming.

Girls were easier, in a way, if you wanted human connection, not just anonymous sex. He understood the rules better. There was something pliable about Alyssa, something he liked. Not too feminist. He'd had some bad run-ins with feminists his first year in college.

Sure, everyone was equal—from the gods' point of view, maybe. He didn't make a show of it, but he had a small shrine to Odin on top of his bookcase. Though Odin wasn't an egalitarian. But he liked that difference; he liked the maleness of men and the femaleness of women. Trans folk, fine, you be you, but that was his taste.

Talk of male privilege made him twitchy. Both men and women were kept down in different ways. He'd never felt privileged. The men's rights activists went overboard, but they made a few good points. Though he wasn't a racist or a sexist or anything.

He finished the joint and stashed the roach.

This girl didn't seem like someone who'd get into the usual PC kind of conversation. Something about her, her pale-pink nails, her girlishness, said otherwise. Sweet, a little submissive maybe.

The thought of sinking his cock into someone made him leap up and take a turn around his room.

Maybe he could check out Grindr. Guys were usually down to fuck.

"What did you think of him?" Cleo asked.

Though Joanie worked at the coffee shop, she continued to hang out there. Now she leaned over the blond-wood table and took her lover's hand. Sun fell across the wood and lit their folded fingers. The air smelled of coffee and cinnamon. Her beautiful girl wore her demi-afro bound up in a big orange-and-chartreuse sash today.

"I hardly got an impression. He seemed kind of blank."

"Your face is saying you didn't like him."

"I hate it when people say they always trust their first impression. I don't. We have so many biases. I felt like he was well-hidden, but then so are lots of us."

"Mmm." Cleo pursed her orchid-lush lips, today a dark shade of purple. "You don't like him."

"It was a fleeting impression."

"Girl, you need to hang onto those. I thought you

learned that." Time and time again, Joanie had discarded her intuitions about her former sugar daddy, and she'd nearly died for it.

Joanie grimaced. "I guess."

"Well, maybe you're wrong. Who knows? All we can do is keep our eyes open." Cleo sipped her iced coffee. At the end of September, the leaves were just beginning to turn. It was a hot day. "Heard from Clayton lately?"

"Not for a bit." Clayton was Joanie's other partner— they'd met when Clayton was her escort client, but they'd formed a connection. Now he'd gone to California to get his master's in engineering. "We're trying to keep it chill. I want him to see other people. He's too good at eating his heart out; I don't want to encourage it."

"Yeah, I get that." Cleo looked at her phone. "I gotta go." Cleo was taking a semester to finish her master's thesis in anthropology. After that, she didn't know. She'd told Joanie she had applications out to various Ph.D. programs, was considering getting a law degree. She wanted to stay in Seattle. In the meantime, the thesis loomed.

At the teahouse, scarlet Turkish lanterns hung over butcher-block tables. Fairy lights sparkled at the ceiling's edge. Along the yellow-ochre wall sat a squat, squishy leather couch. Their server's hair was a cascade of blues, her pierced eyebrows blue-green. Gus let his eyes flicker across her before he turned back to Alyssa.

She'd dressed up a bit, a candy-pink summer sweater

that brought out the flush in her cheeks, with tight on-purpose-ripped jeans. He let her walk a little in front of him so he could watch her ass.

He imagined her bent over a table, submitting to his wish.

The server brought them a pot of Russian caravan tea, smoky-tasting. They sat on the couch. Her perfume smelled like candy, caramel with a hint of musk.

"Tell me about yourself," Gus said.

"I'm a college student. Not at the university, though. I'm getting through my requirements at Seattle Central. How about you?"

Gus gave her the run-down, watching her closely. She would meet his eyes, then her gaze would flutter away. It gave him hope.

"I always liked biology in high school! I did a paper on the grey squirrel. My friend actually had a squirrel that he raised from a baby." Then her face closed in on itself.

"What's wrong?"

"Oh, nothing. I don't see a lot of my old friends anymore, or my family."

"I wish I could say the same about mine."

"Tell me." She seemed genuinely interested, so he did.

Below the conversation, he sensed their bodies and energies aligning. Of her own accord, she moved closer to him on the couch. He touched her gently on the wrist and back. When she leaned over to get her phone from her purse, stray strands of fine blonde hair tickled his arm. They finished their tea.

"Do you want to come back to my place and smoke weed?"

"Sure!" She turned pink.

It was a ten-minute walk. Wednesday evening—he'd made it a weeknight date; he didn't want it to read as too important. They had to dodge the people who crowded the street, all there to get in his way. He lived northeast of the university, in a warren of student apartment houses; his was low, tan, nineteen-seventies-looking, nondescript, but cheap.

Past the university, among residential streets, the crowd thinned. Leaves of maples and oaks filtered the streetlight, which fell dappling the sidewalk. The breeze brought him her perfume, sugar and musk.

Almost without thinking, as if he'd done it a thousand times, he took her hand, pulled her to him, and kissed her.

She yielded easily, kissing him back, throwing her arms around his shoulders. Her breasts pressed his chest, her nipples hard. She slipped him her tongue, and he got hard, and he knew.

Up his steps, he scrabbled with the key in the lock. He lit a candle, but they didn't get as far as his stash. They fell onto his bed, kissing.

He kissed her as if he could eat her, like food.

"Are you—we should at least—" He'd known guys who'd gotten in trouble by not discussing things up front.

"Yeah, we should have a basic talk. But just—" she launched herself at him, kissing him, tangling her tongue with his. He shoved his hands up her candy-pink sweater to grab her breasts. The feel of them, nipples against his palms, a wave of almost visible lust poured over both of them. She was humping his leg.

"Get a condom," she said, indistinctly. She pulled off her top, bra with it. He bit her nipple, hard, and she cried out.

"Was that—"

"It's okay, it's okay, please get a condom!" She shucked off her jeans and tugged at his belt.

He opened his bedside table's drawer and grabbed a condom package. Then it was on. A scramble; he pushed her down, shoved inside her.

"Omigod, yes!" she cried.

The smell of her hair, her perfume, the heat of her body. She kissed his face at random, dragging at his ass as if she could pull him further inside her. He pushed her legs onto his shoulders to fuck her deeper. "Yes!"

He tried to hold back, but it had been... it felt like years. He exploded, releasing himself.

She held him, kissing the sweat along his hairline.

A small breeze insinuated itself through the cracked-open window. The wind rose, shuffling the leaves. A leaf fell spinning.

"That was—I'm usually not that fast."

"I wanted it."

"Can I go down on you?"

She scrunched up her nose. "I'm going to taste like condom."

"I don't care. Let me."

"Okay."

Shadow painted the room greys and blacks, except for the yellow sphere around the candle. Her skin felt like silk under his fingers. He slid down, spreading her thighs gently. She was all shaved, which he didn't care for—too childlike —but he let that pass, focusing on her. He put his tongue to her. This was something he'd been careful to learn, girl-on-girl porn as a tutorial.

She was right, she tasted like condom. He let that pass also. He felt the connection thrill through her body. He propped her buttocks in his hands and licked, feeling her energy rise.

She began to move, moaning under her breath. Her hands clasped and unclasped the sheets. She grabbed his hair. Did she want him to stop? "Keep going!"

She trembled, gasped, and cried out. He continued till her hand pressed his head to stop.

"Omigod, that was awesome! Where'd you learn to do that?"

"I've had a little practice."

"Well, I thank whoever helped, wherever they are!"

He sat up, smiling, and wiped his mouth on the sheet. "Has no one ever done that for you before?"

She lay on her back, staring at the ceiling. "They have. But not like that."

He slid up next to her, burrowed in beside her, and took her in his arms still feeling the post-orgasmic glow.

A breeze circled the room, and the candle wavered. He sat up to check, but it looked fine. The flame returned to its former length, and he let it go.

Chapter 5

"Text me," Alyssa said, standing in the hall light, in the margin of the door.

"Sure."

That was never in question, though he didn't say that.

Eleven p.m., chilly. Gus shut the window, turned on the space heater, lay back down on the rumpled bed.

Having had a girl was good, but it didn't give him what it used to. He craved the feeling that the world was opening up, that it could be his oyster. Though that never lasted.

With this girl, though, something teased at his desires. Maybe they could get into Dom/sub stuff. Something in him ached to bend her to his will.

After a few minutes of arguing with himself, he leaped up and started the computer. Online, he fucked around with a couple high-school-friend gamers, multiplayer on a war game, talking trash. Like someone could take something like Pepe, a cartoon frog, as a serious political statement. It was deep sarcasm, not fascism.

Fuck 'em all.

Suddenly it was two a.m., past time for bed. He had class in the morning, luckily not till eleven. Still, tired and wired, he couldn't fall asleep.

No one could deny things were falling apart. His dad's time was gone, when a man could have the world handed to him like a fried egg on a plate. Not that he wanted to be his dad.

Part of him knew that this world had never been fair. He'd seen how his older sister Liz had struggled. She was the family intellect, but she still had that one teacher who told her, "The only chemistry you need is to bake brownies, honey." No wonder she'd left for the East Coast. No one heard from her now.

But he didn't get the whole white-male privilege thing, when nothing was ever given him for free. His dad could just walk in a room and people would fawn over him. Blond, blue-eyed, high school football star, Dad had become a cop—a good one, people thought. His mother served his father as if he were God.

That all-doors-open pass didn't work for Gus, the middle kid, between two sisters, with Todd the baby. Todd was a little off, a little slow; if Mom paid attention to anyone, it was Todd.

Gus got the mantle of being the son, and somehow he always failed at it.

He was a runner but wasn't the fastest. He played football one year but didn't make varsity. He got good grades but not straight As like Liz. His friends were suspect—"I don't want you hanging out with that druggie crowd."

It was hard to pinpoint what made home so oppressive. The deep Mormon roots didn't help. But his parents didn't fight; his father laid down the law, and so it was. Though the rules weren't fair. He wasn't Liz, to make her own rules, fighting on all fronts at once. He wasn't Todd, who simply flopped. Sallie had gymnastics, cheerleading, and her best friend Jenna, and she escaped. Somehow he, Gus, got stuck trying to rise to his father's expectations and failing in front of everyone.

There was another Gus, a front man, who could deal with that, a cardboard cutout who could say yes to everyone. Behind that face, different people fought. A child who wanted love, a madman, a scholar. He hid online. His nihilist self ruled there—fuck everyone.

He tried not to get too mean. The inner sadist could only come out to play sometimes.

Unhappily, staring at the ceiling patched with streetlight, he drifted off.

He'd made no friends, really, at college. One half-friend, maybe. Chris.

Outside Chemistry class, he stood with Chris in a shuffling mob of students, straggling along a concrete hallway flanked by whiteboards, its pale-brown tile floor shining. A big window at the hall's end opened to white light, half-blocked by the leaves of a big oak starting to turn flame-yellow. Chris and he walked out onto the grass, then off-campus toward a sandwich shop for lunch.

Chris pointed to a black-and-white poster on a telephone pole. "You wanna go see Blood and Nightsoil?" he asked.

"Sure, why not?"

"I'm thinking of going with my friend Kevin. Meet up at my place, say at seven, do some predrinking, head for the Leviathan?" The Leviathan was a local dive bar that hosted live punk and metal.

"Sure." Kevin and Gus had spent a few evenings in each other's company. Kevin was okay.

Gus knew nothing about the band. Back in his room, he did some internet digging. Here they were all in corpse paint, faces daubed black and white, black dripping from their eyes, demonic. He guessed that was cool. Was that a white power cross?

He just wanted to go out, get drunk, and listen to music. He didn't want to second-guess everyone's ideologies. People pulled out that stuff for shock value.

He had Alyssa's phone number taped to his monitor and was counting the days till he could call her. He didn't want to seem too eager.

He had an X-Acto knife he liked. But he hadn't used it on himself recently.

He needed to not think about it.

Some part of him would say success was a problem. You didn't want to challenge the powers that be. Stay safe; be amiable and pliable.

But he didn't want to be.

The voices in his head needed to shut the fuck up.

Porn, sex, drinking, weed, gaming, online trolling, running, he was always running.

He went to his closet, grabbed one of several nondescript tan-plastic shopping bags, got out the shoebox it contained. He'd deliberately not let this box be special.

There was also the X-Acto knife shoebox, in an identical tan-plastic bag.

He slid out his butt plugs, wrapped each in its own plastic bag, and his lube.

There was a hierarchy of desperation. If it worked, a butt plug was better than the X-Acto knife.

If he thought of Brett, he was going to cry.

That overcast twilight, a chilly wind scattered dust in the air. He'd put on something vaguely threatening but nondescript: black jeans, black t-shirt, black hoodie, black combat boots. He hunched into the hoodie against the wind as he crossed the University District.

Chris's was a brick building with elaborate plaster moldings, dating maybe from the nineteen-thirties, surprisingly not yet a condo. He buzzed Chris's apartment. "It's Gus."

"Come on in."

Tan-painted hallways passed; at Chris's door, he knocked. Chris opened and waved him in. He and Kevin were drinking cheap vodka out of the bottle.

Class act. Gus would've at least gotten some orange juice. Maybe that was the fag in him.

The single person who knew about the gay part of his life, besides the guys involved, was his sister Liz. Now her voice spoke in his head: *internalized homophobia.*

He knew self-hatred fed his anger, but he told the voice to fuck off.

Though Chris's apartment wasn't cheap (parents paying for their proto-doctor), he wasn't much of a decorator. There was one piece of furniture, a ripped faux-leather couch. Gus threw himself on the strip of tan carpet in front of it, since the couch clearly only fit two people. The off-white walls sported one big poster, from a Norwegian metal band with links to heathenry.

Maybe Chris was interested in Norse paganism. He didn't want to ask in front of Kevin.

As night fell, they polished off the bottle. Slurring and stumbling, they piled out the door toward the Leviathan, five blocks away. A hole in the wall, its windows were painted over. A bouncer on a stool outside the door checked IDs. He flashed his Maglite into Gus's face, as if Gus could be dangerous. Gus let it wash over him.

Inside, it had black-painted wooden walls, a row of tables with red metal chairs and a long wooden bench against the wall, and in an alcove, a couple of antiquated pinball machines. The stage lay at the end of the deep, narrow space. Gus and friends had managed to get there early.

At least he didn't have to drink straight vodka now.

He bought a round of beer and settled with the guys at a table, a few rows back from the space around the stage.

Kevin surprised them. "Hey, guys. Lemme add something." He slipped out a flask and poured a shot into each beer. "You got a boilermaker now."

"What was that?"

"Old Overholt."

Gus raised an eyebrow.

"Cheap whiskey. Drink up."

Chug, repeat. The night broke into a montage of images. Onto black dark, lights shone, red, purple, and white; bodies slammed. Three acts played; he didn't remember the first two. Blood and Nightsoil hit the stage at midnight.

Full blackout started, then red and white spotlights slashed the black. A scratching voice sung lyrics. The singer wore corpse paint. His long black hair swung. Something in Gus ripped and bled.

The music was like a razor. Better than a razor: it offered more relief. He could barely make out the lyrics, but those he could cut into him.

"Pray to the dark/The darkness takes/Your soul forever/The darkness wakes."

Yes. He gave way to utter darkness.

He swayed with the music, almost dancing, something he never did, but he was as drunk as he'd ever been in his life. Chris and Kevin had disappeared into the crowd. No part of him was worried. He could walk home. Right now, he could fly home.

"Sacrifice the self to the self!" the singer screamed into the microphone.

Gus saw Odin hanging on Yggdrasil.

These guys had the current. It wasn't an accident he'd come to this show.

Skipping across the crowd, his glance caught on a muscular man, shaved-headed, bare-chested, heavily tattooed, probably in his thirties. This man stood a little back from the crowd, head bobbing to the music.

He met Gus's gaze and stared.

Gus let desire pull him across the room—running into moshers, stepped on, slammed into. He pushed, slipped through, stepped on feet.

"Hi," he said.

"Hello." The man nodded. "I'm Max."

He didn't remember their conversation from that first night. Nor his stumbling excuses to his friends, nor his exit with Max, nor any details of their walk to Max's place.

He remembered the sex.

He remembered their first kiss, in the alley behind the Leviathan. Max crushed him into the brick wall, kissed him, biting him. Gus wriggled, bit back, drawing blood.

Max grinned. "You're a fighter."

Gus bit him again, marked his lip, licked his blood.

That wasn't safe. He was tired of being safe.

Staggering up the flight of stairs to Max's apartment, he fell and slid. Max picked him up bodily, slung him over his shoulder.

Max's bed had a gunmetal coverlet and gunmetal sheets. "I'm going to fuck you," Max said.

"Yes."

"Go clean yourself up."

Brutal words in a gruff voice. They were perfect. Gus's heart sang.

Gus stumbled into the bathroom. He used the toilet,

dropped his clothes, took a shower as fast as he could. Grabbing a towel, he re-emerged.

"Get over here."

Max unearthed lube and a condom. "Go slow," Gus whispered.

Max explored his anus with a finger, then two.

"You'll be fine."

Max did go slow at first, slow but inexorably, pausing to let Gus adjust. Then he rammed in.

Gus's whole body convulsed; he cried out.

"Hush," Max said, and put his hand over Gus's mouth.

He rode him, spreading his butt cheeks for better depth, in and in and in. Climbing a mountain of fire. Gus wriggled his hand under and touched his own aching cock.

Pulling out, Max flipped him so they were face to face, bent him almost in half so his knees were by his shoulders, and mounted him again, leaning in to kiss him, savagely, biting. Gus bit back and drew blood. Flecks of blood flew over the grey sheets and Gus's naked chest. Max leaned back, hands on the backs of Gus's thighs, fucking him, watching Gus as he jerked off, catching the rhythm and riding it like he rode him.

Up and up and up. Gus closed his eyes and saw a trail of lava flowing down a mountain of hell, red on black. He felt Max watching.

Then he lost it.

He came.

He yelled.

Max came, shouting. "Fuck! Fuck! Fuck!"

A tornado of energy blew up, blew across the room, then was gone.

Max pulled out with surprising gentleness. "Go clean yourself up."

"Gimme a sec."

He was still breathing, still alive.

The sweet smell of sex floated in the air, below it a breeze hinting of rain.

Max let him sleep there that night, gave him glass after glass of water so he didn't wake up too sick. "Protecting my sheets," he said, which was a lie, because flecks of blood and come and shit were flung across them.

In the morning when Gus woke up, Max was gone, but he'd left a note and a plate of currant scones. The note had Max's phone number.

Chapter 6

irebird House's living room, full of bright-yellow sunflower paintings, could hold a circle of twenty people. That was how many took part in the small intentional community: ten in the house itself, another ten scattered in nearby apartments. Joanie had wangled a small room in the house's daylight basement.

Right now, a gathering was breaking up, a conversation about race and status led by Trisha, who, like Cleo, was one of the few people of color in the group. Joanie stood on the group's edge, nursing an iced coffee.

It was good that she'd wanted to lead it. They had to include people of color. They were trying to build a better future.

In another hour, the living room would be taken over by a meeting about starting a permaculture farming co-op. Joanie had attended a few of these gatherings, but not today.

She wasn't a back-to-the-land girl, though maybe they could put in an edible garden. She was tied to the city at least till she finished her degree. Not that she knew what she was going to do with it.

The gerbil wheel of worry started in her head again. She turned abruptly and found Alyssa standing beside her. "Hi!"

Alyssa lived a short bus ride away, at Hannah's house. Hannah had visited Firebird House, but her connection to Joanie had more to do with the Inanna temples they put on together. Through these temples, Joanie had realized her connection to the goddess. She wished she could just do them, and them alone, for money. It was a great good for the universe, sexual healing.

Joanie peered at Alyssa. "How did your date go?"

Alyssa turned pink. "It was awesome!"

"What did you end up doing?"

"We met for tea. Then we went to his house."

Joanie took this in. "How'd it go?"

"It was great! He's going to text me, I think in a few days."

Joanie inclined her head. "He'd be lucky to get with a girl like you."

"You think so?"

"Sweet, pretty, smart. Why not?"

What Joanie wished for Alyssa was for her to find a passion, a métier. Alyssa was considering early childhood development as a career, but Joanie had a hunch that was because one of her few regular-economy jobs was working in daycare.

If she did it for love, great. Looking after kids was important. But if she did it out of lack of imagination—not so great.

She gave the younger girl a gentle half-hug. "Do you want to stay for the permaculture conversation?"

"I was wondering—could you give me a Tarot reading?"

"Sure."

They went downstairs to the basement, to a room that had been a garage and still had a garage door that didn't open. Across its four windows, a grapevine climbed a trellis, still leafy in early autumn with a few reddening bunches of grapes.

They pushed through the curtain that separated Joanie's room from the rest of the basement. Joanie had only a few pieces of furniture there—a queen bed covered with a family quilt, a couple packing crates for a desk, and a folding chair.

"Sit on the bed, why don't you?"

Alyssa obediently sat.

At the edge of her desk, Joanie lit a coral-pink candle to help create the space for the reading. Beside the bed, she found her Tarot deck in its black silk bag. The bag was ancient, found years ago at a garage sale; the deck was, too.

She didn't collect decks, like some people did. She didn't collect much of anything. She'd had to clear out in a hurry from her last apartment, which her sugar daddy had paid for. She'd brought almost nothing with her. The only things she had from her (dysfunctional) childhood were a quilt that her favorite aunt had made her, a set of glass unicorns, and her old journals; the unicorns and journals were still packed for lack of space.

She handed the deck to Alyssa, who took it gingerly. "Go ahead and let your mind drift, or focus on the here and now, whichever's easier. I like to do a first quick reading about whatever your subconscious brings up, so that doesn't color the main reading."

"Okay." Alyssa shuffled, frowning slightly.

Joanie had started reading cards at thirteen, drawn by—who knows what? Part was opposition to her ultra-Christian mom, who hadn't managed to protect her from her uncle's predation. It still hurt that her mother thought she'd lied about that.

After that she'd wanted to fit that picture, out of defiance: the bad seed.

"How do I know when I'm done?"

"You're done when you feel done." She smiled reassuringly. "Don't overthink it."

"Now, I guess." Alyssa set the deck down on Joanie's quilt.

A breath of breeze circled the room, making the candle flame wave. "Cut the deck into thirds with your left hand, and then put the deck back together." Alyssa did, and Joanie laid out three cards.

She pondered a moment, then began.

"There's a lot of hope here." She tapped the Star, which led off the reading. "And a tendency toward excess." Alyssa blushed at that. "But there's a lot of work for you right now, a lot going on."

Alyssa nodded vehemently. "I know! School, and work,

and... possibilities... and I'm supposed to go home for a bit, at the end of the month. My mother's having a birthday party." She looked aside, her mouth pinched.

"You don't have to go if you don't want to."

"I know. It's a lot easier since she broke up with my step-dad. But they're all still—I don't know, they want to live in the nineteen-fifties!"

"Believe me, I understand. Is there anything more you want to know about this reading?" Alyssa shook her head. Joanie picked the cards up from the quilt and slid them back in the deck. "Get your main question firmly in your mind, and shuffle again." She handed the deck back to Alyssa.

"It's about Gus."

Into the silence fell the flip and tap of shuffling. Green light filtered through the grape leaves. The candle was scented with vanilla, rose, and an undertone of—what? Pine, maybe.

"Okay. Here you go."

Joanie took the deck, hefted it in her hand a moment (old, patient, full of history) and laid out the cards.

"Huh. There's a lot of Major Arcana."

A settling in her stomach. So this thing with this boy was serious. These lightning attractions were like gods' work, messing with poor humans.

"This is a balanced reading—big baddies, but big good, too."

Alyssa's eyes went wide. Joanie reached out and took her hands. They were cold.

"There's nothing here you can't handle with your

friends' help." Joanie scanned the cards, their faded colors warm in the candlelight. "Right now everything's wonderful." She pointed to the Four of Wands with a green-polished fingernail, luminous in the indirect light. "But in your way is the Tower."

"Oh!" Alyssa was new to the Tarot, but even she knew this was one of the baddies.

"I think it's partly the times we live in. But the troubles now are somehow going to touch you closely through this relationship."

The girl trembled.

"But there's hope! And potential. It looks like a positive change of circumstance threw this boy in your lap. The Empress is at the base of the reading, here. Her shield has the sign of Venus—she can shield you in this. She is Venus, Aphrodite, Inanna. And you are aligned with her." Briefly she touched the Queen of Cups. "You also have help—around you is a company of friends, almost a household."

"That's true. You and Hannah saved my ass. I'd stopped believing things like that could happen."

"Your hopes are for love. But the outcome is a long and troubled path. Nothing easy." She pointed with a green fingernail to the Moon.

The yellow orb dropped light on a night landscape. In the foreground, a scaly creature rose from the water.

Watching, curled in a corner wreathed in smoke, Puabi-Ekur pulled out the tiny deer skull.

Around Joanie, all they saw was Inanna girls. No huntresses. No boys.

Where did the skull come in?

Chapter 7

$\mathcal{D}$aegal proved a three-days' hero for bringing home the buck. Afterward, people looked at him differently. They said "little Daegal" still, but less often, more jokingly.

His Briton foster-brother, Maelan, was still the closest thing he had to a friend in that household, with the exception of his foster-father, who was always kind. Ronec was his uncle, his mother's brother. Years before, Daegal's mother had married Daegal's Angle father to weave peace between their tribes. To further weave the bond, at ten years old Daegal was fostered with Ronec.

Ruler of a large estate, Ronec was a good lord, generous to those under him, firm if he had to be, in looks big, red, handsome of a sort. Maelan was his second son of three, born for a partial inheritance. The youngest son inherited the house; the second might stay and farm his own stead or go off and seek his fortune.

Maelan had been fostered, but it hadn't worked out. A daughter of the household, promised elsewhere, had fallen for Maelan, who'd been fetched home. Maelan took after his father, tall and broad-shouldered, hair red-gold.

That summer, a new fosterling was taken in, a boy of only eight summers; his father had been killed in a dispute. To make room, Daegal moved in with Maelan.

They were within a year in age. In the long summer, when dawn came moments after your eyes shut, Maelan and Daegal trained for war with the household master-of-arms, an older man past his days of heavy farming. They fed the dogs, hunted together for the pot: squirrels, partridge, grouse. They chased the young and foolish ducks of summer, in streams and ponds and along golden-green meadows shimmering under the sun.

That afternoon, they'd shot a brace of them. Now they lay in the shade waiting out the heat—if they returned, someone would put them to work.

A spattering of sunlight fell through oak leaves. The forest's green smell underlay the rising scent of the pond. Daegal's sweat cooled.

"Tell me about this girl, then," he said.

"You mean last year, when I was fostering?"

"You have had girls since?"

Unwillingly, Maelan said, "No.... It was clear she wanted me."

"Did you—"

"Yes! But we were careful. No child."

"What was it like?"

"Like the Land of the Blessed," Maelan said dreamily.

Daegal chewed on a stem of grass. A lark called.

Maelan's eyes stared upward, toward the tree canopy, oak mixed with hazel and birch. The leaves fluttered in the wind with a sighing.

"My father wants me to be a warrior," Maelan said. "But my heart lies with love."

"Can you not do both?" That was all the tales: war and hunting in the day, women at night. "You are a good swordsman, almost as good with an axe."

"A great swordsman." Maelan gave him a sideways glance. "It is a thing you should know about."

Daegal didn't understand that—at battle practice, they were fairly evenly matched—but then Maelan reached across and lifted a lock of hair off his forehead.

Maelan met Daegal's eyes, and Daegal's heart moved.

The Britons were easy with such things, the Angles not so much—at least if you took the passive role, if you became a woman. Though even Woden had done it.

Daegal wanted it. No one needed to know.

He captured Maelan's hand, brought the palm to his lips, and kissed it.

Maelan rolled over and kissed him back, on the lips.

"I have been wanting to do this forever."

A breeze rose among the oak leaves, carrying the scent of the pond. Forever afterward, the scent of pond water reminded him of this.

They kissed as if they had invented kissing: sucking, biting, licking, playing, locked in embrace. Maelan smelled like spices from the East, expensive things from far away.

"Let me—"

"What? Oh—" Maelan slid down, reached inside Daegal's trousers, unleashed his straining cock.

Maelan's mouth on him was warm and liquid.

Something fell into place, like fate.

He came faster than he expected. Maelan sat up wiping his lips, and Daegal kissed him, tasted semen on his tongue, a taste somehow both salt and mint.

The sun slipped westward, falling toward the trees.

"Now for me." Maelan's hand cupped his ass, fingers exploring his hole.

"You have done this before."

"I have had it done to me."

"Does it hurt?"

"It doesn't have to."

Maelan pulled off his own trousers, spat in his hand, wiped the spit on Daegal.

"You are sure about this."

"It feels good. Trust me."

"Who did you do it with?"

Maelan only smiled and drew Daegal toward him, positioning himself. Gentle, slow, unstoppable, he pushed his cock in, and paused, then pushed in further. It was amazing. Then he took Daegal's cock in his palm, squeezing and stroking till Daegal cried out, coming. Maelan came moments afterward, filling him with warm liquid.

The late sunlight fell red-gold through the trees onto Maelan's red-gold hair. Daegal drowsed. Warm feeling poured through him like honey: comfort and the retreating tingle of sex.

Maelan snored gently. The smell of sweat floated, and that spiciness, and the smell of warm grass.

Then Maelan was shaking him awake. The sun had set, purple twilight thrown down over them like a net. This time of year, twilight lasted a long time, but not forever.

"If we go now, we can get back before the gates close. No one will notice."

One more kiss, and they were tramping homeward, in the humming shadow full of gnats.

They slept together, in the same bed. It was a Briton household; nobody cared.

It was a long summer, the best summer of his life.

Amid birdsong at dawn they fucked, trying to be quiet; there was no privacy. They fought together; they hunted the meadows. Deer-stalking became a passion for them.

They half-hid their relationship, but anytime they were alone, they were all over each other, lips, tongues, fingers, pricks. Maelan liked taking chances. Behind a haystack, he'd fall to his knees and take Daegal in his mouth. Daegal bit his tongue not to cry out as he climaxed.

"You are bleeding. Let me taste your blood."

It was easier in the forest. Often they stalked deer or hunted smaller game in earnest—the household needed food. But often they lazed in the long grass, kissing, sleeping, fucking. Daegal tried what Maelan had done: sheathing himself in his friend, fucking his beautiful ass.

"It *is* divine."

One night, Maelan went to bed early—they'd been up at dawn. Before Daegal rose from his food to follow, Maelan's father motioned to him. "Come sit with me. Did you have some of the new beer?"

"I did."

"Have a little more." The serving girl filled his horn again.

The roundhouse lay low and dark. A fire in its center gave the only light; such rush lights as had been lit were out. Ronec's wife was abed. The serving girl was waiting for them to finish.

"Your father and I were good friends in our youth, very good friends, before he married your mother." Ronec watched the smoke rise, full of sparks, to the hole in the roof. A star winked through. "Such friends as you and Maelan are."

Daegal sipped his beer—tasty stuff, thick and red. Ronec's wife was known for it. "I see."

"We of Rheged do not care. You Cumbrians do. Yet 'tis not as if you forgo it."

Was that so? It was worth knowing.

"For us and ours, there is no shame in it. But do not turn your mind from women. Your parents will want you to wed."

This seemed to require an answer. "Yes, sir."

"If it is something in your youth, something that stays here, no one will care." He turned to eye the serving lass, who looked aside. "That one wants to go to sleep. Drink up."

Daegal tipped back his horn.

In the smoky darkness, in his bedding under the eaves, Daegal lay down by Maelan. The fire muttered in its ashes; wooden bowls rattled as the girl put them away.

In the darkness, he took Maelan in his arms. Maelan wriggled, burrowing in.

With the sweetness of it, pure feeling poured through him. Love.

It wasn't something he wanted to forget.

In the smoky darkness, in the bedding under the eaves, a sandy-haired young man wrapped around him—he who Puabi-Ekur was in that life.

They had been Maelan.

Later, then, came the fight to the death, the two men locked in mortal combat, several days.

How did the two of them get there? Some kind of duel? Did Daegal die? Did Maelan die?

Why were they given these memories here, now?

The tiny deer skull, carved of bone, was not much bigger than a bead. You could thread it and wear it around your neck on a leather thong.

Something fell into place.

You could wear it all your life, if your true love was your foster-brother, who you left when you were twenty to go to the place they called your home.

Chapter 8

Gus stumbled home, his head pounding, his mind confused.

He was starting two things at once. He couldn't tell if this was amazingly good or heinously stupid. Or both.

In his room, he threw off his clothes, wrapped in a towel walked to the bathroom, and took a hot shower, steaming up the mirror and windows. Stepping out dripping, he studied himself. Sandy hair, narrow but muscular shoulders, surprisingly serious face.

On impulse, he drew a heart on the mirror with his fingertip, then paused.

Whose initials would he put in it?

Should he draw a second heart?

He rubbed it away with his palm.

That autumn, he had a hard time keeping up.

He'd never fallen for two people at once before.

That wasn't entirely true. But not like this.

His next date with Alyssa was more conventional. They saw a big comic-book-based action movie, ate popcorn, drank cola. She wore a pink gingham sundress. Frail, slender, pale, she looked breakable. He loved that.

Someone giving herself into his hands, the Dom/sub thing—he'd never done it before. It spoke to him.

On his bed, he held her down by her wrists and bit her neck and breasts, leaving red weals that would turn to bruises. She didn't protest, only whimpered and twisted.

Pinning her hands with one arm, he found her clit with two fingers and rubbed viciously. She moaned. He dove down and licked, sucked, and bit the nub of flesh. Grabbing his head, she buried his face in her vulva.

"Oh my god!" She shuddered as she came.

After a few moments, he drew away and sat up.

"You liked that, huh?" He wiped his mouth on the sheet. "What are you going to do for me? You going to take my big cock?"

He did have a big cock—his last girl had said it was almost too big. She could have been exaggerating.

Mouth hanging open—pretty lips, he could fuck that—Alyssa nodded.

"Ask for it, baby. Ask nice."

"Please," she whispered.

They stared at each other. Out the window, the wind shook the maple branches. Shadows flickered across her body.

"Take me in your mouth."

"Have you read Aristophanes?"

"No."

"Ovid? The Eddas?"

Gus shook his head.

He thought he'd picked the perfect restaurant, inexpensive but excellent Italian. During the wait, they each had a drink, Max a martini and Gus a stout. Settled on stools in the restaurant's low-lit bar, under a poster for Campari, it was perfect. But now there was this interrogation. Gus was used to being quizzed about his favorite shows and movies, occasionally about gay novels, not about pagan texts.

"What pagan stuff I've done is mostly hedge-witch stuff. I went to an Asatru blót back at home once."

"Tell me about that."

The ritual itself had been dumb. His friends knew nothing. One of them read something in halting Icelandic off a sheet of paper; they poured out beer to Odin and barbecued a sacrifice.

But the fire at night in the forest, the moon rising over spruce and aspen, that had moved him. As the libation sank into the earth, a coyote had howled. Another had answered.

"It was like the wild spoke to us. That part I liked."

"I see." Max took another mouthful of martini. "It seems like you have some heathen in you."

Gus's face went blank.

That's ridiculously condescending, old guy.

"I hope so," he said.

They had a bottle of Chianti at dinner, and Max told the story of his own heathen odyssey.

"I grew up in New York State, in the Adirondacks." He looked across the tiny restaurant, full of animated couples gesturing over checkered tablecloths. "It's beautiful country, one of the last places in the United States where the natural world is bigger than the world of men."

"There are places in Utah like that."

Max continued his story. In the wild country, where snow piled up to three feet and more in the winters, he met spirits. "Landvættir, spirits of place. But, being a gay man, I moved to New York City. I lived on Avenue A before it got too expensive. It was the nineteen-nineties—I was a club kid, I stayed out all night dancing. But the wild kept calling me."

At his parents' for Christmas, Max went out the night of winter solstice to greet the woods. In the dark lit by moonlight on snow, he blazed a trail, working hard through several feet of drifts, to a pond ringed in pines at the edge of his parents' property. The wind threw bits of snowdrift stinging into his face.

"I just wanted to be out in the snow, but when I got to the frozen pond, I saw this magnificent stag across it."

Silhouetted against a gibbous moon, he stood like a god, an eight-point buck.

"He stared at me for a moment, then he leaped away."

Max looked again across the room, and Gus got the chance to study his face: hooked nose, hazel eyes, high cheekbones. A good-looking man. Brett had been a boy.

"The wind rose, and I heard echoes in it. The solstice is the culmination of the time of the Wild Hunt." Gus nodded. The Wild Hunt in ancient Europe, dangerous for mortals, ranged the skies in winter. In the Norse and Germanic lands, it was led by Odin, or Woden.

"The next morning at dawn, I got my crossbow, and I hunted and killed him. I gave him a prayer, an old one I knew." He shut his eyes and spoke it.

All-Father, thank you for sharing life with life. Bless this flesh for me and mine. Give fair travels to this spirit.

"Then I dedicated myself with the blood to Odin."

Max was a hunter. Of course.

A fistful of reactions exploded in Gus.

Gus's dad and uncles were hunters. He'd hated it. Getting up way too early, getting harassed and made fun of, sitting in a tree or behind a blind forever, wet, cold, trapped. And then when the wild comes up to you, gentle and curious, you kill it.

At least a crossbow took more skill than a rifle.

But he felt admiration for the skill, and below that, wistfulness. It'd been forever since he'd been out on the land.

In high school, he'd go camping in the desert, run away a week at a time. His father was an ally here. "Let the boy grow up," he'd say to Gus's mother.

Grass and scrub broiled under the blazing sun; rock formations stood like a circle of watchers. He'd pitch his tent in the shadows, for the cool. You had to be careful of grizzlies, but it was worth it to be away from home.

He'd never met a gay man who'd wanted that. The guys he'd hooked up with had all been city dwellers.

"We should go camping," he said, impulsively.

"You should come to one of our blóts. We do eight a year, plus smaller rituals."

It was full night as they walked back to Max's. The wind shook the trees, shaking down flights of leaves to join the shuffling piles along the street. The smell of woodsmoke and leaf-rot filled the air.

They entered the half-dark of the apartment entrance way. Max turned on the stove light in the kitchen, which threw their shadows sideways: two men, one taller than the other.

In the bedroom, Max lit a side lamp on the bedside table. "I want to see you," he said.

It was like before; it was better. No foreplay, and he wanted none, only to give way. Lube, a condom, and Max was inside him. "Oh my god! Yes, yes!" His face in the pillow, Max looming over him like a god. Hard, harder.

"I want to see you."

Max turned him, face to face, pushing his legs up by his shoulders, bending him in half. Then Max closed his eyes, riding him; throwing back his head, he cried out, a wordless cry. Hand on himself, Gus came a moment after, spilling semen on his stomach. Max crumpled on top of him, holding him.

After a while, Max got up. "Do you want to stay over? We could watch something."

"I'd like that."

~

Joanie's coven met for the fall equinox in Hannah's finished basement. The ritual room there was big, with alcoves, a couple of couches, and a big Celtic hanging, a tree of life with branches woven together. Hannah, Cleo, and Joanie also held their Inanna temples here—changing the drapery, bringing the Inanna altar out.

At the room's center, the witch altar now stood draped with seasonal colors. A big orange candle burned for the god. For the equinox, they called Herne the Hunter. For Hannah's coven, Herne was a later English version of Woden, here a god of hunting and the forest, associated with the Wild Hunt.

Alyssa, who rented a room at Hannah's, didn't come to all the coven rituals—she was a coven friend, not an initiate. But this one she did.

Joanie went to stand by her in the circle and took her hand. Alyssa smiled and dipped her head.

Joanie was part of the coven, in the outer court, taking witch-classes. Alyssa had flirted with the idea, then backed away. This was typical. Sometimes Alyssa didn't seem signed up for life.

A short ritual, it was mainly celebratory, but with a meditation.

Hannah introduced this: "Now, in these times, we ask the forest god, the lord of animals, to help and support us. Show us what we need to protect the wild, both inside and outside us, in these times of trouble, as the earth grows hotter and the human world gets more dangerous."

They shut their eyes. Hannah relaxed them and brought them to light trance.

"Within the circular tower, you find a flight of spiral steps. As you take each step down, you grow more relaxed." She brought them each into a twilight meadow to sit with Herne. With each in their own space, he told them things, what they needed to know.

For Joanie, a path from the meadow led to a glade, where rays of late sunlight shot through tall maples. Herne, antler-headed, sat on a wicker-wood throne twined with morning-glories. His face was kind, but his antlers were a thorn fence above him, with dangerous tines.

"Yes?" he asked her.

She fell in a lump at his feet. "I don't know what I'm doing with my life. I used to be so certain. But now, when I have to make decisions, all my certainty has flown away."

"Follow the path you are taking. When it's needful, the further journey will be made clear."

She gazed into his face, wanting to say something, to protest, but his look quelled her, not by fear but by utter reassurance.

Knowledge soaked into her. She was on the right path. However strange, uncomfortable, and sometimes dangerous it was.

Hannah's voice called her back.

Next, cakes and wine or juice would usually go around the circle, but someone had forgotten them. One of the coven ran upstairs. Joanie sat up from where she'd lain on the floor, stretching her legs. Beside her, Alyssa sat with a worried frown.

"Mmm?"

"My meditation wasn't what I expected. Herne turned really scary. But then Hekate swept in to protect me."

"Scary how?"

"It was the Wild Hunt, like Hannah was saying. I saw Herne as part of that, on a white horse in the sky on a dark night. And he was tall and covered with tattoos. And he reached down for me, like I was supposed to be getting on his horse. And Gus was there. He was already on the horse."

"Then Hekate appeared?"

Alyssa nodded fiercely. "She swept in and saved me." She bit her lip. "I'm not sure what happened to Gus."

Puabi-Ekur attended the ritual as well.

They didn't yet see how this all connected, but they were getting there.

Puabi-Ekur was Maelan, but who had been Daegal?

Perhaps they would find him at the ritual. There were guests. But no one in the circle, neither male nor female, had the scent of the Angle boy.

When it came to the meditation, the trance sent them into the ether. Their vision was of a bright tangle, webs of connection past and future, all threaded together.

They almost wanted to seek out Hekate.

But she'd sent them on a mission, which they were clearly supposed to figure out for themselves. She wouldn't want them returning till they had something.

Where was this Daegal?

Chapter 9

When Daegal was twenty, he went home— home to the place he hadn't been since he was six, home to his father and mother. They seemed smaller than they had before, husks of their former selves. Of course they were older.

The town and hall seemed smaller too, and unfamiliar. Not the round Briton houses, but square-edged, timbered or wattle and daub, with thatched roofs. His father was a gesith, one of the king's war-companions, and lived in a hall more imposing than these smaller houses, but equally smoky. At night, the thick smoke almost sent him out into the darkness.

He was home to be a pawn in his father's plots—it was the price of power, among Angle kings and their retainers, to always be plotting, always be watching and maneuvering against the others. Daegal had failed in finding a high-ranking Briton wife, if that had been the intention.

His choices were to find a rich wife or be a warrior, for his father or someone else. Or both.

He slept with his brothers and fed from the common mess with the hearth-guard, his father's men at arms. Having not much to do, he spent his time weapons training. The border with Rheged was always disputed; there was always room for fighters.

He hunted, too, something that was always needful. The woods of Cumbria were like Rheged: tall oaks, green and quiet spaces. It cleared his mind to stalk deer in the woods. He missed his hunting companion, but there was no help for that.

He had to turn his mind to women now—to a particular woman, the daughter of whoever his father wanted as an ally. That would be no hardship, if she were young and pretty.

He'd caught the glad eye of the serving girl on him, and finding her throwing grain to the geese in the yard stroked her hair, planted a kiss on her cheek. She turned suddenly, setting her basket down, and kissed him fully, and he took her breasts in his hands. Then, hearing someone coming, she batted him away.

But it was a slow time, full of pangs of sorrow, and mostly he hunted. He tried not to sit too long with his thoughts, waiting in the brush for game. The hunt usually gave him a distraction, seeing a doe far away among leaves. She'd catch scent of him, leap away with a bounce, and the chase would begin.

If he could match the two, if he could find an enchanted hind, a fairy woman, entice her to lie with him... fairy lovers were good luck. Once he'd dreamed of them.

Now, if he dreamed, he dreamed of Maelan, but he set that away.

The leaves fell, and the snows came, not heavy. "We will spend this Yule in the hall of Ealdorman Ecgric in Berenicia," his father announced. "He is a worthy friend." Daegal's older brother was already betrothed to a Cumbrian girl of good family, with the wedding to come at midsummer. Daegal would be next.

That mid-December, only a dusting of snow had fallen on the trees. He and his father and brothers led the group of travelers, riding horses. Both nights of the two-night journey, Daegal sat with the other young men by the fire, drinking ale, listening to snow fall in the flames with a hiss, dreaming and wondering.

When they arrived at Ecgric's hall, the yard in front was churned to mud, but the hall itself was imposing, tall and timbered. Two young men came forward to stable the horses. Daegal looked out from under his eyelids.

Who was this daughter, who was this prospect?

He saw her that evening, as she served ale to the company. Tall, with long dark hair, she wasn't a great beauty, but she had intelligent eyes, a slender and pleasing form. The idea of possession was itself sexual. His to serve him, his to please him. He could get used to that.

The next day dawned overcast, with pink light behind the cloud and snow in the air. "Take a walk with her," his father said. "A serving woman will accompany you."

Her name was Ethelreda, known as Reda. She stepped

forward toward him in the yard, lifting her skirt away from the mud, frowning-smiling, long dark hair under a ribbon crown.

They took a path into the forest. The oaks still held a scatter of leaves. A sprinkling of snow fell, touching his cheek with tiny bits of ice. The serving woman walked far behind.

"Lady Ethelreda." Was he to make love to her?

"Lord Daegal."

The title did him more than justice. He wondered what his father had promised hers.

Her sideways glance assessed him. It seemed she did not dislike him. He took her hand, in its leather glove, with its long and slender fingers.

"Will you allow me to court you?"

"It is my father's wish."

"Could it be your own?"

The dark hair shook in a wave, flicking off snowflakes. "It is not mine to say."

"But if it were?"

She gave another sideways glance. She bit her lip, chapped and rose-pink.

He could bite that lip.

"The idea would not displease me."

It was good as he'd get. She was no serving-maid to throw herself at him.

They wed toward the end of summer—his father was

considered lucky to marry both his elder sons well, within a season of each other. Daegal had a dozen fields and an apple orchard from his father, and good fishing in a stream that ran through them, and all the forest to hunt. For a morning-gift, he gave Ethelreda a necklace of heavy gold, three flocks of sheep, and a lump of raw amber that trapped a mayfly.

His wedding night was not his first time with a woman. He'd found the goose-girl and lain with her, twice, making no promises, for the pleasure in it, and to be sure he knew how.

That night, after the laughing company let them sleep, Ethelreda let him do as he would. They had the best room of the house, though small, decorated by the manor's maidens with bell-flowers and corn-flowers, blue and pale. The lights burned to nothing, though he made sure to keep one aflame. He wanted to see her body, so long hidden under bulky clothes: her nakedness, her truth.

The scent of lavender rose from the sheets in the box-bed. Her hair spread across the pillow like a wave on the shore.

He began with kisses, wanting to draw out her desire. Gentle kisses on her face, stroking her hair, till she kissed back. She was in a long nightgown; he untied the lace at its neck, kissed further. Her pale skin almost blue in shadow. Nipples flat, dark red. The nest of dark hair between her legs. He touched the bud nestled there, as the goose-girl had showed him. She closed her eyes. He stroked her, then slipped his fingers further in. She was wet.

But afterward, with blood on the sheets, holding her close to him, he felt her shuddering.

He stroked her hair, fondled her wet cheek. "My lady, why do you weep?"

"I miss my freedom. I am in a strange land with no friends."

"I shall be your friend, Reda."

She turned and in the half-light, from the candle he'd kept burning, he caught a trembling smile.

After the equinox ritual, looking for Daegal, Puabi-Ekur climbed and climbed higher. Pictures of Daegal's life fell, image after image.

She gave him three children in five years, a boy and two girls. One hot, dank summer they died of fever. She blamed him. As if he'd brought the heat, or ill-wished them, when he loved them above all things.

But even before that, he had intimations his marriage might fail. They went back to her father's hall for Yule two years after their wedding, with their daughter still a baby. The day before the banquet, he went searching for Reda. But in their room, the baby was with the nurse, who gave him a long look.

"She went walking with her cousin," the nurse said.

This cousin was Cynric, a tall, black-haired man, who

had always been curt with Daegal. Now he understood why. Reda did not come back till nightfall.

That night before supper, a scop played the harp in the high hall with its carven rafters and great wheels of candles. Just before supper she appeared, cheeks flushed, and came to sit on the bench beside Daegal, enclosed in a silence. He caught a smell on her, something strange, like some herb he didn't recognize.

From across the hall, he saw Cynric watching her.

She must have loved him before they met. But it served her father to have an alliance in Cumbria.

He could be a jealous husband. He could beat her to make her lose her will to stray. He could ambush Cynric and fight him. He could divorce her for adultery.

But she was rarely here in her father's hall; she was most often home with him. There, she smiled on him. She was a good mother to her children. Life was not getting what you want every day. She knew this.

It made him angry, but he kept his counsel.

He wanted her allegiance. He wanted her heart. Beating her would not get him that.

After that, he kept Yuletide at his father's house.

But after the children died, she blamed him for everything, and he lashed out in return. "You would rather be at your father's hall, with your cousin Cynric!"

Finally, they could barely be in the same room together, and they both knew the marriage was broken. No children would bring them together; she would not share his bed. They returned to spend Yuletide again at her father's hall, and when he left, he left without her.

His mother found him an old woman to keep house; he farmed with a couple of his father's men, working from dawn till after sundown. But everywhere he turned, he saw Reda and the children, as if they were ghosts. Only in the forest could he forget, on summer mornings waiting for a deer.

Now he could use a fairy lover, in earnest.

But no enchanted doe appeared, only dun-colored ones who ran from him, who were deer and only deer. Even the goose-girl had gotten married.

In November, after his household brought harvest in and killed the cattle that wouldn't last the winter, he went to his father. Late at night in the hall, over the ribs of a roast pig, they sat with the winter ale. Firelight lit the rafters. The house dogs chewed bones by their feet.

"Have your men farm my portion. I cannot do this, Father. I need not to be here, where I keep remembering."

"Where would you go?"

"I am a strong warrior. Surely there is some ealdorman north or south who needs a fighting man?"

"Go west, if that is what you have a mind to do." The western Cumbrians defended an uneasy border with Rheged, crossed by cattle-raiders and sometimes larger war-bands. "Lord Adel has been a friend to me. He can use such a man."

Looking down as from a great height, Puabi-Ekur held these scenes like cards from a deck.

But following the threads from this past life into present time got Puabi-Ekur nowhere. The filaments spun to nothing, as if Puabi-Ekur were being teased.

They were close, but they didn't see Daegal in the here and now.

Almost it was as if there were a fog between them—the fog of the djinn? Though the djinn were hardly the only challengers in the many worlds.

Chapter 10

On their third date, Gus took Alyssa out for a beer and a burger before they went to a movie.

He needed more than Max. Max was twenty years older than him and ran everything. Max conspired to know everything, and Max was always on top in bed. Gus was a switch, not made to always bottom.

They found a shadowy brew-pub, with red-topped tables and pub food. They split nachos. She had a garden burger; she was a vegetarian.

"So the people I live with—" she hesitated.

He hadn't heard much about her life. And she didn't know much about his.

At some point, he needed to tell her about Max. She couldn't think they were exclusive. But that didn't mean she'd expect him to be dating a guy.

"So, well, they're witches. At least Hannah is. She's kind

of the house mom. Property manager, I guess, though it's not very formal. She's like in her fifties and runs things."

She looked up, her face full of anxiety, to see how this fell for him.

He grinned. "I've done some witch stuff too, back at home in Utah." He took a deep breath. "A friend of mine said he'd take me to a heathen blót, coming up."

"Oh, how cool!" There was relief in her voice.

It was time to tell.

"So…" He leaned forward and took her hand. "You know I'm not dating just you."

"You never said you were." But disappointment sounded in her voice.

"I'm dating a man. He's older. I'm bisexual."

He almost said, "I hope that's okay with you." But that wasn't her call. Though she wasn't asking for that. He liked that Alyssa was a natural sub, used to giving way to stronger personalities.

"I don't have any problem with that." She looked down. "I should tell you a few things about myself too."

He raised his eyebrows.

"So—I don't do this anymore—but I used to smoke heroin. Also, I was a street hooker. I'm clean, though, my tests are all negative, like I said."

He blinked. It wasn't what he'd expected.

The heroin he didn't care about. Back in rural Utah, he'd known plenty of people who'd tried plenty of drugs. People got bored there.

She'd been a whore, though. Part of him recoiled. Part of

him thought it was hot. He tried to keep his opinions off his face.

"No worries. We've both been around the block."

"Yes." She took his hand, gripped it hard. "I really don't care about the bi thing. I mean—" she blushed a little —"maybe it's even a little hot."

He barked, a shout of laughter.

He picked up their folded hands, bit the back of hers gently. "Is that so."

She looked away, now blushing almost fuchsia.

He picked up her arm, bit along its length. Glancing up to see her reaction, he bit hard, then harder, nearly breaking the skin. She gasped.

His story had made her horny. He hadn't expected that.

Joanie woke up in Cleo's bed, in Cleo's arms.

In the middle of the night, with the window cracked, a breath of cool air floated through. The air was heavy, left from the last few hot, muggy days. She twisted, seeking cool in the sheets.

Beside her lay her lover's body, the long slender limbs. She let herself gaze, enraptured, in full possession as her lover slept. She felt at home, as she'd never felt.

In part, that was the community. It wasn't perfect. Sometimes it felt like it took forever to get anything done, like questions circled and circled through various conversations and meetings, never getting settled. Sometimes Forum's attempt at transparent conversation seemed like drama of the bad kind; sometimes the several life coaches in the community seemed only to be making money, not helping.

Then a breakthrough would come, and she'd have hope. It was a group of people trying to consciously create a better world.

She sat up. The breeze ruffled the sari tented above the bed. Streetlight shone off one of the many mirrors stitched to a pillow. Cleo was fast asleep, eyelids tight, the globes of her eyes hidden, moving slightly.

Joanie had been trying to keep track of her dreams, though lately they'd just been wisps and oddments, mulled-over happenings of the day.

She tried too to keep in touch with Puabi-Ekur, as a guide. The previous year, Puabi-Ekur had briefly possessed her partner Clayton before realizing that Puabi-Ekur and Joanie had shared a relationship in ancient Sumer. They'd made a connection, and now she worked to retain it. Joanie performed a morning practice of prayer, visualizations, and thanks to Puabi-Ekur and her deities. Her practice took into account the Wheel of the Year; in the past few days she'd lit a candle to Herne.

In her witchiness, she felt on the edge of the community. Cleo was there too, with a focus on the spiritual, but the coven wasn't as central for Cleo. Cleo's passion was her dedication to Inanna. Cleo, Joanie, and Hannah had done Inanna temples monthly through the spring, but that had tapered off as Cleo finished her thesis.

Joanie also was a child of Inanna. And a sacred whore. But what did that mean, here and now?

For some reason, her thoughts went to Alyssa.

She didn't trust this new guy Alyssa seeing. It was a feeling more than a thought, something about his blankness, his silence, his withdrawal.

A fear whirled up within her. Standing, she kissed Cleo softly on the cheek and tiptoed out, down to her basement room.

Kneeling on her bed, she lit her coral-pink Inanna candle. The basement room was chilly and airless. But in each of the room's four corners, she'd put tiny polished stones, amethyst and obsidian for grounding and protection, blessed and consecrated as wards.

Sitting cross-legged on the bed, she brought herself to present time and space.

As when her sugar daddy was around, a sense of foreboding lurked, as if nasty spirits were messing with her and her friends again. But she didn't want to be paranoid.

Closing her eyes, she ran a red grounding cord from the center of her abdomen down through the floor, the dirt, the rocks and underground streams, to the center of the earth. She imagined it hot and compressed, vibrating with the earth's spin. She ran a silver cord up through her body, neck, and head, through the house, into the night sky, and up, connecting to universal energy.

In the stillness of the night, the connection relaxed her, deepened her into the energy, connecting with magic. Reaching to the corner of her desk, in her incense burner she lit mugwort incense, for psychic work. She'd grown the mugwort in a corner of Firebird House's herb garden.

Then she called out into the ether.

Puabi-Ekur, come to me. I need your guidance.

From far away, a haunt in the upper atmosphere bathed in the light of nebulae, Puabi-Ekur heard the call.

"What is it, my beloved?"

"There's something up," Joanie said, whispering into the darkness. She was the only one who slept in the basement, but it was second nature to whisper, after a childhood hiding her magic. "It has to do with that new boy Alyssa's seeing, Gus. Could you take a look at him for me?"

The vision came like swimming through layers of veils, as if all the self-perceptions and stories were thicker and thicker layers.

Puabi-Ekur focused on Alyssa's young man. Complicated and self-harming and dark. A black streak of nihilism.

They were tripped into a memory: the darkness of the Briton house, chilly and smelling of woodsmoke.

Warm hands in the darkness touched the young man that Puabi-Ekur had been.

Something resonated in Alyssa's man's energy. His look had a similarity too: the sandy hair, the naturally slender body, a runner's body, heavier in the shoulders from hunting and practice of arms.

His hands on them, stroking their hair as he breathed their name: Maelan.

They had been Maelan then.

Gus had been his lover, Daegal.

After Puabi-Ekur and her friends had freed Joanie by running off her sugar daddy and his djinni woman comrade, Puabi-Ekur knew they had returned to the pull and push of karma. Nevertheless that didn't mean Puabi-Ekur had entirely altered their leisurely, measured approach to life. There need not be any time, on the spirit level. They could just float away. The closer one got to living humans, the more pushy time and karma got.

Nothing for it but to tell it straight.

"I know him from a past life, like I know you."

"You were lovers?"

A mugwort seed flared up on the incense charcoal and burned out.

"Yes. In that life, we were both men."

"Can you see when it was? What he's doing here now?"

On the etheric plane, Puabi-Ekur pulled out the deer-skull bead carved of bone that Hekate had given them: tiny, ivory-colored, darker brown at the indentations of eyes and hollow of the mouth.

"The goddess said it was a life far away, in the northern woods. I don't know when. I have some place-names."

"We could Google them!" Joanie said, excited.

"More interesting to me is, what is he doing here now, and why is he connected to all of us?"

Puabi-Ekur had lost Joanie long ago. As Iltani, she'd been taken away and killed. Puabi-Ekur blamed themselves for that. They'd longed to make up for it.

There was a longing here, too, but Puabi-Ekur felt differently about Daegal.

Or Gus. Or whoever he was.

Metal pounded on metal, sword on sword, thrust and counter-thrust. They danced around each other, clashing. They watched each other, circling. Of the three-days fight, this was the second day.

In a cleared field between two small armies, a space had been created, marked off by a line scraped in the dirt, circled with a rope barrier.

Above, against a high overcast, a hawk reeled.

The air had a nip of cold; it smelled like snow. Men in boiled leather armor or mail stood to either side of the roped space, watching closely, speaking in low voices. Maelan knew they commented on the moves, who was tiring, who might be winning.

He, Maelan, the champion, had demanded the single fight, testing the mettle of his adversary. It was to prevent a bloody battle, which neither side wanted. The man they had set against him was Daegal. Their best warrior, he gathered, and the one he least wanted to kill.

The fighters were evenly matched. The first day had been spears, but both had gotten off light. Maelan had a long slash on his leg, which periodically opened and bled, but not deep, only annoying. Daegal had gotten one worse, a deep gouge to his shoulder that had begun to hamper his strength and reach. Maelan watched the blood rise and stain the fabric of his linen shirt.

The memory faded.

Was the fight to the death? Had Daegal died? Or Maelan?

Maybe Puabi-Ekur wasn't supposed to know.

Overwhelming, up rose love and then regret, a long grief.

And an undertow of anger. You couldn't fight a man for three days, even a man you loved, without anger.

Maybe a half-hour had passed. The coral-red candle had melted, filling its dish.

"It was a fight, supposedly to the death, but you don't know if anyone died, or who it was if they did," Joanie said, in an exasperated tone. "And it's in Rheged. Historians have no idea if Rheged really existed." She'd looked it up on her phone. "All you can tell is that you cared about him, and if there are evil spirits around, he's probably not one of them, though he could be aligned with them."

Puabi-Ekur wriggled in the spirit equivalent of a shrug. "Just because I'm on the astral plane doesn't mean I can answer all your questions."

Joanie sighed. "Apparently not."

"I believe information is being hidden from us. There's a lot of complications on all levels right now. We're being fought. Or hadn't you noticed?"

"I noticed."

The machinations of the djinn were subtle, but once you learned how to see them they stood out.

Gus fell into a pattern of seeing each of his lovers once a week—sometimes more often, for Alyssa, since she was easy to get hold of and pliable to his will. Grinding his way into her, hearing her whimpering cries, falling asleep in her arms was a kind of heaven. His bed was their playground on the early autumn nights, the window open to the wind.

They worked into light D/s. Sometimes he blindfolded her and used her that way. Sometimes he tied her up, sometimes made her beg. He liked to go down on her and stop right before she came, then fuck her—by the time he got back to her clit, she'd come nearly instantly.

But he was always drawn back to Max. Shoved into the pillow, with Max he was the one who made the whimpering cries. He gave way, full submission, letting go of the voices in his head.

As the leaves started falling, at the end of September, Gus met Max at a local brew-pub with a Germanic theme. It was all brick and beer posters, shelves lined with white-china steins, inscribed personally for locals. They traded greetings and small talk.

Clearing his throat, Max said, "You should come to our Winter Nights ritual. It's one of our big ones."

Gus took a sip of ale. "I'd like that. When?"

"Overnight, first weekend in October, on our land. It's outside Yelm."

"Where's Yelm?"

"Near Olympia, midstate, this side of the mountains. I'll drive you down. Bring a tent and rain gear. I have responsibilities to the ritual, so I can't spend all the time with you. The group is friendly, though."

It made him nervous, the idea of going such a long way without his own means of driving. But he didn't have a car or money to rent one. Max, again reading his mind, grinned.

"If we really freak you out, it's a short walk to the highway, and about a ten-mile hike from there to Yelm. But I don't think it'll be that bad."

Gus smirked. "I'm not worried."

It wasn't like anyone would try to kill him.

He thought of the shoebox with the X-Acto knife.

If anyone was likely to kill him, it was himself.

Clouds puffed and blundered, forming and breaking, sailing the high, pale-blue sky. The air felt washed by yesterday's rain, soft as old cotton, and on it drifted the scent of woodsmoke.

Driving down Friday morning, the breeze made by their passage carried just the beginning of chill, more wet than crisp. The big-leaf maples shone golden in sunlight. Joy shone out, obscuring Gus's fears.

His jeans-covered leg rested by Max's on the bench seat of Max's truck. Max reached over and squeezed his thigh. Gus traced the line of tattooed runes that ringed Max's forearm, above them a band of black. Gus had studied the runes during his high-school Northern worship.

Douglas fir and alder scrub loomed to either side of Yelm Highway, interspersed with maple. Below the upper story, the underbrush tangled brown and yellow, the vine maple in it scarlet.

"Tell me about this blót."

"I can give you background. I want parts of it to be a surprise, for the mystery of it." Gus nodded. "Winter Nights is one of the three major feasts of the heathen year. It's a time to honor the Alfar and the Disir, our forefathers and foremothers—our ancestors. It's also the turn from summer to winter, the time when the Wild Hunt begins." Here he gave Gus a significant look. Gus had learned that Odin's Hunt, or Odensjakt, was what Max's group called itself—the Scandinavian name for the Wild Hunt.

"What is Odin's Hunt's take on the Wild Hunt?" Each pagan group could mean something slightly different by a term.

"It's said to be led by Odin. It's the dead and spirits, joined sometimes by those who make magic. It can mean war, or the death of someone who witnesses it."

"What are they hunting?"

"That's not for humans to know. Wild animals, maybe. Or humans. For humans it means catastrophe."

"So you do ritual to ward it off?"

Max grinned. "Something like that."

The way he said it made it sound like he meant something entirely different. They exchanged a look. It was clear Max had no intention of telling Gus what he meant.

Chapter 11

They drove through the quiet, low-slung town of Yelm and into the woods of the back country. They took a turn, then another, onto a side-road that some miles along lost its paving. Under tall yellow alders, vine maple blushed red, always with a background of evergreen.

For a moment, among the greenery, the dun-colored flank of a deer flashed. Gus looked up to dark eyes and a rack of antlers. Then, with a flurry, the buck bounded away.

"There're some bumps," Max said, of the gravel road after that, as they jounced, teeth rattling.

Under the branches of Douglas firs, they came to a turnoff, with a posted sign, simple black on white lettering: Odinshof. Under the lettering, runes spelled out what Gus pieced together was the same thing.

"What does that mean?"

"A hof is a ritual hall. This is Odin's hall. As I say, it's not done yet—we're in the process of building it." On the way down, Max had described the setup. The group had pooled their money and run an online fund drive, raising enough to buy twenty acres of land and build a timbered hall. After a long search they bought land and laid foundations. But the hall was yet to come. This ritual, Winter Nights, would be held under the stars or the rain.

The afternoon was clear. The truck bounced along a dirt road shaded by young alder trees, leaves butter-yellow. Max pulled up and parked beside a handful of other cars and trucks.

"Jump out. I'll introduce you around, get you set with a camping space. Then I have to go do ritual setup."

Gus slid out of the cab and followed Max up a gravel road to a clearing ringed by alder and Douglas fir. To one side, set off with orange caution tape, he saw the recently poured foundations of the hall.

Max strode forward to a group of men ranged around a woodpile. A teenage boy was chopping wood but stopped and leaned on his axe as Max came up.

"Greetings, men of Odin!"

A burly, muscled man, long dark hair in a ponytail, wearing a black t-shirt and blue jeans, came to give Max a bear-hug. "This is Gus. Gus, this is Jake. He's one of the priests of our Odin's rite—a gothi."

Jake looked over Gus closely. Gus couldn't tell if Jake liked what he saw or not.

Behind Jake, other men stood staring. Some were nondescript, in jeans and t-shirts; some wore leather or denim vests or jackets patched for Odin's Hunt, with the silhouette of a skull-headed rider on a rearing horse, holding a torch.

"Where do we have the Pack tents?" The Hunting Pack was a loose group of friends of and prospects for Odin's Hunt, affiliated but not in the central group. "Gus should camp by them."

Jake's face cleared. He pointed. "Over by the further alder meadow, past Thor's altar." Gus could just see the altar, a wooden plank balanced on boulder piles, with Thor's-hammer banners to either side.

"I'll walk you over," Max told Gus.

What had Jake been thinking? Some homophobic thing?

Blue sky vaulted over sun-colored alder backed by ranks of dark firs. They passed the Thor altar, on its two rough-mortared piles of boulders, gold-on-red banners waving.

"That's a good space," Max said, pointing to a flat area that was a bit secluded, set between four young firs. Gus went over and tossed some sticks aside to clear space for the tent. Max helped Gus set up his tent as if they'd done it together dozens of times.

Once it was up, Max scratched the back of his shaved head, a gesture that usually meant he felt impatient.

"I'll put on the fly," Gus said.

"I have to go. Ritual responsibilities," Max said, and briefly hugged him. It was only for a moment, but in Max's personal space, Gus relaxed.

A handful of tents, green, yellow, and orange, squatted in the forest. They didn't show much regalia—camping at a Renaissance Fair, as his sister had, there'd be more frippery, carpets and lanterns. One big yellow tent had a rune painted in black on each of its long sides.

Othala. Land of my fathers. The blood and soil rune. It had an association with the Nazi past slightly less clear-cut than a swastika's, but not much.

Gus had a bag of runes, stone ones a Utah Asatru friend had given him. Once he'd finished staking his tent and spreading his sleeping bag, he dug out the leather pouch.

He felt nervous, uncertain, off-balance.

Odin's Hunt. Were they Odinists?

He'd poked the edges of the Odinist subculture before. Plenty of people of that bent lived in Utah. His friend Dennis who had given him the runes was an Odinist. Drinking beer, watching some slasher flick, he'd gotten Dennis's thoughts.

"I practice the religion of my fathers. I want to keep the identity of my fathers. Everyone gets to have their own thing, that's fair."

Gus shook his head, disgusted. "It's one thing to say shit to bait people. But for real? Isn't that just racism?"

Dennis had insisted. "It's not a white-majority society anymore, dude. Or anyway, it won't be in a few years. I want to preserve white identity. I'm a white identarian."

A fancy word for racist. But he'd known Dennis since grade school, and he was unwilling to break the friendship.

Now he took out the runes, forming a question in his mind. Should he stay, and learn from these folks? What would it bring him?

He reached into the bag and drew one rune.

Wunjo: Joy. Attainment of desire.

Whatever this was, there was something here for him.

In the afternoon, sun westering, Gus went to a workshop on sigils built from runes. Yellow light poured down on the picnic table as an older man with a braided beard talked. Gus came away with a sigil, an inscribed magic symbol, burned onto a wooden disc for luck and protection.

He made his own lunch from what he'd brought, then watched a couple of fights in an improvised boxing ring, roped off, grass in the ring scraped away by use. The first bout matched two scrappy boys, big red gloves on pale arms thin as pencils. The second one had older men with muscle on them.

As he sat cross-legged in the grass, one of the men by him leaned over. "Want some mead? I made it myself."

"Sure."

He handed it over, in a self-capping bottle, the kind brewers used.

"This is good!"

"Have some more."

"All right." Gus tipped back his head, took several swallows, and handed the bottle back. They grinned at each other.

Someone was reaching out; that was something.

One of the boxing matches was punitive. A Pack member had stolen another's jacket—Gus overheard the story from two Pack members behind him. The leader of

Odin's Hunt, who went by Bruni, for bear, was going to box the thief, who was almost certain to lose.

Max threw himself on the ground beside him. "How're you doing? People being welcoming?"

"Welcoming enough. I got some mead."

They exchanged a glance. He felt the warmth of Max's body, smelled his male scent, bay rum and sweat.

The Pack member came to the ring first, a wiry guy with a shaved head, stripped to the waist. He squatted on his haunches, smoking a cigarette. A friend stood next to him, leaning over to whisper to him and rub his shoulders.

Through the band of spectators, Bruni made his way. He was also bare-chested. Built like the bear he was named for, he was thick-waisted but with shoulders all muscle. A couple of people cheered. A high-pitched whistle hung in the air. Pushing down the rope, Bruni climbed into the ring.

The fighters wore gloves but no helmets; nothing covered their faces. Jake the gothi blew a horn, and the fight started.

The Pack member danced around Bruni, jabbing. A tap here, a tap there, fell on Bruni's thickly muscled arms. A fly buzzing around a bear. Bruni had fifty pounds on his opponent. Bruni waited, saving his energy, moving only a few paces.

Then Bruni hit back, a punch to the face like being hit by the butt-end of a log, enough to knock the Pack member sideways.

Bruni followed with a solid blow to the chin. Then another, to the stomach.

The Pack member fell. He made no cry; the only sound

was the thud of his body on the ground. He covered his face with the gloves, red smearing his cheek.

"It's blood!" someone called.

Bruni turned toward Jake, the gothi. "Is it sufficient?"

Jake stepped forward, pulled the gloves away from the Pack member's face. Blood was gushing from a cut on his cheekbone.

"It is."

Friends drew the Pack member away.

Max sat with arms crossed over his knees, pensive. He eyed Gus. "What did you think?"

"Of what exactly?"

"Tell me what comes up for you."

He looked across the broad open space, the mottled trunks of the alder, the black trunks of Douglas fir. In the sky of early fall, the blue was pale as if mixed with milk.

"I don't know if fighting is the way to settle things. I mean, what if the stronger man is wrong?"

"It's a set fight. The council determined that the theft took place. This was punishment."

"So why do it like that? He could just give back the jacket. Or do some kind of penance."

Max shook his head. "Not penance. We administer justice."

"So this is, what, restorative justice? It doesn't look anything like that."

Gus had been on the edges of a restorative justice process. A girl in one of his biology classes, an acquaintance, had called out a guy for a violation of sexual consent —he'd never heard what exactly. The guy had agreed to take part in an accountability group. It had let them both return to the loose friend-group of biology students with only low-grade animosity. But that process was all about talking.

Max spat into the grass. "Fuck restorative justice. This is something else. The hierarchy judges, and if you want to stay, you accept the judgment. And the punishment."

"All right."

It was easy. Clean, in a way. Not all the talking.

Max reached out and tousled his hair. "You're starting to get it, I think." He leaped to his feet. For an older guy, he moved fast.

And his ass in jeans, and the roll of his tanned shoulders. A twinge went through Gus.

Wunjo. Attainment of desire.

As twilight fell, Odin's Hunt met for food. As asked, Gus had brought cans of chili, and he carried these to the communal cooking area. A big cast-iron pot sat on a grill over flames, all among black trees, under a lavender sky.

For the first time, he saw a full complement of the women of Odin's Hunt; the women's auxiliary camped in the family area, and almost all the Pack he was tenting by were male. Women made up maybe a tenth of the people convened, and most of them were moving around the improvised kitchen. Some wore jeans and t-shirts, a few of them skirts.

A tall woman with dark braided hair seemed to be running things.

"I was supposed to bring some chili?"

With one wrist, she pushed a strand of hair off her forehead. "Set it there. You came with Max?"

"I did, yeah."

She gave him a quick eying-over. "You'll be okay. These boys are respectful once they get to know you."

He was putting it together. Was there anyone else here who was gay, besides Max? He guessed at most one or two.

Friday night, some people weren't there yet. Max had come early to help plan and set up. The main ritual was Saturday. Tonight was a shared meal and a reading of the Poetic Edda, medieval Icelandic mythology, with music by a folk band that did Scandinavian tunes.

Finding a place by the bonfire, Gus filled himself with the chili, which the kitchen crew had put together from what everyone had brought. Max returned and sat down next to him, casually threw an arm around him. They got some blank looks, but someone passed a bottle of homemade mead. Gus took a mouthful, but the passer said, "Drink up!" so he took more. Max drank too.

His warm thigh lay beside Gus's. Gus smelled his skin, with a healthy bit of sweat.

Bruni stood to read from the Eddas. He had a deep, sonorous voice, not quite a bass. He read well, with pauses to let the meaning collect. Then the music started, fiddle in the lead. It sounded surprisingly like Celtic music.

Suddenly it had been a very long day.

"I think I'll go back to my tent," Gus whispered to Max.

"I might come by later. Okay if I wake you up?"

"Okay by me."

The music followed him into the darkness. Away from the fire, the night had gone chilly and damp. He had a flashlight, a big Maglite that was great for camping because it was hard to lose. He waited to turn it on, walking into the darkness using firelight to guide him as long as he could.

Then he stopped. Above the black trees arched a host of stars. The ancients had seen them like this, innumerable.

He flicked on his flashlight. He was almost to his tent when a voice came out of the darkness.

"Hey. Aren't you Max's friend?"

Another flashlight switched on. One scruffy Pack member stood in front; a couple more hung behind him.

"I am."

"Are you a faggot?"

This wasn't the time to fight bisexual erasure.

"I don't like that word used like that, but yeah."

The lead guy grinned, showing a missing tooth. "Max is a big guy, but he's not here to defend you."

"No," said Gus agreeably, "he's not."

If he ran into the forest, he'd get lost. If he ran to the fire for help, it might be no help. If he took them separately, surprised them, he might come out okay.

They were all about violence, all that boxing and wrestling.

They could dish it out, but could they take it?

Stepping up, with his Maglite hand he punched the lead guy in the nose. The guy bent over, spurting blood, and his flashlight fell into the grass.

Gus leaped out of his way, trying to get the other two lined up.

"What do you think you're doing, faggot?" A second Pack member in an Odin-patched vest came forward.

Gus hit him with a jab. This one landed a punch, but Gus gave him a side kick and he went down.

The first guy was back, the third guy beside him. Gus took a few steps to put the first Pack member between him and the third. His Maglite hand was getting battered, knuckles bloodied, but he hit the first guy in the nose again.

The Pack member fell to his knees, howling.

The third Pack guy jumped forward. Gus squared himself, eye out for the second guy, still a lump in the grass.

"Hey! What are you shitheads doing?"

The Pack member and Gus both turned toward the voice.

Another flashlight beam crossed Gus's. A burly older man stepped up. His deer-antler headdress said he wasn't a Pack member, but rather part of Odin's Hunt. If he joined the three bruisers, Gus was dead.

"Is this any way to welcome someone? We don't beat up guests in Odin's Hunt."

The third guy instantly dropped back. The older man shone his flashlight on each Pack member in turn. The first guy knelt in the grass, hands to his bleeding nose.

"Fuckin' faggot broke my nose, I think."

"Serves you right," the older man said. "You set on him three to one."

"He started it!"

"You sound like a five-year-old."

Running footsteps came, louder than the faint fiddle-tune. Another flashlight beam bounced across the grass.

It was Max. His gaze leaped from one to another man, taking in the scene.

He clapped Gus hard on the shoulder. "Good job."

He turned to the would-be bruisers. "Get out of here. Go to the medical tent, have them check out your nose." To the man in the deer-antler headdress, he said, "Thanks for stepping in, Hertyr."

"Your friend did all the hard work himself."

The second guy picked himself up and stepped forward.

"Sorry, dude. He's right, we shouldn't have done it. It was—"

"Dishonorable," Hertyr put in.

"Dishonorable. And Jason here paid for it. And so did I." He rubbed his side. "That was a solid kick you gave me."

Good, Gus thought to himself. *Remember that, fucker.*

"Shake hands?"

"Sure."

The older men's gaze heavy on them, the other two Pack members also shook Gus's hand. Then they shambled off toward the fire in search of nursing.

Hertyr turned to Gus and Max. "You can be pretty happy with this young man's performance." He made it sound as if Gus had aced some test. "Now I'm going to bed." Hertyr turned back toward his own tent.

Gus let out a long breath. Max drew him forward. Dropping his flashlight, he hugged him. Near darkness, only the stars for light.

"I didn't know you could fight."

"I took karate as a kid and in high school. Not very seriously."

"Seriously enough. You've got what it takes. You're a man."

Is that what Max called that?

But part of him was pleased.

Chapter 12

*M*ax went out again later—he still had ritual details to sort.

It was stuffy in the tent. After tossing and turning a while, Gus decided to sleep under the stars, mosquitos be damned. He dragged his mattress pad and sleeping bag out, found a flat space among the trees, and applied more insect repellent.

The starfield above glittered, and he held his breath.

He hadn't camped in ages. If nothing else, this was worth it for that.

Would Max be able to find him here?

He laughed to himself.

It was a test.

Unzipping his bag, Max bit him, hard, on the shoulder—deep and soothing, like massage.

Rolling his shoulders, Gus rose into the bite, into Max's body, onto all fours. Max, on all fours above him, grabbed him around the waist and held, pushing his body into Gus's, then stood up on his knees and took Gus's hips in his hands. Gus felt Max's hard cock between them.

"You want it, don't you?"

"Yes," he breathed.

Max grabbed his hair and pulled his head back. "I want to hear you say it."

"I want it!"

Gus could feel Max wanted to make him say it louder. But if he shouted—how much did Max not care that other people heard?

"Okay, boy. You got it."

Max took some lube and a condom out of his back pocket and pulled off Gus's underwear.

"Are you ready for this?"

He nodded.

Max reached forward and massaged Gus's cock, hard as wood. Desire, red-hot lava, flowed over him.

Behind him, Max nudged and pressed; then entered, and paused. Gus moaned under his breath, yearning flooding him. He wanted to be impaled.

The rhythm, the feeling poured over him. Max rocked gently, then harder. Gus put his hand to himself.

"I'll do that." Max took him in his hand, and all the feelings together engulfed him.

He came into Max's hand. A moment later Max

groaned, guttural. Max collapsed on top of him, driving him down into the sleeping bag, still impaled.

Darkness. The green smell of grass rose. In the air drifted a current of woodsmoke. Max on top of him weighed him down, like containment, like love.

After a minute or so, Max moved, wiped his hand on the grass.

They lay in silence a while longer. Then Max rolled off, into the grass, lay on his back staring at the stars.

"There's a perfection here," he said, dreamily. "The stars, Odin's Hunt sleeping around me." Gus saw the flash of the whites of his moving eyes in the darkness. "You here."

Gus mustered all his courage.

"Yeah. I feel it too."

Morning dawned, cold and Pacific Northwest overcast. Condensation made his sleeping bag's skin damp. Yellow alder leaves drooped.

Max was gone.

Gus dragged his bag back into the tent and attempted more sleep.

Enough sleep would be good. It was going to be a big day, with the ritual.

But after tossing and turning perhaps half an hour, he sat up again. No more sleep would come.

Coffee.

He dressed in a flannel shirt and jeans, found wool

socks and hiking boots, dressed, then located his camping food gear.

The smell of cooking smoke and bacon wafted to him. He followed his nose.

Over the cook-fire, a huge aluminum pot of oatmeal simmered. The same tall woman with dark braided hair was running the show, this morning in a Renaissance-fair-style green overdress, a white shift peeping out. He discreetly admired her lightly freckled breasts above the bodice. She caught him at it and grinned.

"Oatmeal?"

"Sure."

He held out his bowl, and she gave him a couple of dollops. Off to the side sat condiments; he added brown sugar, raisins, and milk to his bowl.

"There's some bacon left." With tongs, she laid a couple of rashers on the rim of his bowl. "I heard you got into a fight last night?"

News traveled fast.

"Nothing major."

"I heard you won."

He shrugged.

"I figured you could take care of yourself. Odin's Hunt respects that."

"Well, thanks."

Someone came up behind him, and he moved off, toward the coffee. He filled his cup and took a hot mouthful.

By the fire, a burly older man nodded to him. A few chunks of log made seats; Gus took one.

It was still early. Much of Odin's Hunt seemed to be

asleep, after staying up late drinking beer and mead. He shut his eyes a moment.

When heavy hand fell on his shoulder, he woke with a start.

It was Max, also with oatmeal and bacon. "Too early for you?"

"I'm not a fan of mornings. It's why I don't take early classes."

"Mmm." Sitting down next to him, Max reached out and squeezed his thigh. "I'm proud of you for last night. You proved yourself without any prompting from me. That's good."

"Thanks, I guess."

"Tonight is our big ritual. I wasn't going to ask about this, but I feel like you've stepped up. Are you interested in joining the Hunting Pack?"

"Can I think about it?"

"Sure."

Gus glanced over, but Max's face was neutral. "Get you some more coffee?"

"Sure."

His ass in jeans leaving always made Gus hot, jeans not tight but wrinkled at the knees, holding the shape of his butt. Gus's body still held the feeling of being fucked; his shoulders were pleasantly sore where Max had bitten him.

Max would like it if he joined, but he wanted to know more about the group first. The Hunt tilted right—that was obvious.

But did he have to fall in with the politics? Couldn't it just be social? He liked camping. He liked Northern ritual.

Max came up behind him, rubbed his shoulder, sitting down handed him a full cup of coffee.

He felt connection, the flow of love.

In the camp kitchen area, the kitchen lead stood with hands on hips, her green overdress snug from chest to hips on an hourglass frame. Max's gaze followed his.

"You like our Julia, huh?"

Sheepishly Gus nodded.

"I've sometimes wished I was attracted to women." Gus raised his eyebrows. "But I'm an androphile. I'm happy with that."

Now was the time.

"I do like women. I'm bi. I hope that's not a problem. I'm dating a woman, as a matter of fact, a freshman student."

Max shrugged. "I've been seeing a couple other people myself, not seriously." He looked across at the kitchen lead again. "After all, if you want children of your own body, the easiest way to do that is with a woman. I've certainly thought about that part." He grinned. "As it is, I travel light. I don't even own a dog."

You have me, Gus thought.

Was that true?

Rather than speaking, Gus leaned his body into Max's, the closest he wanted to come to snuggling in this space.

At twilight, everyone gathered at the main fire. Most wore some kind of Viking gear: heavy boots with fleece lining, cloaks pinned with iron-work brooches, men with long hair braided. Drumming started, on simple hide drums on wooden frames, a heartbeat.

Down a hill in a hollow, at another fire, the ritualists gathered. Two or three more drums beat there. Gus could hear toning—a low hum that rose, fell, and rose again, full of shouts and howls.

The crowd, maybe a hundred people, moved restlessly. Gus found himself beside Julia. "What happens next?" he asked.

"They'll give the signal, and we'll go down there, to the vé."

"The what?"

"The shrine."

The drumming at the vé picked up. A horn blew, and a man's voice called out, like a song: "Koma!" And twice again, "Koma! Koma!"

"He's calling us."

The gathered crowd walked down the long hill. The blue sky had darkened to indigo at the zenith, with no stars yet. Tall trees hemmed the space around the vé, alder leaves a flash of yellow. Behind the alders stood dark firs. At the crowd's edge, men held lit torches.

In the hollow, an altar stood, two piles of stones that between them held up a board. The center section held utensils: knives, a bowl, bottles of mead, and a couple of pitchers. To the sides, the altar was stacked in deer antlers. Against it lay a spear, by that a tin washtub. In front, between the altar and the people, a small fire flickered.

The bare-chested ritualists wore runes and sigils drawn

in black on faces, chests, arms. A black streak ran across their eyes; streaks of blood dripped from cuts on their arms.

Blood-magic.

Jake, his gothi name Ganefard, stepped forward, long dark hair braided under an antlered headdress. On his fore-hand and chest someone had drawn the rune Othala.

Blood and soil.

"We are gathered here for the ritual of Winter Nights."

He touched the altar with his hand. "This is the space of our ritual, always sacred to Odin, Thor, Freya, and the Northern gods." He raised the spear by the altar and pointed it aloft. "But I reaffirm our connection." He called the directions with the spear, pointing each way one by one, then set it aside.

"Now I call in our gods." A young woman stepped up, her mass of blonde hair firelit, holding a bottle of mead.

"I call Father Odin, All-Father," Ganefard continued. "Fráríði, the one who rides forth. Come to us for Winter Nights." He took the bottle of mead and poured a cup's worth, splashing, on the altar, then handed it back. "We give you our good mead." From the altar, he picked up the bowl, and tipped it; from it dripped something dark. "We give you our blood, symbol of our oaths. Hail the All-Father!"

"Hail the All-Father!" the crowd echoed.

He called Thor and Freya and continued, "For Winter Nights, we honor the spirits of the land and our ancestors. We open the door for the Wild Hunt, Odin's Hunt. We do this as makers of magic, who travel with the One-Eyed Hunter."

Raising the spear, he gave a blood-curdling shriek.

"We are Odin's Hunt!" The crowd replied. Twice more—the last time, even Gus yelled.

The girl with the mass of blonde hair stepped forward again, with another girl, her dark hair streaked with flame-color. From the bottles on the altar, they poured mead into two rune-painted pitchers.

A man stepped forward, another priest from his antler headpiece and regalia.

"Over this mead, I sing sacred songs to reclaim our fabled past." He raised his voice in what Gus guessed was Old Norse. Afterward, the girls walked the sanctified mead around to fill drinking horns and paper cups.

Gus took one. Twilight had turned to darkness; against it, the white cup shone blue. Lit torches ringed the vé now.

He tossed back the mead, tasting of original honey.

"The next step is to honor our ancestors and our gods with a sacrifice." The girls brought up the pitchers; Ganefard poured one into the other and raised the second above his head. "To the ancestors!" The crowd shouted in reply. Ganefard poured the mead onto a small stone side-altar and set the pitcher aside.

"Earlier today, our sacrifice was dedicated to the gods." Several men stepped forward to the altar from the crowd: Bruni the bear, Max, who went by Sigewulf for the Hunt, and a third who Gus didn't recognize.

"Move," Julia said to Gus, nudging him. He stepped aside to make way for a fourth man.

This man led a young male goat, not much more than a kid, with brown short fur and a black-striped face. The goat came easily on a rope leash; he knew the man who led him.

Ganefard pulled out the washtub, and the fourth man gently put the goat into it. The goat looked trustingly up into the man's eyes. Ganefard took the goat's horns, Max and the third man the goat's legs. Bruni picked up the big knife.

"We make this sacrifice," Ganefard said, "to Odin, to Freya, to Thor, and to our ancestors, with this gift ushering in the time of the Wild Hunt."

In the torchlight, Bruin raised a big knife, runes etched into the blade.

He sliced the goat's neck, once, twice. The blood ran down.

Held inverted above the tub by the men, the goat shuddered, and his eyes shut.

A wave of emotion passed over Gus, a heat of physical revulsion mixed with sorrow and anger. This was not okay. They couldn't do this.

Another voice spoke inside him. His ancestors had killed goats for food. He ate meat himself, probably prepared less humanely.

The goat bled into the tub. Ganefard bowed his head.

"We thank you, child of earth, for giving us the greatest gift. You honor us and our gods." Reaching into the pooling blood in the tub, with a fingerful he touched Bruni's forehead, drawing a rune, spear-shaped Tiwaz.

"King of the Hunt, leader of our warband, I name you Bruni Odin's son."

He turned to Max, dipped his finger again. "Strong fighter, brave leader, I name you Sigewulf Odin's son."

A ripple crossed the crowd. Those fully part of the Hunt, men and women, stepped forward to be blessed with blood.

Julia turned to Gus. "They will bless Odin's Hunt first," she said, "but then the Hunting Pack can come up. Or even the right visitors." Gus was about to draw back, but she put her hand on his arm. "You've shown you could be one of us. Come up with me. I will sponsor you."

He stared at her. The flame of a torch reflected in her eyes.

It wasn't a vow, or an oath. It was just goat's blood.

He didn't believe that. But he let the knowledge go.

Max wanted this.

He let Julia draw him forward.

Chapter 13

On a Sunday morning in late October, Joanie and Alyssa worked the coffee shop's opening shift. Outside hung an overcast sky, a winy scent of autumn in the heavy, wet air.

Inside, the chocolate-brown walls lay in half-shadow. Alyssa swept up front. She pushed a fall of blonde hair off her forehead and sighed. She seemed glum, but she'd never looked better—high color in her cheeks, form filled out from the bone-thin girl Joanie had met. Like a pre-Raphaelite Cinderella.

Technically Joanie was Alyssa's supervisor, though Alyssa did her job without much direction. "That's fine, Alyssa. Come help me in back."

Alyssa slid behind the counter. The back kitchen was just a long worktop for prep and some half-refrigerators to keep things handy. Joanie was patting chicken salad onto sandwiches.

"What do you need help with?" Alyssa asked.

"Nothing, really. I'm half-tempted to send you home. Though we might get a rush midday." She stared at the girl, frowning. "It's mostly—what's up with you? You look like someone died."

"Do I?" She collapsed onto a stool. "I guess I feel like that."

"What happened?"

"Gus disappeared."

Joanie's body revved up, a stress reaction.

"Why?"

"I don't know. That's the problem. Everything was going perfectly, and then he was just gone."

"Oh, honey." Wiping her hands on her apron, Joanie stood and hugged the girl. "How long ago did you guys talk last?"

"A couple weeks ago. We saw a movie; I slept over at his place. We left it that he was going to contact me. I didn't hear from him for a week, so I finally texted him. Nothing in return."

"Was he seeing someone else?"

"Yeah, actually, some guy." Alyssa looked down: pale-blue polish on her nails, moderately bitten. "I told him I didn't mind. I'm fine with being poly."

"Has he ghosted you before?" Alyssa shook her head. "I don't like it, but it could be a lot of things. I'd text him again. Especially since it's making you so miserable."

Alyssa scrunched up her face. "I don't want to run after him."

"If he likes you, it won't hurt anything. If he doesn't, and he's an asshole, who cares?"

Leaning, Joanie peered out at the cafe. The only two customers had been there an hour. "If you want to leave early, I can cover."

Sitting on his bed, window propped open, Gus had just lit a joint when he got Alyssa's text.

<He owed her some kind of explanation.>

But what? He didn't know how to explain things to himself. He felt like the god of his life had lifted him up, into unknown places, then suddenly let him drop.

That night at the blót, among the torches, he'd gone up to the gothi, gotten a rune in goat blood on his forehead. For all he'd told himself otherwise, it meant something. The energy had thrilled through him; he'd felt a change. Max had fucked him that night like never before, leaving him bruised and satisfied.

But the next morning, Max sent him home with some other Pack members.

At Odinshof, midmorning, yellow sun blazed on the last alder leaves.

"This second night is only for initiated members of Odin's Hunt, with a very few members of the Pack. Then I'm going to stay down here a week or so, do some work on the longhouse before the rains set in."

"So it'll be a bit."

"You'll survive. You're a man." Max wore half a smile, but he meant it. Gus didn't know what to say.

Someone else might have thrown himself into classes and made dates with Alyssa. Gus spent two weeks drinking, watching porn, barely making his classes, and cutting marks into his legs.

That wasn't on Alyssa, though. She deserved better.

He made himself pick up his phone.

<Not a lot. Got plans for dinner? I'd like to see you, if you're into it>

And, after a moment: <*Sorry to disappear, a lot going on*>

That was a lie. But he didn't want to tell her he was depressed.

He wished he knew himself what was wrong. He knew Max wanted to see him, just needed to get some building done.

<Sure, I can do dinner>

He'd found the place in a restaurant app, Italian, with mirrors and chandeliers. He got there early and snagged a corner booth upholstered in red vinyl.

The door opened; light from the street poured in, and then she walked through the light. She wore an off-the-shoulder white bell-sleeved blouse, pink lipstick, and blue jeans. Her body language was hesitant, but when she saw him, she broke into a smile.

Why had he put this off? Why had he not wanted to

see her?

Relief made him loose. She was in a goofy mood. She made the breadsticks talk to each other and walk over and sniff him. She'd come in flip-flops, slipped them off, and massaged his crotch with her bare foot.

"So what did you do, disappearing for two weeks?" she asked.

"I went to my friend's pagan thing in the woods."

"How was it?"

He took another sip of house wine. A drop of red bled onto the white tablecloth. He looked away.

"Not good?"

He told the story. Her rapt gaze, her wide blue eyes on him held him up.

"The emotional lift and drop messed with you?" she asked. "And Max disappearing afterward?"

"I guess. And I don't know, I went into it backward. Usually, I don't insist on knowing everything ahead of time. But this time it wasn't good."

"The goat? I would be sad about the goat."

"Partly that, but not just that."

"Were they—I mean, they're your boyfriend's friends, but—"

"But they're not my friends. Except Max. And Max is—well, we're more sex partners than friends, really." He twirled the wine in his glass, pretending he cared about its scent (he'd been drinking it since he got there). "I think it's the combination of things. The ritual opened something." The connection with Max had also. "And then just as quickly, the door closed. And, honestly, I'm not quite sure what it opened to."

He knew she'd started to ask, were they white supremacists?

He didn't want to look at that now.

Back in his room, he left it dark but for a candle and streetlight. Drawing her to sit beside him on the bed, he lifted her hair with both hands, bound it together as she watched him, mouth open in an O. He tucked stray strands into the mass, then let it go and pulled her close to kiss her, eating her mouth as if he could enter her through it, a doorway, her lips.

He didn't have the energy for domination. Lying back, he pushed her head toward his crotch; sliding down the bed, she unzipped him and her mouth was on his cock. Heaven.

After a while she sat up, slipped a condom on him, and mounted him. He put up his hands to help her balance. He rocked his hips and she rode him. He reached up and cupped her small, perfect breasts.

A fall of streetlight, a wet breeze smelling of rain. "Chilly," she said, and lay down on top of him. He enveloped her in his arms. Rolling on top, he replanted his cock in her, riding till she cried out. Then he cried out too, spilling into her, release that was connection. He let himself down onto her warm and pliant body.

After, he wanted to tell her he was sorry for making her wait, but she'd fallen asleep.

He paused before blowing out the candle to watch her sleep a few moments: slender pale limbs, flushed cheeks, long lashes, half-open pale-pink lips. Like an angel on a card. If the angel were a great fuck.

Chapter 14

In spring, Daegal went to western Cumbria, to Ealdorman Adel, with a boy from his farm whose parents wanted him to see the world. Daegal was known as a good master.

They rode slowly through woods covering low hills. The oak forests shone in their new green leaves. They passed through small villages of thatched houses, where in the dooryards lambs leaped and played. Crossing the fells, Daegal and the boy scared a herd of wild ponies, long-forelocked, and watched them run. Each evening, they camped by one of the small lakes, mirrors that reflected moonrise, a pale moon on a pale pink sunset sky. Daegal's spirits lifted in spite of himself.

It marked a new beginning, a second chance. A new household. He would not let himself think, new women.

He didn't consider something like he'd had with Maelan —that was a thing apart. Though it appeared in his dreams.

The sun slipping westward, falling toward the trees. Semen on his tongue, a taste both salt and mint.

Once, twice, again, at night he cried out, woke sweating, hoping the boy hadn't heard him. But the boy slept soundly. The last coals murmured in ash; in his bedding he touched a sticky mess as orgasm waned.

Puabi-Ekur saw Daegal crossing Cumbria, and these dreams.

Sometimes the gods gave you problems that were too hard for you.

But the hints piled up.

This boy, this Gus, who once was Daegal, this fuck of that blonde girl's. Herne frightened her, the night of fall equinox. Hekate saved her.

From what?

Coming around a neck of trees, the sight hit him suddenly. A built hill, green-sided, rose up and up and up. On top stood Ealdorman Adel's hall, the biggest building Daegal had ever seen, at the center of the ealdorman's hill-fort.

The fort held a double-handful of buildings besides the great hall, and a double-walled stockade. The ealdorman traveled from place to place around his territory dispensing justice and collecting rents; this was his main seat and the finest of his halls. Perhaps fifty people lived in the hill-fort itself, another hundred and fifty or so in the village on the hill's lee side.

Daegal's father had sent ahead a letter, laboriously written out by the clerk, telling of Daegal's coming. Nevertheless he might have been forgotten.

A foot-soldier challenged Daegal at the gate of the stockade. "I am Daegal, son of Cedric, of east Cumbria. My father sent ahead. I am to pledge myself to Lord Adel."

The man looked him over appraisingly. "We can use good fighting men."

Daegal and his traveling companion stabled the horses. He took his time combing down his chestnut gelding. He didn't know what came next. As he got the horse a second forkful of hay, a small boy ran up. "Lord Daegal, you will be staying in the main hall, the boy with you as well."

At nightfall, he went to supper in the great hall.

High-braced arches held up pinewood rafters, leaving a middle aisle. Platforms stood to either side with trencher tables, now only half-full, mostly with the fighting men who would be his peers. The head table faced these, at which a tall, wrought chair, almost a throne, stood for the ealdorman. A smaller chair sat beside it for his lady wife.

As Daegal stepped through the main door at the hall's far end, the ealdorman entered too, from a door closer to his seat. Adel raised his arm and waved in greeting. "You must be Lord Daegal! Come sit with me."

Daegal sat down at his right hand. Adel was a muscular

man, broad-chested, probably in his thirties, heavily tattooed in the style of the northern tribes, unusual but not unheard of. He had a hooked nose, hazel eyes, and high cheekbones—a good-looking man.

"I have come to pledge to you, my lord."

"Yes. I had your father's letter. We will do the oath later, with the priest." A serving-woman set down before him a wooden bowl, roast pork with apricot jelly, in a bed of carrots, onions, and nuts. Another woman found him a mead-horn, silver-tipped like his host's.

He glanced across at the empty seat, where Adel's wife would sit.

"You may have heard, Lady Ermelind is about to bear my child. The midwives have kept her abed this fortnight."

"No, I had not heard, lord. All blessings."

"Thank you! Take some mead." Adel waved, and a woman poured out for Daegal. "This is one my personal steward makes, a pigment-mead, with imported spices. Try it." Daegal took a sip. He tasted cinnamon and clove. "Fine, is it not?"

"It is."

The hazel eyes, lit by the central fire, studied him.

"I like you, Daegal son of Cedric. The formal pledge is later, with the priest. But it moves me to ask you pledge to me now, man to man, with a toast."

It came now, before he had any measure of him. But perhaps this was how it must be.

"Very well, my lord." Daegal raised the horn, recalling the oath that his father's men made. "With these words, I make my pledge and become your man, giving you life and limb and truth and earthly honors, bearing arms to you against all men, so help me all the gods."

Adel raised his horn as well.

"I accept your allegiance and will do my part, supporting you and protecting you in all things, as is the ancient agreement, so help me all the gods."

They drank, each finishing his horn. A flush of heat rose from his belly as the alcohol hit. He glanced across at his host, who was staring at him.

A handsome man, a strong face. Adel had a reputation as a fair judge and a strong fighter.

His father wouldn't have sent him if he hadn't felt right about him.

But there are things one couldn't know, as with Reda—things underlying, that came out only over time. Shadow things.

uabi-Ekur stared at them. The oath of a warrior to his lord. Here they made it in mead. Earlier, it might have been blood: the blood of an animal, blood from one's own body.

Many times Puabi-Ekur had been a soldier. As Ekur, he'd been a general, fighting Inanna's wars. As Maelan, he'd been a warrior and ended up fighting his lover.

What did the deer charm mean?

They needed to know more about this boy Gus.

Who was Daegal, who was Gus now?

The answer wanted to rise. They could feel it. But then it would fog and blur.

"It's kind of fascinating, the problem you had with Herne. Because scholars think Herne links back to Wotan, who was the father god of the Anglo-Saxons. Who is another version of Odin, who is, obviously, the god ruling Odin's Hunt."

Alyssa and Gus had begun to approach each other, gingerly, about their mutual interest in pagan topics. Gus had wrung from Alyssa that her family were, in fact, German and Anglo-Saxon in heritage, in other words Germanic three times over.

That late Friday night, at Gus's apartment, he'd got her stoned; they got silly and flirty. They kissed like it was going out of style. They had a stupid half-kidding argument about karaoke—"I would never do it," he said.

"I bet you have a good voice."

"I don't."

"You should come sing pagan carols with us."

"Never." Finally he just put his hand over her mouth and unzipped her jeans, sliding his fingers past her underwear into her sticky wetness, and she went silent, whimpering.

As the candle burned, he fucked her slowly, twice. At last they were both exhausted. He had only enough energy to blow out the candle.

They woke to an overcast end-of-October morning. Winds pushed around white-edged clouds, which ripped to tatters, till blue sky showed.

She yawned and sat up. He loved her sweet breasts, with their pale-pink puffy nipples. "Have I asked you to Samhain?" she asked.

"I don't think so. Let's go get breakfast. I'm starving."

They stumbled out to find his favorite breakfast nook, all red-checked vinyl tablecloths and white-painted booths.

He had eggs, bacon, and hash browns. She had pancakes. He kissed her when the waitress wasn't looking.

"You should come to Samhain," she said. "It will be good. All about Hekate."

"Sure, I can do that."

"Halloween night. Then after that I know of a party."

"Sure."

He wasn't paying attention to a word she said, just looking at the way her tight white t-shirt hugged her chest. The form of her bra (candy-pink edged in lace) showed through the cloth.

She glanced one way then the other, then picked up her plate and licked it.

"Silly girl." He wanted to lick her and bite her. "Come back with me."

Back in bed, he laid his palm on her warm back, beside the mole there, and licked the line along her spine, down to her sweet ass. Flipping her over, he dove into her warm, wet pussy, licking. He felt utter closeness, breathing the same air. Her anticipation was edged with fear. His touch made her shiver. The feeling built and built till she came.

Sheathed in latex, he mounted her, riding, catching the rhythm. He orgasmed, a small explosion, shuddering. As the feeling melted, he let himself down to lie on top of her, amid a sweet fishy smell of sex. For a few moments he slept.

The movement of her checking her phone woke him. "I have to go," she said.

"I'll walk you to your bus stop." He kept thinking he'd get a motor scooter, but he was broke. He could get some kind of service job, but he'd rather live cheap while he could. But he and Alyssa had gone out four times that week. He needed at least to pay his own way.

The overcast had returned. It started to sprinkle. She only had on a thin hoodie; he took off his rain jacket and bundled her into it. On her, it bunched like a paper sack. At the bus shelter, he wrapped himself around her, kissing her.

"I do love you, you girl."

Her face was so close, her big blue eyes. "I love you too."

The coven held their Samhain ritual a couple of days early, in Hannah and Alyssa's basement. They'd draped the room in black and set out somber Halloween decorations, skulls and bones. Coveners had brought ancestor pictures, of dead parents and grandparents; some brought pictures of dead heroes or pets. People gathering brought down spiced cider or mulled wine in witch mugs.

Joanie came in quietly, wanting to be invisible, but Alyssa saw her.

"Joanie, this is Gus!" Alyssa, in a tight black velvet minidress, drew him forward, her arm linked into his. To Gus, she said, "You have Joanie to thank for my going to talk to you originally. And for texting you so we got back in touch. Really, you have Joanie to thank for our entire relationship."

"Well, thanks," Gus said, turning toward Joanie. He extended his hand.

She shook it. "Pleased to meet you!" She turned on a

shiny smile, wattage designed to cover hesitancy. She still was dubious about Gus. She couldn't say why.

Cleo, seeing them all together, came over and was introduced, her dark-brown eyes like searchlights on Gus. "So you're the new boy? Nice meeting you. We expect you to keep Alyssa happy, now."

"Cleo," Alyssa said, embarrassed.

A covener looked in from the top of the stairs. "Preritual discussion, five minutes!"

Joanie retreated, shutting herself into the half-bath—simple, white-walled. Hannah had hung up a pen-and-ink of a deer-antlered girl.

It wouldn't be the end of the world if she were late to the discussion.

Sitting on the closed toilet, she grounded and called in Puabi-Ekur, waiting till she felt their presence, almost saw them, a smoky ball in a ceiling corner.

"What do you think of Alyssa's new boy?"

"There is a pattern here. I just can't read it yet."

"I thought that was one of the benefits of being in the spirit world, that you can see things more clearly! Didn't you say that at some point?"

"Not always. But Hekate is here."

"Yeah? The ritual is for her."

"Listen to what she tells you, when she speaks."

After the circle calling, a covener doused the lights. Somber music played. One by one the circle members and Gus gave herb-offerings for the ancestors to the fire-cauldron. Lavender, myrrh, mugwort, and mint scented the air with sweet burning.

It was the Witches' New Year. Traditionally in the witch calendar, loosely based on the Celtic or Briton one, it was the last harvest festival, the culling of herds. It was also a time to honor the dead.

A bell rang; feet stepped down the stairs. A covener led in a figure draped in a sheer black veil.

Hekate. The goddess of witches.

One alcove was curtained off with a black hanging embroidered with a Hekate wheel, a winding serpent surrounding a spiral. The covener led the goddess behind the curtain.

Hannah stepped forward. "The goddess Hekate will give oracles. Before you enter her space, please burn some incense as an offering. She may wait for you to ask a question, or she may simply speak. While everyone comes before the goddess, please meditate quietly."

Dark ambient music played on a loop. The fire cauldron was out; a few candles burned.

Gus hung back, waiting. Alyssa sat cross-legged next to him. He contented himself with looking down her scooped neckline. Mostly he tried to meditate.

He hadn't been to a ritual in a long time. Once he'd been be a pretty good pagan boy, but that was a long time ago.

Then everyone had gone to see the goddess but him.

He stepped up to the draped curtain and shook resin onto the incense brazier, releasing a plume of smoke. Then he drew the cloth aside and entered.

The goddess sat on a draped chair, herself draped, with black candles to either side. He knelt.

He hadn't thought what to ask, but a question came to him.

"Lady Hekate, I recently began a new pagan path. But I'm torn about it. Someone I'm starting to care for is part of it. But I don't know that person well, and I don't know the group, and I have doubts. And yet what I get for guidance seems is to go forward."

Silence held for a moment, and then her voice came, low.

"There is something here, my child, a challenge for you from the gods. Choose wisely. Use discernment."

That was pretty generic.

"We each have many paths laid out for us. Sometimes the learning is to go through, to go down to the stones below the dark river, dive deep, and return to be reborn. You are a soul that has chosen this. And yet there are risks along the way. Even deadly risks. I shall give you a token."

Behind her in a basket lay a handful of black stones, he guessed basalt, each with a Hekate wheel cut into them. She reached for these and put one, cool and smooth, into his hand.

"Keep this on your person at all times, until you know you are safe to let it go." She folded his fingers over the stone in his palm. "You will know when." He gazed up into her veiled face.

The black sheer cloth obscured all but a shadow of her features. Yet he felt her gaze at him, as the goddess.

Chapter 16

fter the ritual ended, in the kitchen and shadowy living room a few people stood, drinking wine. A mix of scents arose, mulled wine and apple cider. Gus had thought that Alyssa would be in a hurry to go to her party. But she poured herself a glass of red wine, so he did too.

"What did Hekate tell you?" she asked him.

He didn't want to say. Because he thought he knew what it meant.

Eh, some pagan chick who thought she was possessed by a goddess, what did she know? He fingered the stone in his pocket. "What did she tell you?"

But he had paused too long, and she'd turned aside to ask Joanie. "What did Hekate tell you, if you want to say?"

Joanie had been late in the line to Hekate's darkened space. Now she entered.

The twin candles flickered. She knew the woman under the veil, and she knew too that she faced not that woman but Hekate.

"My lady," she said, and knelt.

"My child," the goddess said. "What would you ask of me?"

"I feel as if you helped save my life. I want to thank you again."

"You're welcome, my child."

Silence fell. The bittersweet scent of myrrh filled the space.

"I feel at a crossroads," Joanie said.

Of course, crossroads traditionally belonged to Hekate.

"I don't know what to do with my life. My goddess Inanna calls me, but I want to do something practical. I identify as a sacred whore, but I need something to make money, and it becomes less and less possible to do that kind of work."

"Is it?" the Lady asked. "If you have a goddess's blessing?"

"Maybe not. But also, I'm going to have this economics degree, and I don't know what to do with it. I was going to go on and get a master's, and do something to help map the economy of the future. But now I don't know."

A rustle as the lady moved. She placed a cool, smooth engraved stone in Joanie's palm.

"Go to a crossroads next new moon night and make the

traditional offering to me. At the appointed time, you will receive your answer."

In the pause, silence collected.

"Speak to your priestess. She will start you on your path. Never forget—you are for your people."

"Thank you, Lady Hekate."

Joanie bowed her head and folded her fingers around the stone.

"I asked about my future," Joanie said to Alyssa. Behind her head, over the sink, a couple of silly pagan plaques hung: "The witch is in!" "Beware: kitchen witch!" Hannah, when she put her mind to it, was a fabulous cook in the Southern tradition. "I want to know what to do with my degree. She suggested I talk to Hannah."

Hannah held court in the living room on her couch, under a Celtic-knot hanging. A few candles shed a golden half-light. One of the coveners was saying her goodbyes. After a flurry of hugs, Joanie sat down next to Hannah.

"Trisha did a great job as Hekate!" Joanie said.

"I was so proud. But you look like you're fixin' to ask a question."

"When I talked to Hekate, I asked about what I was going to do with my degree. You know I'd planned to go on and get a master's, but I'm doubting that now."

Hannah leveled a gaze at her. "Since you lost your income." Before her sugar daddy, Joanie had worked through an escort service, but that was gone too.

"Exactly. The oracle said a couple of things. She said I was for my people. And she said you'd have an opinion about what I should do."

"Huh." Hannah picked up her glass of white wine from the coffee table. Droplets beaded on the outside of the glass's bowl, catching bits of candlelight. "I guess I do. When you get this bachelor's degree, you know you have a number of options. Work in finance and so on. If I had to choose, I'd say you should do something for your community, for the witches."

Hannah hitched forward, pointing her finger for emphasis. "You know pagans and witches by and large are crap with money. So many people living on the edge! There must be something you can do in finance to help them. Even basic accounting would help."

Joanie turned it over in her mind.

"That work doesn't have to be everything. I know your heart's with Inanna. But having a couple strings to your bow's not a bad thing."

A dark throne sat among the stars, twin torches to either side. Flames flickered at the feet of the seated lady, reflecting redly from the key at her neck.

"Lady Hekate," said Puabi-Ekur, and made obeisance, kneeling before her.

"Puabi-Ekur." Dark humor hid in the tone. "It is understood, is it not, that one may ask for help?"

Puabi-Ekur bowed their head in answer.

The goddess rose from her throne. Her human form, like the throne hanging in space, was only a reference point, but even spirits made use of these anchors. "Come with me," she said. "I wish you to see something."

Taking the form of pure spirit, she gathered Puabi-Ekur to her. They went up and up and up, seeing below the web of interactions of all beings on earth, human, animal, plant, laid out like a golden net below them. The net was a field, dense in many dimensions, one being time. Even for a spirit, full comprehension of the field was fleeting. The goddess indicated one strand, which dove toward a nexus point.

"This direction," she said, "is the past, this the future." In the direction of the future, the whole field grew more dense and narrow, itself aiming for a nexus point.

"This thread is Gus, who was Daegal; this one yourself, who was Maelan. Here is where you fought, in human time centuries ago."

"Who died?"

"What concerns me is that it created this." She drew them closer to the golden net. "Here, this ball of karma, with all its attendant snarls. You see how it is linked —" she showed the linkage—"to Gus, Alyssa, and Joanie."

"Yes."

"And this." A thread less golden, glowing a smoky bronze, no less beautiful but different in kind, wound through. "A djinni, a challenger. You see this thread links back, too."

Puabi-Ekur studied this new thread.

She'd said they should ask for help.

"It's at the heart of the tangle," Puabi-Ekur said. "Perhaps it created it. Who is it?"

"As Soteira, I am concerned with the spiritual growth of all. The answer is yours to learn. But know this—once you find it, you have the means for change."

"Then this is my next task."

With a gentle push, the goddess sent Puabi-Ekur spinning, and the web of light and the space among the stars disappeared. Puabi-Ekur once again hovered over Joanie as she sipped wine.

"What do you think?" Joanie whispered.

Puabi-Ekur thought that Hekate hadn't told them much. Typical goddess approach.

"I think there's big ball of karma, and you, Alyssa, and Gus are all caught up with it. And there's someone else, who's central, who I haven't seen yet."

Joanie turned to Alyssa.

"What did Hekate tell you?"

Alyssa rubbed a finger along the top of her glass, releasing a ringing tone.

"It wasn't like a conversation," she said. "As soon as I was behind the curtain, I went into trance."

In the night journey, a waning moon hung over the earth. A howl rose in the distance, a dog or a wolf. The moonlight illumined a long path of gritty white sand. She was barefoot, in dark ragged clothing and cloak. In the distance, dark hills lay against a translucent black sky.

At the crossroads stood a small shrine, just an altar, the column upholding it marked with Hekate's wheel. On the altar, she put items as offerings: an onion, a chunk of bread, a metal cup with wine, some incense and its brazier.

Then she sat beside her offering, praying for the goddess to appear.

When the goddess did, she was a woman of late middle age, not a crone. She wore dark ragged clothing and bare feet. She motioned to Alyssa to follow her.

They climbed into the dark hills. Footsteps released spicy smells from herbs in the undergrowth. They came to a cave, a black mouth. The goddess lit a lamp, handed it to her, and gestured that she should enter.

She went forward. A little way from the mouth, a stream divided the cave floor. The gold lamp flame reflected in the black water. She entered a huge room, covered in ancient cave paintings of animals, especially deer, with an altar at the back. On the altar was a giant deer skull.

In a sphere of darkness, her tiny lamp held all light. Below passed a half-silent trickle of black water. Movements caught her eye, at the sides of her vision, but when she turned to face them they were gone.

Something moved up front, by the skull. The lamp didn't show much, so she went closer.

The skull was crying tears of blood.

A rustle, a slow release. Almost-silence. The flicker of the lamp flame, the coppery smell of blood. An impulse drew her closer, and she put her fingers into the blood.

It was warm, as if from a living body. As she touched it, a whisper rose, something trying to speak.

Subliminal, carried on thought, came a wish, a complication. "This is your blood too. You can help carry this."

Then the cave tore away like paper, and she was at the crossroads again.

A wind whispered around her, lifting and shaking her tattered skirts.

The goddess beside her spoke: "You stand again at a crossroads, one you have seen before. You have been here in other lives. You return to claim your power. And yet all power requires tests."

"And then?" Joanie asked. Gus didn't speak, willing to let Joanie drive.

"Then it was over," Alyssa said. "I was back in the alcove, with the goddess drawn down, sitting in front of me, silent. She handed me a stone, and I said good-bye and went out."

Joanie sipped her wine. Gus watched her.

"This is the second time in two sabbats you've gone into trance like this. Visionary streak, much? Come talk to Hannah."

They explained to Hannah, who turned things over in her mind, sitting in state on her bulgy couch under the Celtic knot hanging. "Alyssa, come here, darlin', sit by me." Alyssa did, shyly, stroking the grey velveteen couch with her fingers. Candlelight threaded gold through her hair. Gus perched on the wide arm of the couch next to her.

"I see a connection between the two visions." Alyssa looked blank. "You have a scary Herne, who is connected with deer, in one, and Hekate saves you from him. Then in the next you have Hekate, who leads you to a cave with a deer altar."

"I can see it," Alyssa said.

Now more than ever, Gus saw she needed to be with him. And maybe with the Hunting Pack. She could be a volva. In the northern traditions, a volva was a female diviner.

"I'm supposed to carry blood," Alyssa whispered. "I don't know what that means." Sliding close behind her, Gus put his arm around her. She started but then relaxed into him.

"The other part is clearer," Joanie said. "There's a test."

"That's not gonna make her feel better," Hannah said. "Alyssa, you may be gettin' a test, but like the goddess told you, you get a test to strengthen and prove your power. And it's not you alone. You have help. You have your coven, and you have your deities. Hekate is standing beside you, honey."

"I suppose," Alyssa whispered. "I feel like she's on my side. But she's also pretty frightening." Her fingers clutched the fabric of the couch.

"She's truly awesome, in the old sense," Hannah said. "She's a goddess. But I think you got an amazing vision! And of Hekate, goddess of the witches. It's got to be good luck." She turned to Joanie. "Joanie, honey, will you get me a bit more of that pinot grigio?" She held out her glass. "We can toast our Alyssa!"

Her glass filled, Hannah raised it. "To Alyssa, and her visions."

"To Alyssa!"

Light reflected off the clinked glasses, and Alyssa smiled tremulously.

Chapter 17

I'm glad we finally got out of there," Gus said.

They stood at a corner of the living room in a large University District house. A student house, its fireplace was decorated with orange and black streamers, and in the big bay window paper skeletons hung. Jack o' lanterns sat on nearly every surface. The room smelled of marijuana and slightly burnt pumpkin.

Around them, costumed people talked: a tiger, a cowboy, a pink fairy. Alyssa had thrown on a black cape lined with red satin and a witch's hat, Gus an evil clown mask, now at the back of his head. They had beer in red Solo cups from the back-porch keg, some kind of amber ale.

"Sure," said Alyssa. "I wanted to go out." She looked around vaguely. "There's Marjorie."

Wading through the room with apologies, they found one of two hostesses in the brightly lit kitchen, washing out a glass in the sink.

"Marjorie!"

"Alyssa!"

The girls hugged.

"What happened to Christa?"

"She got started too early, doing tequila shots with her boyfriend. They're both passed out in her room."

A purple zombie leaned in. "Hey, can you grab a towel? Dan spilled beer on the couch."

"Excuse me." Marjorie turned away.

Alyssa grimaced. "So much for introducing you to Christa."

"Yeah, I guess not." He caught sight of the door to the back porch. "Kind of hot in here. Want to go outside?"

In the corner of the narrow backyard, stood a portable firepit, cast-iron cut out with stars. They found lawn chairs and sat. Firelight flickered across Alyssa's face, which was blank.

Setting his beer in the scraggly grass, Gus picked up Alyssa's hand. "Where'd you go, baby girl?"

"What? Oh. Just zoning out."

"You do that a lot."

"I guess I do. Old self-protection device, from when I was a kid. It doesn't necessarily work."

All the girls he'd dated were damaged. Why should she be any different? He was damaged himself.

"Tell me about it."

"What do you want to know?"

~

She was her mother's only child. Early on, she'd thought her stepfather didn't like her. Later, he liked her too much.

Almost the worst of it was that it was in her own bedroom.

It tainted her poster of rainbow unicorns and the pale-pink walls. Her mother never understood her constant desire to sleep elsewhere: a closet, the living room couch, anywhere. The first magic she learned was cleansing, from wanting to cleanse her room.

She learned to go elsewhere, during. "I liked to go to a place I called fairytale dreamland, where the fairies took care of me. I got used to going away."

A tear trailed down her cheek.

Her stepfather had threatened to throw her out if she ever told. Finally, at fifteen she told and wasn't believed. That was when she ran away.

"Oh, Alyssa. I'm so sorry." Gus stood up from his chair and moved behind her, folding his arms around her, wrapping her and her lawn chair both in his embrace, leaning his cheek on her hair.

"It's in the past now. I don't have to see those people if I don't want to." Her mother had broken up with him, but never had believed her. She claimed not to understand why her daughter rarely came home for holidays.

Gus nodded, his cheek against her back, the plush of the velvet cape.

"You didn't have an easy time of it either," she said to him.

"No. But I was never raped."

"Anyway, that's how I learned to go away."

"You really are a visionary, though."

"I guess so. Other people have visions."

"This is the gift you got. No one should go through what you did. But at least you got something out of it."

"I guess."

They didn't stay much longer. After hugs good-bye for Marjorie, he walked Alyssa to the bus stop. The smoke smell of dead leaves floated on the night air. They traveled mostly in silence.

At the bus shelter, the overhanging roof shone wet from earlier drizzle. "You can come over if you like."

"I'm not in the mood." She threw her arms around him. "It's just—the vision, and the talk. I feel a bit down."

"I get it." He dove in, nuzzled her neck, squeezed her butt. "You're just candy to me. But I love you and want the best for you."

"I know." She cleared her throat and met his eyes. "I do know that. I just—"

She needed time alone.

"I understand."

The bus heaved into sight, lit blue-green, groaning and hissing, pulling to a stop with a squeal of brakes. A last hug, and she climbed the steps, slender form draped in black velvet disappearing behind the shut doors.

Back at his apartment, he pulled out his shoebox and got stoned.

He didn't feel done with the evening yet.

He was enough of a witch that he wanted something more, some magic. Lying on his bed, he opened his window to the night. The moon was a smudge of light behind slate-blue clouds.

After a few minutes watching the moon's hide-and-seek, he texted Max: <you around?>

Still in his clothes, black oxford shirt and black jeans, he fell asleep.

He woke at two a.m. to his phone ringing.

"You wanted to know if I was here? I just got back from Odinshof. You awake?"

"I am now."

The interior of Gus's room lay matte black. The window was open. The air was cold and smelled of weed.

"You should come over."

Almost, but not quite, it was an order.

He could say no. But he didn't want to.

"I'll be there in half an hour."

After a moment, he levered himself to standing, stumbled into his bathroom, and turned on his shower. He wanted the hot water to wake him up, to clean him for Max, and to wash off the smell of Alyssa's perfume.

He climbed the stairs to Max's apartment. A single bulb threw light sideways, long shadows falling from the bannister. In the stairwell, darkness floated like a kind of fog. Down the hall, he found the grey door that gave no information but a number. He knocked.

The door swung open, and Max stood there, silhouetted against the light thrown by a torchiere in the living room behind him.

Gus fell into Max's arms.

The feel of him, his strong arms, the warm healthy smell of a man underlying the spicy scent of bay rum.

He didn't have to pull any punches with Max. Max wasn't delicate. Whatever abuse he'd survived, the breaks had healed stronger.

"You're cleaned up?"

Gus nodded, his head against Max's shoulder.

He shucked his clothes; Max did too. Max pushed him onto the bed, covering him. The gunmetal coverlet lay sheened and smooth. Max's warm and hairy body, solid as warm stone.

Max got up. A container top flicked open, slick of lube on the condom.

Gently, slowly, Max entered, letting Gus's body ready itself.

Then he rammed in, and Gus gasped.

He'd needed this so much.

Max grabbed his cock and pumped. Barely two minutes, and he exploded: blue-white light like a Roman candle in his head, in his body, coursing through him. Max came too, shouting. They fell together to the bed.

Max pulled off the condom and tossed it.

Grabbing Max's arms, he drew them around him, and they slept.

Puabi-Ekur watched the sleeping lovers from several dimensions away.

The fog of darkness through which Gus made his way to this place—it had a djinni feel.

Along the way to their current alliance with Hekate, Puabi-Ekur had fought the djinn, one personified as Joanie's sugar daddy. Djinn were often challengers, not always evil —Puabi-Ekur could be described as a djinni. Puabi-Ekur had gotten a sense for these challengers.

They couldn't be too hasty, though.

Gus woke midmorning to the smell of bacon and stared a moment at the white ceiling.

After a moment, he realized he was at Max's.

Grabbing his phone, he sat up. Eight a.m. He didn't need to be in class till twelve-thirty. He let himself fall back to the bed again.

The sweet smell of ass sex hung in the air. He luxuriated on sheets clean and smooth, fluffy comforter lapping him, letting his eyes shut again, feigning sleep.

A creak, the bed indented; Max sat beside him with a plate of bacon and a cup of coffee. "Ready to get up?"

Gus pushed himself up sitting, leaning against the pillow. "For you, anytime."

Max grinned. "Eat as much bacon as you want. I can always make more." He set the bacon on the side table. "I figured you'd want this, too." He handed Gus the cup.

He took a hot sip. "Thank you."

Warmth radiated through him.

Coffee is life.

Max sat watching him.

"Tell me about the work at Odinshof. Did you finish the hall?"

"We got the walls up and put on a tarp to cover the roof. We'll put on the actual roof next spring. We also had a small council of elders, which is what kept me so long."

"About?"

"Business. A lot is boring. Full members pay dues, and we have a fund. We decide what to do with it. In this case, one of our members is a roofer, and he fell off a roof and won't be able to work for six months. We voted to give his family money."

"How did you take so much time off work?" Max had been gone nearly three weeks. He was a part-time fitness trainer and tattoo artist, both jobs with a lot of flex, but he was still an employee.

"I had some vacation at the CrossFit place, and I had someone cover some shifts, both places." Max smacked Gus's hip, hard, possessively. "Speaking of work, I've got to get out of here, but can you meet me for dinner here tonight? Now that you're part of the Pack, I have some ideas for you."

"Okay. Give me a hint?"

"Wait for tonight."

The next to last night in October, it was overcast and windy. Rain hung in the air, but only a few sprinkles fell. On the walk to Max's, the streets were full of shadows. Gus kept seeing movement in his peripheral vision, but when he turned nothing was there.

The witches said that the veils were thin, this time of year.

Whatever.

Coming in to Max's building, on Max's stairway, the bannister threw long striped shadows, very film noir. The darkness in the corners hung like fog. It set his nerves on edge.

His grandma would have said there was evil in this house. But then, she'd also have said Max, his big hot gay man, was evil.

Max served him pasta with marinara sauce he'd made himself. They ate propped on stools at the kitchen counter. They were both hungry, and dinner was nearly silent. Half-light fell from the living-room torchiere, and Max lit a big three-wicked orange candle that cast flickering shadows.

Afterward, Max gave him a beer in the living room, which was tiny, besides the light just a charcoal-grey leather couch, a glass-topped coffee table, and a bookcase, mostly philosophy and fiction. Gus snuggled up to Max on the couch.

"Don't get too comfortable," Max said. "There may be something to do tonight." He took a sip from his bottle, then set it down on the table, turning toward Gus.

"You've seen Odinshof and our ritual there. You see we haven't excluded anyone, though our rituals are based on Northern models and naturally attract people with roots in that culture. Yes?" Gus nodded.

"I'm interested in people of strong moral fiber, who are willing to fight for what they care about, physically as well as talking about it, interested in living in what I'd call the old, tribal way. I'm not interested in what the media calls white nationalism. Most white nationalists I've met are spineless morons who only want to fight among themselves. It's disgusting."

Gus nodded again, not sure where this was going.

"Take a look at this." Max tapped his phone and called up a story on a local Antifa blog. The headline read, "Odin's Hunt: a Fascist 'Tribe' in Seattle."

Gus scanned the story.

The term seemed a bit harsh. Nothing the Hunt had said or done was overtly about fascism. Though to be fair, he'd barely seen what they did, and there was almost certainly a lot hidden.

"It's bad press, but everyone gets that. What's the deal?"

Something in Max's face told him Max didn't plan to write a letter to the editor. "This man, Rob, who wrote this —" Max pointed a finger at the name on-screen— "he used to be a friend of mine. He knows very well I'm not a fascist. I think I need to teach him a lesson."

Uh-oh.

Max eyed him, glowering. "I know what you're thinking. And I wouldn't mind knocking his head against the wall. But I'm more interested in sending a message." He grinned. "Come with me."

Tucked beside the kitchen counter was a cooler. Max flung the lid open. In it was a plastic bag of what looked like rump roast, the bag's interior daubed thickly with blood. Max took this to the empty kitchen sink.

He pulled out a severed goat's head. It dripped blood and smelled like rotting meat.

"That's pretty gross."

"I'm going to leave it on his pillow."

Gus wrinkled his nose, from the smell and from the idea. Did Max really want to do this? It was a cinematic reference, sure. But it was still over the line. "That's barbaric."

Max glared. "Barbaric?! You're missing the point. Yes, it's barbaric! What do you think getting back to the tribal level means? It's not for pussies."

Tossing the head back in the bag, he turned back to the living room. Gus followed him, at his gesture dropped back onto the couch. The smell of rotting meat traveled with them.

"Are you with me or not? If we're really going to be tribal —we're really going to be tribal. Understand? I'm not kidding. What do you think these next years are going to look like? We all know the world is falling apart. I want a tribe, a strong tribe, who knows the old ways, who are loyal to each other. That's what I want, and that's what I'm building."

Gus stared at him.

Max in his vehemence was hotter than ever.

"Sure. I want a tribe myself." Who doesn't? "I believe in the old gods. And you're right. We all know the world is falling apart."

"Then come with me tonight. I know where this guy lives. No one's getting hurt. He just gets a message."

This was just wrong. If you had a difference with someone, you worked it out, or tried to. You didn't leave an animal head in their bed.

A moment, two moments passed. They gazed at each other.

He saw, with diamond clarity, that if he didn't come with Max now, there'd be no Max in his life.

He wasn't ready for that.

Chapter 18

Gus had done his share of night vandalism in high school. He turned off his mind and let go.

Max, dressed all in black, gave him a black pullover to wear. He was already wearing black jeans. "I've got a pretty good idea of how to get into his apartment. It's an old building. I can jimmy the lock with my kit. I need you to play lookout."

"How do I let you know if someone's coming?"

"How about, 'Your laundry's done'?"

They trundled down the stairs, Max with the wrapped goat head in a black-cloth grocery bag. In Max's aura, the stairwell seemed even more witchy, long black tendrils of shadow cast from the bannister. But Max himself felt protective.

They dove out into the windy night. Streetlights cast shadows; leaves unpiled themselves, rustling, traveling on the wind. Max walked fast. Gus half-ran to stay beside him.

Gus had just started to warm up from the exercise when they came to a nineteen-twenties-era apartment building, yellow brick, copperplate-font name above its polished oak door. They lounged, talking, in front, till someone opened that door. Max caught it as it hung half-open, and Gus followed him into the building.

Incandescent bulbs lit the long halls yellow. Gus smelled onions cooking.

"There." Apartment 212.

Over the knob lock, the door had a deadbolt. Kneeling, Max pulled out a tool from his lock kit and picked at the lock—clicks and tapping, but no opening.

Steps sounded on the stairs.

Shit.

"Dude, your laundry is ready."

Max dropped his lock kit in the bag. "Did you want to get a load in?"

A weary-looking grey man passed carrying a load of groceries. He shut his apartment door behind him. Gus smirked. "I didn't think that was an option."

"It's not." Max bit him hard on the shoulder and went back to work.

Several other people passed, forcing them to pause. The whole thing was taking too long. "Plan B."

They retreated out to a narrow walkway between the yellow-brick building and the next. "See that window?" On the second story, it was half-open. A narrow juniper tree leaned by it, trained against the wall. "I can get up the tree. Pretty easy to get inside. Keep a lookout."

"What's our signal now?"

"How about, 'You proved your point! You can climb a tree.'"

"And if you're coming down?"

Max thought a moment. "'You're a lunatic. That's why we have stairs.' I can jump it."

Tall laurels cast shadow, sealing the walkway into darkness. In ninety seconds, using the tree and the wall, Max laddered up. With a yank, he opened the window and was half-through. A few seconds more, and his wiggling legs disappeared.

On the sidewalk, Gus watched the apartment house as if waiting for someone, periodically glancing at his phone. A car parked, and a man jumped out and went into the building. A woman stepped by in high heels, walking a pug that eyed Gus distrustfully but didn't bark.

Max poked his head out. The woman wasn't clear. "You're a lunatic, dude," Gus said.

They locked eyes. This was sexy—partners in crime.

Then Gus heard a door open behind Max.

Max's eyes went wide. He glanced backward, then turned and jumped. He hit hard on the grass, falling into a crouch, then stood shaking his head. The woman at the corner didn't notice.

"Run!" Max gasped.

They ran. Behind them, a man's voice yelled, "You fucker, what did you do to my bed?!"

Down an alley, turn, down another street. They turned the corner into a flare of blue-green streetlight. They were coming to a major thoroughfare. "Keep going?"

"Yes."

One block along the well-lit road, they ducked again into the trees.

Gus was wearing out, but Max just kept going. He had to run all the time. Gus kept up. Four blocks, five blocks, they ran, getting sideways glances from passers-by. They should have worn running clothes.

Max led him into an alley between two buildings, square-built new construction, and stopped. Gus leaned over, panting. Max went to the corner of the building.

"See anything?"

"No."

"Do you think he knew who you were?"

"Hard to tell." A moment or two. Max scanned the street. "I don't think he's after us."

"What do you think he'll do?"

"Eh, he's a leftist wimp. He'll do nothing." He stood up, breathing hard, and coughed. "Come on, let's go."

At the corner of the alley, Max stuffed the cloth bag into a dumpster. Walking fast, they doubled back to the university-area main drag. It took some time for Gus's breathing to even out.

"Buy you a beer?" Max asked.

"Sure."

They ducked into the Leviathan, lit only by a few beer signs and fluorescent strips above the bar. In the shadows, conversation murmured, people leaning over their drinks.

Max took a mouthful of beer and wiped his lips. Scanning Gus, he said, "You're good in a tight spot."

Gus felt his face go warm. "Thanks."

Chapter 19

Mid-morning, mist lay in the valley below the hill-fort, floating in wisps above the trees' new green. A lamb's loud baaing carried on the breeze. On the hilltop, a space was set aside, with straw thrown down for traction in the mud.

When he left home, Daegal had brought the sword his father's smith had made him, one of his few possessions: patterned iron, lovingly sharpened. Now he settled himself, sword in hand, scuffing a place in the straw with his feet.

His opponent was Romulf, master of arms to Ealdorman Adel's fifty-odd personal fighters. Romulf walked up, without swagger, strong, an easy movement.

"Show me what you are made of," he said.

Then Romulf came at him.

Sword rang on sword. They traded thrust and parry. Daegal moved from guard to guard, occasionally going on the offensive. They tried each other's weaknesses. Daegal knew it was just a trial; Romulf didn't intend to wound him.

As they fought, Romulf talked.

"You are good. Have you fought in battle?"

"Once." He'd been in a skirmish, fighting off a raid on his father's cattle, one summer years before.

"Have you killed a man?"

"I have."

The lands next to his father's belonged to a gesith who was a known bully and thief. This man put it about that Daegal's father had stolen his cows. Everyone knew it was a lie, a premise for a raid. Daegal's father's men made a practice of bringing the cattle home at night, and Daegal and his father's men set watch.

One night they came.

In the darkness, suddenly shouting erupted. He ran up, wading into the fray. As his father's other men beat raiders back, a big red-faced fighter charged him. One lop of his sword and the man was on the ground, bleeding from a nearly severed arm. He'd been told the man died of the wound.

Daegal narrowly avoided a swipe of Romulf's sword.

"Keep your head in the fight!"

How long was he going to keep going? Maybe he wanted to know about Daegal's stamina.

With a grunt, he pressed Romulf hard. Now there was no talking, only the clang of metal. Back, and back, and back, till they were about to go too far, to the common outdoor space, where people passed and in the sun a couple of women, sat on a bit of cloth, sewing.

"Stop!" Romulf called.

Daegal sensed movement behind him. A hand clapped his shoulder.

"Good work!"

It was Ealdorman Adel.

Despite the morning, the tall blue sky, the smell of fresh grass, somehow Adel's hazel eyes said darkness.

Seeing nothing else to do, Daegal bowed.

That night, supper was served in the great hall after sunset, to perhaps forty men and a few women, several of them noble ladies who companioned the ealdorman's wife. Many of the ealdorman's fighting men lived in the village with families and ate there; only a double handful lived in the annexes and ate with the ealdorman.

The great wagon-wheel hanging lamps, full of tallow candles, were half-lit, and the room was full of shadows. Daegal took a place at one of the tables on a side platform. He had a nodding acquaintance with the fighting man beside whom he sat.

A serving woman gave him a wooden bowl with the night's meal, nothing fancy—venison stew with onions and turnips, bread, the salad greens plentiful in middle spring. The fire in the center of the hall radiated heat, and he began to warm up. He'd been moving all day, outside in the spring chill, continuing to train after his sparring match with Romulf. Now he let himself be lulled into a haze of warmth and food.

But when the ealdorman entered at the head of the hall, he called to Daegal.

"Come! Lord Daegal! Come sit by me."

He wished Adel wouldn't single him out. The other men would be envious.

His current neighbor gave him a raised eyebrow as he stood. Daegal shrugged and went to the head table, carrying his bowl.

He sat, and another serving woman brought him a horn, silver-tipped like the ealdorman's. Leaning, she filled his and the lord's with mead. He'd seen her around, a tall girl with strawberry blonde hair; catching half a smile on her face as she served him, he smiled back, not letting his eyes slip to the bosom tenting her bodice. She stepped away.

The ealdorman had caught the look. "Do you like our Heidelinde? I am sure something can be arranged."

Did he have to say that so loud?

Daegal glanced under his eyelids to see if the woman was out of earshot. "Thank you, my lord."

Tonight again the ealdorman had come to the table without his wife, who was still abed resting so she could bear a healthy child. Adel stared a moment at the mead in his horn, then tipped it back, waving at the girl for more. "Are you one for the women, Lord Daegal?"

There was no good answer for this.

"I was married, my lord, but my children died of fever, and my wife left me. It is why I decided to leave my father's land and be a fighter."

"I see. Do you miss being married?"

Daegal thought back to his marriage.

If Reda had only told him the truth to start, she could have saved them both a lot of pain. Perhaps she didn't know. "I try not to spend time regretting the past."

The tallow lights struck gold into the hazel eyes as the ealdorman studied Daegal.

"I understand that. I hope you can make a new start here. If you like fighting, there is no shortage of that!" He took another mouthful of mead. "Thanks to our neighbors to the west, in Rheged."

Adel seemed to need no response, so Daegal kept silent.

The dusk deepened. The hall had only a couple of windows, shutters propped for air, but somehow the darkness entered. Adel insisted Daegal he take second and third helpings of food, till he pushed back from the table. "No more."

"Very well. Yet drink with me, Daegal."

Was he always like this? He couldn't be. Adel and his men fought often and won. If Adel were a drunkard, he'd lose more regularly.

"Yes, my lord."

The tables slowly cleared as men went to bed, finding pallets along the walls. The serving women banked the fire. Then Heidelinde brought to the head table a big ceramic jar full of the mead they'd been drinking. "My lord, I must be up early. Kindly may I leave this with you?"

Adel nodded, eyelids lazy and low. "You have given fine service, Heidelinde. Get to your rest."

Heidelinde filled their horns again, curtseyed, and left out the door at the end of the hall. When she opened it to leave, it showed black night.

A wet spring air blew in, making the flames bow. Then the door closed.

An image passed, of her in his bed, strawberry blonde hair wrapped around his fist, those full breasts heaving. But not tonight.

"Tell me of yourself, Lord Daegal. You have been married, then. And before that, you were fostered in Rheged. Do you know that country well?"

"I was fostered due west of here, in the land of Lord Ronec."

"Ronec is a frequent foe of ours. Not this season, though. How did your father come to foster you there?"

"They had been friends as boys and kept the friendship. As you know, my lord, peace held then, more than now."

"Peace will come if the Britons of Rheged stop raiding, Lord Daegal."

Daegal was hardly going to argue that. "Just so, my lord."

Adel filled his own horn again, from the jar Heidelinde had left, and also Daegal's. If Daegal kept drinking like this, he wouldn't be able to walk to bed.

"Come, drink with me," Adel repeated, and tossed back a new mouthful.

The talk circled. The hazel eyes, a little blurred, fixed again on Daegal.

"Among the people of Rheged, it is said, the men have sexual congress with one another. Have you found that to be true, Daegal?"

He met Lord Adel's eyes.

"I know that such occurs, my lord."

They traded a long stare. "Mmm," Adel said, noncommittally. He stood, swaying a little. "I find myself unsteady on my feet, Daegal. I would ask you to help me to my bedchamber."

So this was where they were going.

The outside door had been left cracked. A breath of wet night wind slipped in again, circling the hall, the lights bending and flickering in its wake.

Daegal stood. He was a little less drunk than Adel. He put his shoulder into his lord's armpit, and they staggered for the nearest door.

Outside, in the chilly night, spring stars winked. Adel smelled of mead, not unpleasantly. The idea of Maelan flashed across Daegal's mind, and he set it aside.

Adel's bedchamber was in a nearby side-hall, separate from his wife's. Rushes lay on its floor, in its center a box bed with a fox-fur coverlet.

He could tip him in and run away.

But no. He lowered Adel gently among the linens, and as he expected, Adel grabbed his arm.

"Lie with me tonight, Daegal."

"My lord, I—"

"Do not say me nay, Daegal. It is a needful thing."

He wished Adel would use his hand and go to sleep.

But he didn't say that. Instead, he pulled his tunic over his head and stepped out of his boots.

Afterward, he silently left the bedchamber. The moon had set, to a scattering of stars. The hilltop where the fort stood was easy to navigate. He found the hall and his own bedding.

There he lay awake.

When he was a boy, they'd talked of serving a poor master as whoring themselves. But this was different.

It wasn't without pleasure, the act. And he didn't hate Adel.

But his heart stung.

There was pleasure, and a little caring. He'd taken care of Adel.

But to be made into a thing?

Chapter 20

$\mathcal{A}$t the beginning of November, Max invited Gus to the upcoming monthly meeting of Odin's Hunt with the Hunting Pack. This time, Gus wanted to invite Alyssa.

He walked to Max's apartment through November mist. The trees loomed out of it, black against fog lit white by streetlights. The night held a feeling of waiting.

Now was the time to bring Alyssa in. He wanted her to be part of his spirituality. She was a medium. Maybe she could be a volva.

Max buzzed him in. On the scary staircase, the bannister shadows reached for him like claws. He ran up quickly, ignoring them, found Max's anonymous door, knocked.

Max opened it with one hand, with the other tapping his phone with his thumb. He gave Gus a one-armed hug. "I was just talking to my lawyer," he said casually.

Gus swallowed hard. This kind of thing wasn't in his experience. "What about?"

"Take a look at this."

He handed Gus the phone. The Antifa blog displayed. The headline was "Break-in by White Nationalists," and the story named Max as potentially the person who broke in.

A cold trickle ran over Gus's heart. He hoped no one had seen him at the apartment.

He handed the phone back to Max.

"That's libel, if he can't make it stick."

"Yeah. That's why I was talking to my lawyer."

"Do you think this guy is going to press breaking and entering charges?"

"Nah. He's all talk. You want to go have dinner?"

"Um—" Gus was flat broke, living on beans and rice till his next student loan installment came. Scanning his face, Max half-smirked.

"I'll buy you dinner, if I can fuck you later."

They were breathing the same air. Max's scent hovered, mixed with bay rum.

"You can always fuck me," Gus whispered. Since it was true, it didn't matter about dinner.

Max laughed.

They walked out into the November early evening, dusted with fog. Lights had an aureole. Red taillights shone like Christmas in the mist. Everything was quieter, set at a remove, though the sidewalks were full of people.

Max wanted a burger, so they went to a burger place. The restaurant was a long narrow space, with distressed wood stained grey, a shining aluminum open kitchen, and old-time sepia Seattle pictures on the walls. Max got a classic cheeseburger with bacon; Gus got the California burger, which featured avocado.

"Avocado is lawyer in Italian," Max said, "or, well, avvocato is. Though the etymology is different."

"You've got lawyering on the brain," Gus observed. "Do you think it'll come to that?"

Max shook his head. Gus had been starving, so he devoted himself to his food for a while.

"You asked me to the next Pack meeting, and I'm excited to come, and I know it has a ritual piece to it. How would you feel about me bringing Alyssa? She's definitely got the witch thing going on." He described her vision at the coven Samhain.

Max mulled it over, sipping the amber ale he'd gotten. "She can't hang out with you the whole time, or even much of it. Pack business is pretty gendered. There's the women's auxiliary, and they'll welcome her, but she can't stay glued to your side."

"I get that. But she's got a talent. Is there a place for a volva, in Odin's Hunt?"

Max took another mouthful of ale. "It is a traditional role. We don't have anyone doing it right now, though. I don't know who could teach her. Our gothi does some seidr, some divination"—he looked up; Gus nodded, he knew the word—"but we've never had a woman train with him." They locked eyes. Max stared at him, intense. Gus wasn't sure what he was trying to get across.

Finally Max spoke. "If I were you, I'd wait a bit, ask Jake the gothi about it. Once you're more established in the group."

Gus turned this over in his mind. In any group, you had to wait a while before you suggested change. That was human nature. You had to bond with the group first.

"Okay."

They split a chocolate malt for dessert, then went out. So much fog, it threatened to condense on their skin. Gus drew close to Max, and Max took him under his arm.

They left the main drag for the quieter, darker side streets. A few leaves fell in a chilly breeze. Max grabbed his ass, squeezed hard; it felt good.

He wanted to bottom to him. He wanted Max inside him. The engine of horniness started, warming his blood.

There came a yell: "There he is!"

Down the street, silhouetted against a glare of headlights from a passing car, stood a group of five men.

Max and Gus exchanged a glance.

Antifa.

It was almost always a better idea to run. They ran.

Clearly he was going to get in shape if he stayed with Max.

"Head back to the apartment," Max said. "They won't fuck with us once we get in."

They both ran, flat out. It was only a handful of blocks. Max pulled ahead, but only barely.

Adrenaline rush. Cold, black air. The apartment building was in sight. They would make it.

Then, a puddle, wet leaves. Despite the rubber on his soles, Gus hit a slick spot, slid, and fell backward. His head hit the concrete.

For a moment, longer maybe, blackness.

He came to with the Antifa guys surrounding him. Again silhouetted against the light, so he could barely see their faces. He felt sick and woozy, limp.

"Who is this fucker?"

"He was with Max."

"His new boyfriend."

One of them nudged his ribs with a steel-toed boot. "Another fucking Nazi."

"Yep."

At the sound of running footsteps, the Antifa turned to look.

Max caught the first with a punch to the jaw, an audible crack. The guy went down.

Another Antifa threw a punch at Max, who socked him. He went sideways, came back up at him.

Come on, wake up, Gus told himself.

He saw another guy about to leap at Max, grabbed him around the ankles. His momentum took him down. Crack of head on the hard pavement. The guy rolled, holding his head. Gus rolled into a ball and got himself standing, though he felt shaky.

Max was trading punches with one of the Antifa, with another of them about to come up from behind. Gus launched himself at him, not much caring how he landed, grabbed him around the waist, spun him to the ground. "Aah!"

Wet street shone in a gleam of streetlight. All the Antifa were down. Max caught his eye.

They ran, Gus lurching and stumbling. Max grabbed him, held him up. Up the steps, into the apartment building, closed the door. Gus stopped just inside, leaning against the yellow-ochre wall, half-folded over.

"I think I'm going to be sick."

"There's blood in your hair." Gus felt it trickling, coming down his neck. "Come upstairs and let me take a look at your head."

In the apartment bathroom, black-and-white checkered floor, simple white porcelain sink—it was a newish apartment, but classic taste—Max got out the rubbing alcohol and cleaned him up a bit.

"Hold still."

"Ow."

"Let me finish. There. How do you feel?"

"Like shit. Really sick to my stomach. But thanks." He didn't want to sound unappreciative.

"I should take you to the ER. When the coast is clear. Here, come out into the hall, there's a balcony that we can see from."

"Won't they be able to see us too?"

"Not if we're smart about it." Max led him into the hall. A shallow balcony lay behind a French door. Someone had set a group of potted palms and philodendron on the balcony. Two palms stood taller than the rest. Max stationed himself and Gus inside, behind these.

"Looks like they're gone," Gus said quietly.

"No, look." Max pointed. A lone man walked down the street, nonchalantly, toward the apartment building. "That's Pete. We used to be friends. He knows where I live."

They watched Pete approach, turn toward the building. A step through the orb of a streetlight showed he had bright red hair, close-cropped. He went out of sight under the balcony, which faced front.

"He's going to try the same trick we did, waiting for someone to let him in—the fucker," Max said. "I'll catch him and teach him a lesson. Wait here."

"Here, not the apartment?"

"There's a distant chance he'll make it to the apartment. Stay here."

Then Max was gone.

Gus was happy enough to stay by the balcony, door cracked for fresh air. The hallway smelled like stale cooked food, which made him a little sick. The air helped.

He heard the door open and close, then Max's footsteps.

"Hello, Pete, did you want something?" Then the sound of a punch.

Pete staggered backward into view. His hands covered his face.

"You motherfucker, Max." Pete dropped his hands. Blood was coming out of one nostril.

"You were going to kick my friend. You could've killed him."

"I wasn't. He was down. Have you entirely forgotten who I am?"

"Fucking Jonathan would've."

"Well, that's Jonathan. Not me." His hands went back to his face. "I was going to tell you something useful. But now I'm not. Fuck you very much, Max. And don't try jumping me as I walk away, or you'll get the fight of your life." Pete turned away and walked down the street, back the way he came. Slight scratch of leather soles on gritty pavement.

The footsteps faded into silence.

Gus heard the weight of someone coming up the stairs. He caught sight of Max before Max saw him.

Max's face sagged. He looked older. He'd jumped the gun on this one.

When Max reached the landing, Gus came forward and took Max in his arms. "Let's go back to the apartment. Even if it is a concussion, there's not much to do about it."

Max scanned him. "I should take you in."

"It's my call. You just need to keep me awake, as I understand it."

Their eyes met, and Max slowly grinned.

"I think I can do that."

In the bedroom, Max had lit a black candle in a dish, throwing shadows on the wall. The shadows were fucking, and so were they.

Max for all his roughness was a good lover, and he knew that Gus was a little broken this evening. So no fast movements, nothing harsh, just the long, slow impaling.

Slow, slow, long strokes, sweetly setting him on fire, Max

at the same time tugging on his cock. Slow and slow and slow. Melting.

Gus came into Max's hand, sticky, everything going white and black, almost passing out. In a dream above him, he heard Max yell.

He drifted off, only to wake to Max shaking him.

The room lay in shadow. A big poster, part red, part black, showed a half-naked, muscled man, from some German play Gus knew nothing about. The clock beside the bed (an antiquated thing, but Max was hitting middle age) in red LED numbers said three a.m.

"Let me see your pupils." Max shone a flashlight in his face.

"Ow. Stop that."

"Your eyes look fine. I wanted to make sure. It's a good idea to check periodically if I can wake you up."

"Internet research, huh? Do you believe everything on the internet?"

"Go back to sleep."

Chapter 21

ᚺ

For Daegal, the next two nights were a repeat, though with less mead.

Each evening, Adel asked him to sit and drink with him. Each night, he left Adel snoring among his fur coverlets and found his way back.

The side-eye from his fellow fighters got more extreme.

He was going to have to go elsewhere to get supper.

He found the head cook the next afternoon, after the midday meal, in the annex where he and his staff worked. "Do you have some bread and maybe dried meat? Or anything. I need to get up early the next few days. I want to go to bed before supper is served." His space in the main hall was screened off from the main aisle; as long he was abed before the meal, he should be fine.

The cook eyed him suspiciously from his pot over the fire. Smoke curled and floated out the open doorway. "Very well. Come here."

Leading him to a nearby building that served as a pantry, he gave him a rough linen bag and a generous amount of bread and, in a wooden tub covered with cheesecloth, goat's-milk cheese. "That should keep a few days." He led him back and gave him a bowlful of the cabbage soup from the earlier meal. "Have another bowl. 'Tis hearty."

Between this and some solo overnights in the woods, Daegal managed to absent himself from the great hall supper for nearly a week.

Spring was warming into summer. Each morning, he got up with the dawn and ran for a bit, through the waking village (menaced by geese and the occasional dog), into the green hills, making a wide loop. To build up strength, he carried a pack on his back, weighting it more each day with rocks.

Then after the usual morning sparring—he threw himself into it, wanting not to think—Romulf stopped him.

The other men wandered off. Nearing noon, the sun beating down, hot. Daegal had been sweating. He kept his peripheral vision engaged. He didn't want Adel sneaking up on him.

"You have been avoiding supper in the great hall," Romulf said. "Lord Adel wished me to ask you about it."

"Did he." He tried his best to keep his tone level.

"I can guess why." Romulf put a hand on Daegal's shoulder. "It is a hard place, where Lord Adel puts young men. One thing I can do to help, though it will put you in danger. I can send you on our raids into Rheged."

After a moment, Daegal nodded. It was why he was here, after all.

"I'll send you to one of our outposts, to Lord Wihtred."

Chapter 22

ᚺ

In early November, the first frosts dusted the grass with ice as the sun rose. Days were nippy and wet; Gus slogged to class through the rain. It had been a brilliant early autumn after a dry summer, the leaves golden and scarlet; now those golden flags fell wetly through the grey days.

Odin's Hunt and the Hunting Pack decided to have their monthly meeting down at Odinshof, over the weekend.

"I'm not sure this is the best one to bring your girl to," Max told Gus.

That night they had an evening in, at Max's. They'd fallen into a rhythm. Gus came over once or twice a week. Max lived within walking distance, which helped. The Pack had a weekly book club, and he accompanied Max to it, reading some recent works on runes. Gus usually saw Alyssa once a week.

Now Gus sat with Max on the charcoal-grey leather couch. They'd been binge-watching a horror show.

"It's generally open to invited people, but certain ones. Closer ones. Not newbies."

"That's kind of awkward. I already told her she was invited." He hadn't, but he wanted her to come. Maybe she could become their volva, over time.

Max shrugged. "If she's a typical feminist college girl, this won't be her thing. Almost any other of our rituals would be better. This won't be remotely vegan, for example. We're more flexible at a lot of them, but not this one."

Was he deliberately trying to make Gus angry?

No, this was just the kind of thing that was inside Max's head.

"She's not like you imagine her, Max." How to explain? "I told you I'm a switch. She fits my other side. She's a subby girl, pretty flexible. I wouldn't call her a feminist. Or at least, not beyond equal rights and so on."

"Odin's Hunt isn't against equal rights." Max took a swig of his beer. "But I'd say we consider the sexes separate but equal. Women have their sphere, and men have theirs. I can point you to a woman blogger on the subject, a poet. She expresses it well."

Separate but equal? That sounded bad.

"Look, why don't you meet her?" he asked Max. "You'll see what I mean. She's not someone who'd get up in arms about, say, a goat sacrifice or something. She might have some kind of reaction, but she won't make a scene. I want to show her the Odin's Hunt ritual. I think she might take to it. I don't want to make her feel blown off."

Max met his eyes. They traded a stare. A breath, two breaths, three passed.

"Okay, invite her. I trust you. You can answer her questions. There's just some ritual pieces we like to keep quiet. Like the goat sacrifice."

"I get it."

Gus and Alyssa met for pho, off the University District main drag, at a tiny shop whose interior walls were a cozy brown-green. The scent of the broth rose into the air as the server set down the bowls. Gus added cilantro, took his first mouthful, and felt the warmth suffuse him. He'd been cold all day, Pacific Northwest cold, the wet getting into his bones.

Alyssa looked at her bowl, stirring with her porcelain spoon. "I don't know. Camping outdoors in November?"

"Don't worry about the winter camping bit. I've got a good tent, and I can get us sleeping bags that work down to subzero temperatures. And I'll warm you up." Gus grinned.

"I hate being wet all the time."

"They keep the fires going. One of their projects is a wood-fired sauna. They may even have it done."

"Mmm." She concentrated on her soup a moment.

It took courage, but he said it. "I'd really like you to come."

They traded a look. He reached over, picked up her hand, and kissed it. She ducked her head—this was hard for her.

"I do want to meet your friends in Odin's Hunt," she said after a pause. "Maybe we can borrow one of my roommate's cars and drive down together."

"Maybe we could have a night beforehand in a motel or something. Somewhere cheap." His parents had given him a credit card to use in an emergency. A special occasion might count, just once.

"I'd like that," she said, smiling up into his eyes. "I'm a little nervous about meeting your Max, I have to say. He sounds intimidating."

"You'll be fine." When Max had to deal with women, he tended toward the courtly—some older training raised its head. Gus imagined aunts or female cousins he had to be polite to. "I can't imagining you guys disagreeing with one another." Because Alyssa wouldn't talk at all.

"What about sleeping arrangements?"

"You'll sleep with me. A lot of the daytime we'll be separate, but we'll be together at night. I told Max that. There're people you'll like. There's this one woman, Julia, who runs the kitchens. She's been really nice to me."

Alyssa eyed him. "Do you like her?"

"She's easily forty!"

She laughed. "You really want this, don't you? I'll go." Picking up his hand, she pressed it to her cheek. "I'll go because you want me to."

Alyssa was able to borrow a car—an older white coupe, Hannah's. They drove down Thursday night as the grey sky went black, unleashing several inches of rain. They planned to stay overnight at a cheap hotel outside Olympia, more or less on the way to Odinshof.

"This is totally an emergency!" Alyssa said, as the elevator doors closed on them, going up to their floor. "Here we are, driving south, on our way to go camping, and it's pouring out and it's late and there's no chance we'll find the campground till tomorrow—"

"None whatsoever." He grabbed her, kissing her.

That night, he didn't dominate her. A wave of emotion rolled between them. When she came, she cried. He held her, kissing her.

The next morning dawned rain-washed and warmer. In the parking lot, the sun flashed off the remaining leaves, the last maple trees stained yellow-orange to red, as if the color had run in the rain.

"We don't have a long drive," he told her. "It doesn't much matter when we get there, as long as it's by nightfall."

"Take me there. We can walk in the woods."

He felt sunny with happiness, and yet the happiness felt fragile.

He wondered if Alyssa and Max would like each other, and if she would take to Odin's Hunt. He'd given her a general idea of the group, with few specifics. He wanted her to experience it for herself. Now he thought of the boxing matches that might greet them. How would she feel about the violence?

The coupe bounced along. They turned onto the side-road that led to the hof. Big maple leaves piled in the road, their golden now brown and wet, like mashed cardboard.

The scarlet leaves of the vine maples lay scattered. The Douglas firs stood tall, wet, and green. Under their draped branches, the sign for the turnoff to Odinshof peered out.

"Turn here."

The dirt road was rutted, full of mud puddles. Gus's tension rose as they came closer.

But when they pulled into the rough parking lot, a muddy square defined by logs on three sides, only one pickup had parked. Gus recognized it as Jake the gothi's.

"I guess we're early."

They climbed out and went up the gravel road to a clearing ringed by alder and Douglas fir. Off to the side, the hall was up now, missing only a formal roof, the hole covered by blue tarps.

Gus smelled smoke. As he walked past the woodpile, he saw in the clearing ahead a campfire, which Jake poked with a long stick.

"Hi!" Gus said, walking forward. "I guess we're a bit early?" Jake glanced from him to Alyssa and back. "This is Alyssa. Alyssa, this is Jake."

Jake nodded to them. "Might as well go put up your tent in the Pack space. You know where that is."

"Alyssa wanted to walk in the woods, since it looks like we have time. Do you have any suggestions?"

"If you go out to the turnoff, and walk up the road a half-mile, you'll come on an old logging road. That goes back into the back country a ways. It's supposed to be a clear day, or relatively clear. Only a little rain." He grinned. "Just keep making noise. There's bear around, but nothing to worry about—black bear."

"Thanks!"

They walked back to the truck to get their packs and sleeping bags.

Jake was a bit more friendly now than when Gus first met him with Max.

Finding a flat spot at the Pack meadow's edge, they set up their tent. Despite Alyssa's inclination not to camp in the rain, her neat, quick work made it clear she'd set up her share of tents.

Blonde hair up in a ponytail, she wore a dark-purple rain jacket and tight pale-blue jeans—eminently fuckable. Stepping around the tent, he grabbed her, took her butt in both hands, dragged her as close to him as he could, and kissed her wide-mouthed.

"So hot. So fucking edible."

He threw down one of the pads, a sleeping bag on top of it, her on top of that, and climbed on her, rubbing up against her. Her eyes shut. He pushed his hands up under her jacket and shirt. She snapped to attention, sat up. "Your hands are cold!"

"They'll warm up." He nuzzled her.

"Come on, we can't have sex here. People will be showing up. Let's take a walk!"

The logging road took a long, slow rise through grey-green lichened alders and thick Douglas fir. Underfoot was brown leaf cover, from dropped alder and maple leaves. The air smelled of rotting leaves and woodsmoke. The sky was a soft blue with intermittent smudges of white cloud. Bird-song warned of their approach.

"It's peaceful," she said. "Been a long time since I've been camping."

"Have you camped much?"

"My mom and stepfather used to take us. I tried to opt out, but because of him more than anything else." She looked aside. Her eyes glittered with tears.

"I'm sorry if it's a bad memory."

"I love the woods, though." She slipped her hand into his.

Among the trees, with her, he dropped some of the stress that always haunted him—his studies, the troubles of the world—and was simply present.

"You want to stop a moment?" Alyssa asked. "It's been a while since I've done so much walking."

"Sure." They settled at the base of a fir. She leaned back against him, head against his shoulder. He stroked her pale blonde hair.

A tock-tock-tocking sounded. "Is that a woodpecker?" she asked.

"There it is." He pointed. "The red head. Pileated wood-pecker. They come in mated pairs."

The woodpecker stopped, as if it had heard them. After a moment, it flew away, an undulating movement. Black, a white streak showed in flight, bright scarlet for its crest. Matching the flight, another bird flew off a close branch, following.

Alyssa snuggled close to him.

He loved Max, but there was something deep in his love

for her, in the possibility of family. He could introduce her to his parents.

But he didn't want to sell out a whole side of himself.

When they returned to camp, midafternoon, the parking lot had begun to fill in. Max's white truck was there. Gus swallowed hard and stepped forward, hand clasped hard on Alyssa's.

He found Max at the fire, sitting on a chunk of log. He had a bottle of mead by him, and as Gus came up, he took a long, contemplative pull on it, staring at the fire.

His eyes turned to Gus, and narrowed.

Gus stepped forward. "Max! This is Alyssa."

Max stood. Alyssa shyly put her hand forward, and they shook hands.

"Hi," she said, brushing a strand of blonde hair out of her eyes.

Max glanced at Gus under his eyebrows, a dark look, complicated.

"I think we're going to meet tonight in the new hall. Did you two get a chance to see it? Let me take you over there."

They entered the shadowy doorway. Looking up, Gus was impressed.

High-braced arches held up pinewood rafters, through which blue tarps showed. The arches left a middle aisle. "It's not nearly as large a hall as early Germanic folk might build," Max said, "say the Angles and the Saxons in Britain. But it's the same design."

"It's beautiful," Alyssa breathed.

"Thank you," Max said.

A set of picnic tables stood end-to-end along the central aisle. "We'll meet in here tonight. A short business meeting, then a ritual." A firepit stood in the center, vented mostly by the doors. "It's traditional. It gets a little smoky." He peered under his eyebrows at Alyssa, but she said nothing.

Blue-tinged light fell on them, the blue cast from the tarps above.

A shout rose outside, many voices together. Max's gaze turned toward it.

"The first boxing match must have started." He turned back to Gus and Alyssa. "I should go watch. I used to be an amateur boxer, briefly, and I coached one of the guys." He headed toward the cheering. Gus and Alyssa followed, more slowly.

Chapter 23

H

Four ropes set off the boxing ring, blond grass ripped up to mud. A couple of young men in their twenties traded blows. Max hunkered in one corner, eyes glued to his trainee, watching every move.

Jealousy flared for Gus. This had to be one of the guys Max was fucking.

One boxer landed a blow to the face. A scrape opened up on the opponent's cheek, and a drip of blood ran down.

The rain had stopped, leaving it warmer than it'd been all day. A god-ray of sun filtered through the firs. Alyssa sat beside Gus on a log, his coat under them to protect from the wet.

"I don't know how long I can watch this," she whispered. "I'm not a fan of blood sports."

"They don't damage each other. The idea is that everyone should learn to protect themselves." They traded a look. "Especially men. Women of course are vulnerable, but men are more likely to get physical assaulted, on the average."

She said nothing, only stroked his arm. Her thigh trembled against his, and he put his arm around her. A couple of times she winced. He was happy when the match ended.

Night came on. Dark slate blue clouds clotted above, streaked in the west with wild pink. The Pack and Hunt shared stew. Alyssa clung to Gus's side as they lined up for food at the improvised kitchen.

She couldn't stay by him all night. The ritual would almost certainly split them up. And he wanted a chance to be with Max, too.

As they shuffled forward in line, Gus saw Julia among the kitchen crew. She stepped forward.

"Hello! Who's this?" Gus introduced them. Alyssa smiled brightly. As she stepped ahead in line to get a hunk of homemade bread, Gus leaned in toward Julia.

"Max said there was a men's ritual tonight. Alyssa might want to go to bed early, but if not, can you make sure she's not stranded on her own?"

Julia's dark-brown eyes met his. "Sure."

The night grew dark. The tribe collected around the campfire. Compared to the last big ritual, Winter Nights, less regalia appeared, more jeans and flannel shirts. There were a few wool cloaks, some clasped with iron pins.

Bottles of mead made their way around. First came someone's metheglin, with cinnamon and clove. Alyssa took a double mouthful. "This is good!" she said. A bearded man across the circle nodded acknowledgement. Then black mead, made with currants.

Dinner finished; they washed and stashed their plates. A horn blew, signaling time to meet in the hall. Lit torches showed the way.

Gus strolled in the hall's direction, hand in Alyssa's, not thinking of much. So far the day had been pleasant, though oddly free of Max. Max had warned Gus that Alyssa couldn't cling to him, but he'd spent the whole time with her.

The door was thrown open. Inside, the fire smoked; the rafters collected darkness. Everyone filed in and sat at the picnic tables. When the door closed and the crowd settled, Bruni stood up before the group.

"Welcome to our new hall! This wouldn't be possible except with a lot of money and help!" He read out the helpers' names. "Now I'm going to ask you for more money." Everyone laughed. "If you followed the saga of the foundations and the building, you'll recall we ran into some unexpected problems." He went into details, and Gus zoned out.

He snapped back to attention when Jake stepped forward as gothi, as Ganefard. "Now we'll start the ritual part of this meeting."

Facing the line of tables where the crowd sat stood an altar, holding a metal bowl full of dark liquid, a mead bottle, a brown porcelain bowl, a drinking horn, and a knife. As at Winter Nights, Ganefard called to each of the directions, then welcomed in Odin, Thor, and Freya, pouring a libation of mead for each into the porcelain bowl.

"Now we have a dedication to do. I ask Josh, whom we call Wulf, to come forward." A tall young man with white-blond hair made his way to the front. "Make your oath."

Josh recited a long oath to Odin. When he finished, Ganefard dropped a leather thong with a rune around his neck. Taking up the bowl of liquid, Ganefard painted the same rune on Josh's forehead. Othala, blood and soil. A favorite of the Nazis.

They were way too fond of that rune.

"With this rune, I name and dedicate you a member of Odin's Hunt."

The gathering cheered for Josh. He sat, and Ganefard cleared his throat.

"We are in the time of the Wild Hunt, for which we're named—Odin's Hunt. We are in the space of makers of magic, makers of change, who travel with the One-Eyed Hunter." He looked around the room, then shouted, "We are Odin's Hunt!"

The crowd roared, "We are Odin's Hunt!"

He continued, "One of our number will come up and read a poem dedicated to Odin, to start getting us into ritual space for the evening to come. As often was so for our fore-bears, we will split into separate groups, one for men and one for women, and do the rest of our ritual separately. If you wish not to continue, there will be mead and music at the main fire."

The poem acted as a long dedication to Odin. Gus's mind wandered, but he saw the images in the air: Odin on Yggdrasil, sacrificed, himself to himself. The Wild Hunt, ghastly, riding the night sky below a full moon. Tonight, the moon was full, though as they'd approached the hall it had hidden behind clouds.

At the end, Ganefard stepped forward once more. "Hail Odin!"

"Hail Odin," the room resounded, in reply.

That seemed to be the cue to file out.

"What happens now?" Alyssa whispered.

"I don't know. Presumably they'll tell us at the door where we go next."

"I guess so." Gently she pulled him out of the line of people.

The firelight cast a moving shadow. He smelled her candy perfume. She kissed him deeply, as if she might never see him again. His mind said that was silly, but his heart felt it too.

He caught Max's eye on him.

"We should go now. I'll catch up with you later."

She nodded. At the doorway, they went their separate ways.

The group of men followed Ganefard, who carried a torch in his hand. Other torchbearers were interspersed along the line, with the final one at the end.

Past the torches, clouds rode, edge-lit pale by the hidden moon. The ragged line followed the path a long walk down into a hollow.

They stopped by a fire pit. One of the men stepped forward and set light to a fire laid there, which flared up.

A ring of men's faces appeared, illuminated from below by firelight.

Almost all the men there were full Odin's Hunt; most of the Pack had dropped out. Max had stepped up beside him, though, and Gus knew he wanted him there.

Bruni and Max had exchanged a look, when Gus joined the group. Max had said, "He's with me."

Now Ganefard said, "There are two levels to the mystery tonight. No one need take part, except if he chooses to."

Young blond Wulf stepped forward immediately. "I choose to!" Chuckles came from the men, and Ganefard smiled. "It's not time yet, Wulf, but I thank you." Wulf stepped back out of the firelight, face in shadow. Gus wondered if he were embarrassed.

"For the first part—we are Odin's Hunt, and tonight if we choose we can make personal blood sacrifice." Another man stepped forward, a big Bowie knife shining in firelight. "Alarad here will help you do this. His knife is sharp, and we make sure it's clean. Passing on disease would weaken Odin's Hunt."

The bearers brought their torches around and planted them in the ground, torchlight illuminating a tree stump made into a rough altar. A wide-mouthed wooden bowl sat prominent in the light, its belly carved with a ring of wolves and bears chasing each another. Beside the stump sat a bottle of rubbing alcohol and a yellow tube of antibiotic lotion.

"With this sacrifice, you can dedicate your work tonight to Odin, dedicate yourself to Odin for the night or for your lifetime, or simply offer the blood to our gods. Or whatever you choose. There is no coercion here."

Something about this last statement made the back of Gus's neck prickle. It sounded like one of those statements that meant its opposite. Like parents saying "I love you," when they meant, "I want to break you."

"Or you can step away. But if you choose to step away, now's the time."

The ring of men's faces lit by firelight didn't move. No one left.

One by one the men went up, received a nick to the finger or a slash on the palm. The latter gave a gush of blood and more pain. They bound up palms and fingers with gauze.

The night air carried whispered words. Some men kept their oaths to themselves. Gus chose to have his finger cut, and simply said, "To Odin," as he let the blood drip into the bowl, before Ganefard caught his finger and bound it.

"Have all made sacrifice?" Ganefard asked, looking around the group.

"All have made sacrifice," Alarad affirmed.

"There is a second level, to go deeper into Odin's mystery. We become his hunters."

All this time, Max had been across the fire from Gus. Gus assumed that meant that each stood alone in the ritual. Now Max crossed to stand behind him. His body's warmth entered Gus's space, and Gus relaxed.

"Hunters often, for practice, release an animal into the field for sport. They give the animal a head start, to make the game fair. We do this too."

He looked around the circle, from face to face.

"This game is not required. But, again, now is the time if you want to step away."

The men shuffled in place. They'd all passed multiple tests to get here; no one wanted to be the one to step away in fear.

Around them, too, were the elders of the group: Max, Ganefard, Bruni the bear, bare to the waist in the cold and wet, his muscled shoulders shining in light drizzle.

Gus hung back.

The warmth of Max's body lay behind him. Max was silent.

Eye glanced to eye, a flash of white against darkness. But no one left.

"Are you in?" Ganefard asked.

Wulf stepped forward immediately. He shone in the firelight, a young man in his beauty: white-blond hair, strong-muscled body, square shoulders. "I am!"

One by one, others joined him in the firelight.

Max continued to stand behind Gus, saying nothing.

A trickle of fear crossed Gus's heart. He was wary of what came next, but he didn't want to lose Max over this.

He stepped in. Another young man followed. The circle was complete.

"We are all here," Ganefard said. There was satisfaction in his voice. "Follow me."

The torchbearers picked up their torches, and the group struck further into the woods.

Their path sloped downward, down a ridge into a hollow. What they followed, Gus guessed, was the remains of an old logging road, unpaved and grown up in ferns and salal but relatively wide and even. Beyond the torches, ragged clouds parted. The full moon flashed through the trees.

Sticks crackled as the men walked. No one spoke. Gus's finger throbbed where it had been cut, and a spot of blood showed black on the bandage. But his heart was lifting. This felt like a quest, the men companionable around him.

It was a challenge, for Odin. Cagey, dark, intelligent Odin, of hundreds of epithets and faces. Always one-eyed, always the father of runes.

They reached a clearing in a ring of young alders, leaves thick on the ground. The torchbearers planted their torches.

Chapter 24

H

At the edge of the ring of trees, tied to a Douglas fir, was a man.

Light from the torches washed across him, trussed with black rope, firmly but not in a way to cause pain. He wore street clothes, blue jeans and a plaid flannel shirt. A pillow-case thrown over his head hid his face.

Hearing them come up, he struggled against his bonds, making muffled grunts.

In the uneven torchlight, face half in shadow, Max stepped forward.

"This man led an attack against me the other night. Five against one."

Against one?

"He and his friends ambushed me, thinking numbers would win the fight. But I got away."

The hooded man had gone silent.

"We are Odin's Hunt. We are not afraid to act with

violence, when violence has been used against us. And yet, we are on the side of justice."

Bruni stepped forward. "Though justice was not done to Sigewulf, we will have justice here."

It took Gus a moment. Sigewulf was Max's Hunt name.

Another man, stepping into the circle of torchlight, threw down ten spears, each a man's height tall. They fell against each other with a rattle and clang. Their steel heads glinted, reflecting flame.

"A simple weapon," Bruni said. "Some of you have practiced with them. Some of you have not. We will pick the hunters by lot. The game will have a head start. And then we will hunt."

Shock poured through Gus, hitting his stomach like a weight.

The men looked at each other. Gus kept his face blank.

What the fuck was going on? Had he heard right?

"The hunt will run all night. If the game escapes us, well and good. Dawn will save him. If not, well and good. He takes whatever wound the spears give him. And then he is free to go."

No.

This was wrong, this was stupid.

What did they want? To scare the guy, to kill him?

It was like some stupid movie. People didn't act like this.

Could he, Gus, stop this?

He wanted to shout, hit somebody, do something, but he pushed the feeling down. He had to think first.

What would happen if this guy got away and went to the

police? Though he hadn't about the goat head—he'd blogged about it instead. Cops treated Antifa like shit.

"We'll choose by the bones." Bruni held forward a black woolen bag. Some bones in the bag would be painted, some left natural; one or the other set would signify the hunters.

Maybe Gus could go back to camp, get Alyssa, get out of here. Call the cops.

When the bag came by, Gus chose, fumbling among smooth bones held in rough cloth. He pulled a red-painted vertebrae, by size a rabbit's.

"Show."

The men put forward palms, each with a bone.

"Red bones are the hunters."

Gus, Max, Bruni, Wulf, and a handful of others held red bones.

Shit.

He bit the inside of his mouth for distraction, to not show fear.

"Very well," Bruni said. "Cuthred will lead the rest of you back. Go with Odin."

The other men gathered and went off into the night, following one of the torches. The yellow light of the torch flame bobbed up the path.

Gus's breath came fast. He felt the warmth of Max, still standing behind him, and consciously relaxed. He needed Max not to know how he felt.

Bruni turned to the remaining men.

"As I say, the rules are simple. You have your spear. Throw it or wield it however you will, from now till dawn."

If they wanted to, tonight, Odin's Hunt could easily kill

this man, their prey. Max, Bruni, and any other experienced Hunt members knew the ground, which their prey didn't.

Did they want this man to die?

Bruni picked up his spear. "Come with me."

Most of the other men followed, each taking a spear.

Gus hung back, hoping Max would walk around him, but he didn't. A torchbearer also hung back, waiting. Max grabbed Gus's elbow.

"Come on. We're not going to hunt yet."

He didn't want to argue with Max, here and now. Twisting away, he followed the line of men. Max walked after him.

They went deeper into the forest, one torchbearer before, one behind, leaving the man tied to the tree.

The new, smaller group came to a further clearing. Bruni said, "Before we start, we need preparation. This is our time to fully get into ritual space."

Toward the edge of the clearing stood a stump, a black bowl on it, next to it a small drum and a half-dozen self-capping bottles, mead probably. Max, behind Gus, noticed the angle of his gaze. "Metheglin. Bruni's special."

"What does that mean?"

"You'll see."

From his tone, Gus guessed it was doctored somehow.

He breathed deeply, trying not to panic, his body cramped with fear, his mind racing.

Shit, shit, shit.

If he protested, they might go after him. That wouldn't help anyone.

He could double back and leave. Report them.

Whispering a magic formula, Bruni smeared a dark, earth-scented mixture on the men's faces. Mud and blood, Gus guessed, as at Winter Nights, maybe some herb sacred to Odin. The runes crossed and crossed again, a sigil on each man's face, till each face was covered with dark glop, a ritual mask.

Then Bruni was dabbing Gus's face, whispering in Old Norse. He didn't understand the words. Finished, Bruni handed him one of the bottles. "Drink up."

Gus took a mouthful.

"More than that. Finish the bottle."

Beside him, Max said, "Drink it." Warmth was in his voice, threat also.

Max wouldn't kill him. But he could knock him out. Gus wanted to stay awake.

He tipped it back.

He just hoped he didn't get totally lost in the forest on whatever drugs they'd dosed him with.

When all had finished, Bruni scanned the group.

"We are in battle form, but we need to be battle ready." He nodded, and one of the men picked up a drum. He began a heartbeat rhythm, slow and deep.

"We are here for Odin. To be his Wild Hunt. Odin's wolves, Odin's men. Feel your way into the fighter that is you. Feel your way into your berserker."

Deep in his throat, Bruni growled, a growl like a bear's.

The drum beat steadily. Other men joined in, a low hum that grew stronger, louder. One man tossed his head back and howled like a wolf.

Max was watching. Gus added his voice. He felt the

metheglin begin to work in him, sparks of light at the edges of his vision, the earth moving and breathing under him.

The toning rose, fell back, rose again, crescendoed to a shout.

It fell to silence. They were in a bowl of trees, black silhouetted branches against the black translucence of the sky. The moon slipped from behind a cloud and shone full-faced down.

Max threw his head back and howled.

"We are Odin's Hunt!" the men shouted.

Two men grabbed the torches, and through the dark trees they walked back to where the man stood tied.

The bearers planted the torches. Bruni walked up to the captive and pulled the pillowcase off. The man looked from painted face to painted face, eyes wide, defiant.

"You heard the rules. We're going to give you a head start. Make the most of it."

The man made frustrated noises against his gag.

Bruni turned to Max. "Take the gag off?"

Max shrugged. "As you like. He'll just spew crap."

Bruni seemed to weigh the options. "Untie him," and two men scrambled to do that. "Take off his gag, too."

The ropes and the cloth gag fell.

Gus got a good look at him for the first time that night. Not a bad-looking guy, tall, with ash-blond hair, well-built.

What was his name, anyway? Rob.

As soon as his gag was off, as predicted, he started to talk.

"You shitheads. You can't do this. You've broken half a dozen laws already. If you kill me, Antifa will know who did it. They'll come against you with the full weight of the law. You'll spend the rest of your life behind bars, all of you." He looked again from face to face.

Bruni pulled a cell phone from his back pocket, tapped over to the timer.

"If I were you, I'd save my breath and start running."

Sweeping their faces with one last look, the man bolted. Running steps disappeared into the dark forest.

Fear jetted through Gus. How could he stop this? How could he help this man?

But he felt disoriented. The trees around him, alders lit to their lower branches by torchlight, moved and waved.

A cold breeze hit his face.

It was the wind. Not the drug.

"How long should we give him?" one of the men asked Bruni.

"Fifteen minutes."

Max shot Bruni a glance but said nothing.

Max wanted it to be less. Max wanted this guy dead.

Gus had wished death on people—teachers, parents, bullies. He'd never considered carrying through with murder. He couldn't explore the thought, off-kilter and slightly sick from the drug as he was.

Max stood next to him, warmth from his body encircling Gus.

He was the only person Gus knew well here. Besides Alyssa. Who was probably asleep in the tent.

With a flare of longing, he wished he were with her.

The trees moved in the wind. He held tightly to the

wooden pole of his spear. Some of the men around him squatted down. Bruni sat down by the stump altar.

He'd throw his spear into the underbrush and get away. It was what half the guys would do—lose their spear immediately.

Max moved up close, putting his hands on Gus's thighs —not as obvious as a hug, but as near. Gus moved to leave a finger's width of air between them, though his body wanted the warmth.

Fifteen minutes seemed like an eternity.

The alarm beeped. Bruni shut it off.

"It's time. The rules are simple. You can hunt singly or in groups. The hunt lasts till dawn." He heaved himself to standing. "I'm off this direction. Wulf, come with me." He turned on a flashlight, and the two went off in the general direction that the prey had.

Most of the others followed, but Max hung back. When Gus moved to go, he grabbed his arm.

"Stay with me."

The full moon shone down, all milky light, enough to see Max's face. Eyes wide, dark obscuring paint, a mask of intensity.

A cold wind shuffled branches. The sound of the others' movement disappeared.

"I know this land pretty well. Unless he has the wit to hide, which he might, if he has any wood-sense at all he'll head up the gully toward the road. If we go straight up the ridge here and cut across, it'll be faster. We can catch him where the gully meets the road."

"I'm not going to help you kill him."

"I just want to scare him."

Gus frowned, looking into Max's face, impossible to read.

"If that's true, how will you shut him up?"

"The gods are with me. And a good lawyer. I want him to understand that if he speaks against Odin's Hunt, there'll be consequences. I want him to understand we take vengeance if we're wronged."

Maybe Max believed it, in the moment. But it wasn't true.

Max's hand tightened on his arm.

"Tonight I want you to stay with me."

A wave of fear brought disorientation. Cold wind touched his face. The stars were pulsing.

Max was going to make sure Gus stayed with him, whatever it took.

He was going to have to ride this out. Like Hekate said, go through it.

Max watched his face.

"Okay," Gus said.

"Good." Max pulled a flashlight out of his pocket, lit it, and gestured with the beam up the ridge. "Straight up there, then across. The climb will be a bitch, but after that it'll be easy."

Up the ridge they clambered, mostly on hands and knees, through ferns, salal, thorns of native blackberry, all in near-pitch dark under the trees—the flashlight would be no help but only give them away. Gus used the butt of the spear to help himself, but the length got tangled in the underbrush. Dirt fell in his face and mouth; roots pulled away in his hands.

They came to a stand of cedar. "Stop here a sec," Gus said, brushing himself off.

"Have some water." Max handed him a water bottle. "We're close. Up by that Doug fir"—he pointed—"we should cut across."

Close to the top of the ridge, they had more moonlight. It had cleared to a brilliant, cold night, a few stars fighting the moon. The scent of frost and fir hung in the air. The full moon stood at zenith, maybe midnight.

"That way," Max said, and started off. Gus followed him. Max found a game trail, which made it easier going, though they had to duck under fir and brush.

After a time, Max said, "Here." In front of them cut a ravine, edged with fir and alder, filled with rocks from an ancient slide, some dense with moss. At the divot's bottom ran a trickle of a stream. "We can wait here, say an hour or so. If he finds his way out, this is the way he'll probably come." He found a cedar tree, propped his spear, and sat down, patting the ground beside him. Gus sat next to him.

All this time, they hadn't encountered anyone. All the other hunters had gone another way.

Gus felt his brain whirling.

Mushrooms, probably. Maybe some weed, or marijuana oil.

Max put his arm around him, but Gus could feel Max was in no mood to make out. There was a tension in his body.

Time passed slowly. The trees in the wind, the earth itself, felt like they heaved in waves. Nausea came and went.

After a time, movement sounded in the forest, crunching. Gus focused. But it seemed too small for a human.

"A raccoon," Max said, and pointed. The moonlight showed the bandit mask.

When he heard movement again, something larger, Gus was half-asleep despite the cold.

It didn't take Max to identify it. Among the trees, in a falling ray of moonlight, a young buck stood. Tall, six pointed antlers, gazing toward them in the bluish light.

Gus stared, transfixed.

The feeling of wild life looking into him pierced him.

Odin of the Wild Hunt. Deer Stalker.

Max drew in a sharp breath.

Perhaps the stag heard it, because he leaped away.

"Amazing," Gus said.

Max put his arm around him, kissed his forehead. Gus let him.

After another wait, a large movement sounded. At this one, Max stood up, quiet, tense.

He shook Gus and whispered, "Come with me."

Grabbing their spears, they climbed again, further up the ravine. They went along the rockfall, which made for cleaner climbing. Closer, closer, then they made the top of the ridge. They hit an actual road, not paved but gravel.

Gus heard the same thing Max heard. His fingers tightened on his spear.

Something moved in the underbrush, something big, deer or human.

A shaking in the bushes, and he emerged—Rob. Moonlight shone on his ash-blond hair. A wind rose in the trees and fell again.

Rob and Max stared at each other. Gus watched them both.

Max moved closer to Rob, slowly. The pale-grey gravel shone in the moonlight.

Rob tensed but didn't run.

"Hi, Max," he said.

"Hi, Rob."

These two had been friends once.

"You know you're a fascist, Max. You're working from the fascist playbook. This just proves that."

This guy wasn't afraid of Max, and he wasn't going to shut up.

"Rob, I'm not a fascist. I'm the Wild Hunt. I'm a follower of Odin. I hunt for the god." He raised his spear, in leisurely fashion. "It's time for you to run."

The two stared at each other another moment.

Rob turned and sprinted away.

Max gave him a decent lead. Then he drew back his hand to cast his spear.

As Max threw, Gus leaped on him, knocking him down. The spear grounded itself about a yard away.

"Fuck you!" Max shoved himself away, Gus rolling off. He jumped up, but Max backhanded him and he fell.

Max grabbed Gus's spear, ran a handful of steps, and cast again. The shot went wide.

Out of the woods burst a handful of men. The other hunters had followed Bruni, who led them now.

Bruni's eyes shot from Max and Gus, in their painted sigil-masks, to the blond man running in the moonlight.

Rob sped up, hearing the commotion behind him.

Two, three, four men threw their spears.

Three went wide.

One caught him in the middle of the back, impaling him.

Chapter 25

H

Gus knew before he knew. There was something final in the way Rob fell, limp as a ragdoll.

The man lay on his chest. The spear stood upright from his back, canted a little, casting a shadow onto the moonlit road. Under the pale body, a pool of black blood spread quickly. A black hole edged in shining wetness went through the center of the torso.

Bruni hunched over Rob, hand on the wrist, feeling for a pulse. He looked up at Max.

"I'm not getting anything."

Gus squatted beside the body.

Blood poured out, shockingly fast, drenching the plaid shirt and the ground below. The meaty smell made him gag a little. The man's face, lying sideways, was pale; the eyes stared, unseeing. Gus touched the flesh, which was warm.

He put his hand in front of the face and felt no breath.

"We could try resuscitating him," one of the men said.

"Fat fucking chance," another said. "There's a spear straight through him. I'm guessing it went through something major."

The blood soaked into the ground. The smell came stronger. Bruni and Max looked at each other.

Cold fear filled Gus's gut. They had a plan.

He stood and stepped away as Bruni tried for the pulse again.

"I think he's dead."

"I'll deal with it," Max said.

They had a plan, and they weren't telling anyone.

Behind him, the other men were whispering. "I didn't think anyone was going to die!"

"Shut *up*."

"Come with me," Max said to Gus. "I know the shortest way back to camp."

Bruni nodded. "I'll get the guys to find the missing spears."

Max grabbed the pole of the spear and pulled the point out of the body. Blood dripped onto the road.

"I'll take that," Bruni reached across for the spear. To the other men, he said, "Let's drag this guy into the bushes. I don't think there's anyone within miles, but I don't want any surprises."

Max and another man each took one end and hauled the body over to the brush. Max looked at the blood on the road dispassionately.

"I'll deal with that," Bruni said. "I'll make sure someone stays with the body till you come back."

So animals didn't get at it.

"He died well," Bruni continued. "We need to show him respect."

It seemed a little late for respect.

Max turned to Gus. "Let's go."

They walked down the moonlit access road toward camp, gravel crunching under their feet. The wind rose and fell, sighing, in the trees.

The peak of Gus's high had passed. He stayed silent, but his mind had plenty to say.

Fuck, fuck, fuck.

This was some really stupid shit.

He eyed his companion, the strong, wide back in front of him in the moonlight.

"Turn left. This is the path to the main camp."

They stopped at Max's truck.

"I'm going to grab some trash bags and duct tape and the cart from the kitchens and go get the body. I want to say a few words over him. He died honorably."

Moonlight fell through a lattice of tree limbs. A highlight bounced from the truck's side mirror. It was hard to read Max's face, still with the black sigil mask, hardened now and cracking in places.

"That was a stupid thing you did," Max said, "trying to stop me."

It took all Gus had not to say exactly what he thought. But he had to throw Max off the track.

"This whole fucking game is stupid, Max. There are laws against murder. Do you want Odin's Hunt to go to jail?"

Max let out a long breath. Gus heard in the sigh an understanding that Gus wanted to protect him, that Gus mostly cared about evading the law.

"Let me take care of it, Gus. Now I'd like some help."

Back at the kitchens, they found the metal cart the crew used to haul supplies in. Moonlight fell in rays between tall stands of Douglas fir and cedar.

They returned through the forest to the access road. The moon had fallen in the sky. A smell of woodsmoke, a crispness in the air said winter to come. Orion had climbed the sky to the south, glinting.

The fear backed off a little.

He couldn't do anything until Alyssa was out of their reach.

Bruni had managed to make the road look as if nothing had happened, though the smell of blood hung in the air. Max and Gus plunged into the woods at the side of the road.

A few of the men had taken off, but a few had stayed: Bruni, Wulf, and two others. They sat in darkness, among ferns and salal, by the body. Bruni waved to hail Max as they came up.

"He was courageous," Max said, "a worthy enemy." Gus heard sorrow in his voice. They'd been friends once.

"Is there any mead left?" Bruni handed over a partial bottle.

Max raised it. "To Robert Ammon, a noble man, now gone to his rest. May the gods and spirits look after him."

"May the gods and spirits look after him," Gus murmured.

Rob hadn't deserved this.

Max poured out the mead in offering.

With the men's help, Max and Gus wrapped the body in two layers of trash bags, splitting the bags and taping them with duct tape to make a watertight container. They loaded the body onto the cart. Bruni stayed to finish cleanup in the woods with Wulf; the others walked back with Gus and Max.

They loaded the wrapped body in the back of the pickup, and the other men went to help Bruni. With help from Gus, Max quickly packed and put his tent and gear around and on top of the body. At the water faucet by the kitchen tent, he washed the ritual mask off his face.

The moon had fallen further in the sky; Gus guessed it was four a.m. He stood with Max beside the truck.

"Bruni's going to finish the ritual in the woods," Max said. "You might join him."

"I think I'm okay."

Bright moonlight filled the bowl of the small clearing where the parking lot sat. Gus realized that he was still wearing dried face paint; it itched.

"You're not going to tell me how you're getting rid of the body. To protect both of us."

"Good-bye, Gus. We'll talk soon."

He stepped once more into Max's arms. It was necessary. Max hugged him hard. The heat of him, the connection. Twisted, painful, still there.

He thought Max was going to say something, but

instead he got into the truck, started the motor, and drove away.

Puabi-Ekur watched, an astral half-step away.

Looming behind them stood Hekate, their patroness, but also another god—Odin, god of the Wild Hunt.

Gods too could be tangled in the web of karma. Gods made promises they had to keep. Odin's Hunt had made offerings, time and time again.

But no death weighs as nothing on the astral, and this one had the potential to create many consequences.

The web and the missing djinn were coming into focus.

By the beam of a flashlight borrowed from Max, Gus trudged back across Odinshof to his tent. On the way, he washed his face in cold water at the kitchen faucet, rubbing himself dry on his shirt.

The moon hung near the tops of trees, an hour away from setting. In November, the dark of the year, it was still a long time before daybreak.

He paused outside the tent, staring across the land. He kept seeing the body in the moonlight. Sorrow prickled his face. He wanted to cry. He wanted to rage.

The guy was dead. He'd had a whole life ahead of him.

Maybe he could call 911. Gus opened the tent flap and leaned in, pawed around, and found his phone.

He was out of cell range. Shit.

He tried walking around to find service, but no luck.

He and Alyssa couldn't leave immediately, either. The Hunt had to keeping believing he was on their side, at least for now.

Back at the tent, he shucked his boots, sat a moment in the moonlight.

It hit him then, the events of the evening. He hugged his knees to himself. A wordless cry circled in his center, horror and sorrow and anger. He rocked back and forth, rustling the leaves. A sudden fear leaped that the Hunt was there, but he was alone.

After a while, he climbed into the tent and took off his clothes, as quietly as he could. But he couldn't open the doubled sleeping bag without waking Alyssa.

Her eyes stayed closed as he curled around her, spooning.

"Hey, baby," she said softly, snuggling into his arms.

Then she sat bolt upright.

"What happened?!"

He opened his eyes blearily. "What?"

"There's some kind of energy on you. Something happened. Don't tell me it didn't."

Gus groaned. It had been such a long night.

But he owed her an answer. She was a visionary. Of course she would pick up on the energy. He sat up, slowly, and she put her arms around him.

"It was hard, huh?" She leaned back, putting him at arm's length. "Did something bad happen?"

He needed to talk to someone. But telling her was a bad idea.

"Did someone get hurt?"

She'd halfway guessed it already. They'd probably assume she knew. Maybe it was better to tell her and to arm her. He needed so much to talk.

"Tell me."

Even if it was stupid, he was going to do it.

"You know the witches' pyramid?" he said. "To know, to will, to dare, and to keep silent?" She nodded. "This is pretty dark. If you want me to tell you, I need you to promise to keep silent. From everyone."

A tremor went through her. "I will."

In the darkness of the tent, enclosed in nylon walls, in the enclosure of her arms as they sat together cross-legged, facing each other, leaning on each other, he told the story.

He felt the tension rise in her body as he talked. She flinched at Rob's death.

When he was done, she said, "That's crazy! We should get out of here and tell someone."

"Not right away. I don't want to tip the Hunt off. They know where I live. We should lie low for now."

"Really?! But they killed somebody!"

"Not so loud!"

She continued in a whisper. "These guys are insane. You don't know what they're going to do next."

"For now, Max thinks I'm on his side. It's a thin edge to walk, I know."

"But it's wrong, what they did, and you know it."

"Yes. It is. Of course. And it won't help this dead guy if they kill us too. I really don't want you hurt."

"I don't want you hurt, either." She was silent a moment. "I saw a man get killed once. When I was a prostitute. He lived near where I was staying. He'd been messing with some gang members. I was sitting on the porch, and he was on the street corner, two houses down. They drove by and shot him."

"It sounds scary."

"It was. It happened really fast. I ran inside."

"What happened to the shooters?"

"Nothing. The guy had a police record. The cops came around and asked about it. Everyone told me to keep my mouth shut, and I did. I was pretty young. Since no one would testify against the gang, no charges were filed."

Gus turned the story over in his mind. "The killers should have gotten justice."

Even in half-darkness, he saw the whites of Alyssa's eyes as she gave him a sidelong look. "I don't know what justice was in this case. People said the dead guy was in a rival gang. Every life is worth something, but I don't know who the bad guy was there. If anyone. It was complicated."

"Mmm." He drew her arms around him tighter and nuzzled her neck. Her body smelled of candy perfume and a little sweat. He wanted to want her, to escape into sex, but a weight of exhaustion and emotion held him trapped.

"This guy and Max knew each other. He wrote an inflammatory article about Max, which is how this started."

"Then it escalated." He nodded, head against her arm.

"Max said he didn't want to kill him, only scare him." He

shut his eyes. "I don't believe him. I don't know who threw the spear that killed the guy. But the responsibility is Max and Bruni's."

"Yes. And with the gang, obviously there's a social background, but it was one bunch of murderers against another. Here, the guy just wrote an article. Murder for vengeance isn't okay."

"No." Max spoke of tribe, but there were post-tribal things worth keeping. "I have to do something. But right now, we should chill."

"Yeah, I don't want you to die. I like having you around." She pulled him down into the silky nylon of the sleeping bag. He hugged her hard.

"Me too."

"What you need now is sleep."

Wrapped around her, he fell into oblivion.

In the morning, he woke to Alyssa shaking him.

"I let you sleep as long as I could, but they're going to put breakfast away."

She grabbed his breakfast gear as he stumbled out and threw on clothes.

They walked across camp, the sky overcast, the day chilly. The alders whispered, moving branches in a cold breeze.

They converged on the cook-fire just as Julia grabbed the huge aluminum pot of oatmeal to take it away, her brunette braid swinging.

"Do you need some of this?" she asked.

"Yes," said Alyssa. She set out two bowls and filled them. Gus added brown sugar, raisins, and milk.

"Is there any bacon left?" he asked Julia.

"That's long gone, boyo."

"Coffee?"

She gestured with her chin toward a pot. "Should be some left."

He filled both cups Alyssa had brought and found a spot for the two of them. Since Winter Nights, someone had installed a pair of picnic tables near the firepit.

Alyssa sat beside Gus, her pale blonde hair glowing in the indirect light.

He tipped back his cup. "Omigods, coffee, and it's hot."

"I thought you'd want to get up."

"I wouldn't go that far."

She grinned and bit his shoulder, lightly, through the cloth of his flannel shirt.

From across the fire, he saw Bruni striding across the camp toward them, now in street clothes but still an imposing mountain of man. It brought back the night before—the body pale in moonlight, the spear rising at a slight angle from its back, the smell of blood.

Gus gulped down his oatmeal and coffee.

Bruni came up. "Come with me for a bit," he said.

Gus stood. "I won't be long," he told Alyssa.

The sun had come out, but mist hung under the far trees. Bruni led Gus across the compound to his own lean-to, the most old-Scandinavian building on the property after the hall. A steep roof, thatched, sat on a structure of rough brown-grey boards. Bruni had hand-hewn all the materials that went into the building.

Inside the lean-to, it was dark, except for the light through the door. A bed lay in the corner, made up with an army blanket, beside it one chair. Bruni took the chair, leaving Gus the bed.

"I think you know what I want to talk about. Last night was a terrible accident. I think Max told you our intentions."

"Yes."

"As the state falls apart, in the United States, we come to a place where we must protect ourselves. We can't let Antifa spread defamation about us, because deeds build on words."

Gus kept his face blank, listening.

That wasn't what was going on, but he'd let Bruni have his say.

"I'm going to ask you what I'm asking everyone else that took part, to keep your mouth shut."

"That was a bad idea last night, Bruni. I want Max to have his vengeance. But it's not safe for the Hunt not to follow the law. I think we should go to the police and tell them it was an accident. Which it was."

He would tell the police the truth.

Bruni shook his head. "I'm afraid not. By and large, the rank and file police are on our side, or at least open to white heritage. But not the judges. If you look at Washington state judges, a fair number of them are black or Mexican. They're not going to rule in our favor. Just keep your mouth shut, and let us take care of it."

Gus pinched his nails into his palms, to keep from reacting. This was such bullshit. But if he didn't agree, he declared himself an enemy.

"Okay."

"I'd like your blood oath on it."

In Northern tradition, there was a special level of hell for oath-breakers.

From a shelf behind the bed, Bruni took a big knife with a leather-wrapped handle and unsheathed it. "Easiest to cut you in the same place."

Gus held out his hand. Bruni tugged the gauze bandage off his finger. Lighting a candle, he ran the knife through the flame to cleanse it.

Gus watched. He'd say the words but not mean them.

Odin, help me.

In the myths, Odin outmaneuvered enemies by lying.

He felt the weight of the engraved basalt stone in his pocket.

Hekate, help me.

"Repeat after me. I, Gus, agree by the blood I give here today—"

He paused and let Gus repeat the words, then continued: "To remain silent about the acts of Odin's Hunt last night." Gus echoed him again.

"—no matter what pressure is brought to bear. This I swear by our gods Odin, Thor, and Freya."

I do not swear this.

As Gus finished, Bruni cut his finger. This time it hurt worse. It burned like fire.

Bruni milked the wound, so blood dripped onto the dirt floor. Then he bound it again, using the same gauze.

"That's done. Listen to me, now."

Bruni leaned close enough that Gus smelled his stale sweat. "What Odin's Hunt does, it does together. If you break your oath, the gods will have vengeance. And so will we."

Chapter 26

ᚺ

*P*uabi-Ekur contemplated this false blood oath, and the evening before, the death. Lines of influence spread outward on the astral, touching lives.

Odin sat in the background, watching all that passed, as did Hekate.

Before Gus and Alyssa even got to Seattle, the wound was hot and red around the bandage.

In stop-and-go traffic coming north, hands on the wheel, Alyssa glanced over at him.

They'd talked it through. He needed to find a lawyer before he spoke to the cops. It would be too easy for the Hunt to paint him as an accomplice. He wasn't willing to let Alyssa endanger herself by stepping forward for him. Besides, he knew more.

"Your hand looks bad. I can see it from here. I want to take you to urgent care."

"Oh, god," Gus groaned. "I don't have time! I have so much homework!" Real life was dawning on him, and with it the familiar tightness in his stomach, the tension of being overwhelmed.

"I had a friend who got sepsis and nearly died. You'll lose a lot more time in school if you're in the hospital. Or dead."

"If I die, I won't have to do homework."

They went to an urgent care clinic on the south edge of Seattle. The waiting room, designed to keep people calm, was all blues. An aquarium full of colorful fish flashed gold and red.

There was an hour wait. "I'm going to go find something to eat," Alyssa said. "Do you want something?" He shook his head.

He poked at his phone a while, playing with social media, memes that friends posted. His mind went around and around, revisiting the night and morning past.

A man had died. Was killed. Not quite murdered.

Max and Bruni thought that was okay.

Possibly Bruni was right that the police were—what did he say? "Open to white heritage." The police did seem to give white-power groups more leeway than Antifa.

Alyssa flopped down next to him, with a kiss on his cheek. "I saved you some fries. Want some?" He took a handful.

A physician's assistant in scrubs stepped into the waiting room. "Gus Masterson?"

An enlarged photo of a waterfall dominated the examination room. The attendant took his blood pressure, height, and weight. "The doctor will be a few minutes."

When the assistant left, Alyssa wrapped herself around him, kissing him, and he let her. Time passed. Alyssa took a magazine from the plastic wall holder.

At last, the doctor came in, a young Asian-American woman. She pulled the scruffy, blood-spotted gauze off his finger.

"How did you get this?"

"I cut myself by accident. I cleaned it up, but I guess the knife was dirty."

"It's definitely infected. Were you outdoors?" He nodded. "How long since you had a tetanus shot?"

"I don't know."

"You probably should get one. I'm going to give you some antibiotics. Please take all of them."

The shot was barely a mosquito sting. The attendant put a round bandage on his triceps. He filled the doctor's prescription at a pharmacy down the street, after more waiting.

They crossed the mall parking lot, black asphalt among brick buildings, under a clean-washed blue sky with pale sun. Avoiding a blinding reflection from a car window, he dove into the car's shadowy interior, the car roof blocking the sun.

It was a retreat back into the ordinary. A sense of escape and redemption flooded him. Leaning across the middle panel, he kissed Alyssa's cheek, and her soft mouth that tasted of bubble gum. "You take good care of me."

"What did you think of Odin's Hunt?" Joanie asked Alyssa.

Back at the coffee shop, in the middle of pumpkin spice season, Halloween's tiny orange pumpkins still sat on top of the espresso machine. Late autumn sun fell across their blond wood table. They'd done a shift together, were hanging out afterward, both with homework.

Alyssa had gotten herself an early eggnog latte in her personal cup. She stirred it, nutmeg circling. "Good and bad both."

"Mmm?"

"I liked the people. They split up the men and women for ritual, and Gus left me with Julia, who led me through. She was really kind. Everyone seemed sincere. I felt like the ritual worked. But I didn't like the gender separation, and I didn't like what I heard about the men's ritual."

"Gus told you?"

"He wanted someone to talk about it with. He asked me not to share it. But it was disturbing. Scary." She bit her lip. "I think Odin's Hunt is dangerous."

"Dangerous how?"

Alyssa's pale blue eyes met Joanie's ink-spot ones.

"Physically dangerous," she said. "Hurting people dangerous."

It took some time for Joanie to finish her homework, peel

away the day, but that night in her basement room she made time for witch practice.

She sat on her queen bed, covered with the quilt that her aunt had made her. She lit the white candle that sat at the edge of her desk, on a small black cloth printed with Hekate's wheel.

She grounded and centered, sending a red cord to the center of the earth, connecting to the sky, to a particular star.

"Lady Hekate, this connection of Alyssa's disturbs me. Perhaps it's not the boy himself that bothers me. At Samhain, he seemed fine. Alyssa says he cares for her and respects her."

From Hekate, all she got was an echoing silence, but something in it made her think of Puabi-Ekur.

An energetic eddy roiled at the ceiling, and she felt Puabi-Ekur come in.

"Yes?" Puabi-Ekur asked.

"I wanted to ask again. What do you see about this Gus that Alyssa's dating, and this group, this Odin's Hunt?"

Puabi-Ekur had been poking at this for a while. It was still covered in fog, sticky fog like spiderweb.

That was the djinn. They'd outwitted them before, but every set had its own tricks.

The djinn were hiding something, quite on purpose.

To Joanie, Puabi-Ekur said, "I'm looking at it, as hard as it will bear. I don't have answers yet."

Joanie frowned. "We need answers. I don't want anyone getting hurt."

Puabi saw a body transfixed by a spear.

For that it might be too late.

Chapter 27

ᚺ

With a handful of men and three horses, the horses to carry supplies, Daegal marched to the farthest outpost of Ealdorman Adel's holding.

In late spring, the trees gloried in their fresh green, oaks still yellow-tinted, beech unfurling their broad leaves, pines and yew dark. They passed dells full of bluebells and the first lilies of the valley. As they passed a lake at dusk, meaning to camp on the far bank, a flight of swans landed, feathers tipped by the lingering rose-pink of the sky. To Daegal, the land was a great peace, a great comfort.

He'd said clearly he traveled west because he wanted to see action, to do the fighting he'd come to Lord Adel to do. That had been sparse where he was, despite the master of arms' promise. Nevertheless, it was well-understood why in truth he was leaving, and for most of the hall's people that did him credit.

"Some would stay and play the favorite," the master of

arms commented, "no matter their feelings for the lord. I find your leave-taking very fitting, myself."

"Thank you," Daegal said, nonplussed. He didn't like being a topic of conversation.

Adel didn't feel the leave-taking was fitting, or wanted. The last night before Daegal left, the lord kept him up drinking mead, with the usual result.

Afterward Daegal slipped out, to a spring night, the scent of flowers in the darkness.

It would have been a lovely night to spend with the right person. In the woods, bringing the May in early.

He remembered the summer he'd spent with Maelan, how his heart would quicken when Maelan's steps approached.

That was then, this was now.

Chapter 28

B ack in Seattle, Gus's classes were in their last weeks, getting ready for finals. He hadn't decided about Thanksgiving. His mother wanted him to come home.

Max hadn't returned to town since the last gathering of Odin's Hunt.

What was taking so long?

He was hiding a body.

Gus needed to focus on classes, but he also needed to find a lawyer. He didn't have any idea how. He searched online a few times but ended up confused. He didn't want to get stuck with a bad lawyer.

Alyssa was working hard at her own classes and the coffee bar and didn't have much time for him. When they had coffee at her shop, at a table by the window, washed in bluish light and the scent of coffee, he was aware of Joanie's brooding gaze on him.

She didn't like him.

He didn't know if he would like him, if he were Joanie. He should never have gotten Alyssa involved in Odin's Hunt. He had to make it up somehow.

One sharp-cold, frosty early evening, the last streaks of red in the western sky, he broke off studying to play a game. After a while, he changed accounts and spent some time messing with guys as a fake girl. Then he got onto a red-state site and trolled a doofus who couldn't tell the difference between "conservative" and "conservation." But it just wasn't fun the way it had been.

He was going stir-crazy. He had to get outside. Maybe go have a beer.

Halfway he was thinking he would look up his friend Chris, who he hadn't seen in a while. He sent a text. No answer.

He could just go bang on his door.

He headed for the University District's main drag, pulling his peacoat close against the sharp cold. Then he saw Wulf, Josh in the mundane world, on the street in front of a smoke shop. "Wulf!" he said. "Josh!"

The young blond man did a double-take. "Gus! Hello!"

"I didn't realize you were a student."

"Yeah, in my first year. I was getting some vape stuff. I was going to go home and smoke weed. Do you partake?"

"Sure. Or, I was thinking I might go have a beer, or maybe buy some beer."

"Sounds good!" Josh clearly thought he was being invited.

He'd wanted company. But this company?

But Chris hadn't answered his texts.

Part of him, too, felt sad about losing Odin's Hunt. Not all of them were asshole racist murderers. He'd liked Julia. He'd liked the community part, too, when they helped the roofer, and the book club.

They doubled back to the nearest grocery for beer. Both of them were broke, so Gus settled for Rainier. Coming out into the fluorescent aura of the grocery doorway, which smelled of ancient vegetables, they stared at each other.

"Where to?" Josh asked. "I live literally two blocks from here."

"That's closer than my place. Let's go."

At a nondescript apartment building, a few blocks off campus, Josh ran up the flight of stairs. Gus followed more slowly.

Josh was a ball of energy. He didn't know if he could keep up.

Josh threw open the door, which hit the inner wall with an audible thump. He looked from side to side as if he were expecting a squad of goons to jump him.

"No one home," he said, and visibly relaxed.

The place was a trash-pit. One low-slung, sagging tan couch, propped up with a cinderblock, took up the back wall of the main room. The rest of the room held a couple of folding chairs, a stack of empty twelve-pack beer cartons piled in a corner, a water pipe at the center of the room, and beside that a plastic bowl filled with ashes.

"I love what you've done with the place," Gus said.

Josh barked a laugh. "Yes! I blame it on Pat, my room-mate. Come in my room, if you want, it's neater." He muttered below his breath, "Pat won't come in if the door's shut."

Clearly there was something up between him and his roommate.

A huge heathen poster dominated Josh's room, considerably cleaner than the main room. The poster, white on black, wrapped small-font commentary around the valknut, the Viking sign of triple interlocking triangles. Gus strolled up to read. The text enumerated the nine noble virtues.

Josh threw himself on the bed, neatly made with a grey coverlet. From a desk drawer, he retrieved a glass pipe and a baggie of weed, then cracked the window slightly. It was full night outside now, the sky matte black, the air sparkling with cold.

"It's not that big a deal," he said, "but keep by the window, if you don't mind." Pulling his chair to the window, Gus grabbed the bag with the twelve-pack, took out a can of beer for himself, and handed one to Josh.

Josh took a hit from the pipe and handed it to Gus, who did also and passed it back.

"What's up with you and your roommate?"

"Pat's not so bad. He's just—well, he's kind of a pig. I didn't realize how much that would bug me." Josh sucked in a big mouthful of smoke and paused, then let out a trickle. "He'll walk in, in the middle of the night, and crank the tunes when I'm sleeping. He doesn't think about anyone but himself."

Typical bad-roommate behavior.

"Also, there was this girl I was dating. I brought her over, and he was totally picking up on her."

"Rude."

"It didn't work. I mean, she didn't get with him. Though she broke it off with me. He was a friend from high school. We've signed a year lease, and I'm not sure if our friendship is going to make it. Anyway, I don't want to be here when he comes in."

"Mmm." Gus tipped back his beer. Josh put some music on, streaming on his computer—Scandinavian folk songs, eerie and cold.

He asked Josh how he'd come to heathenism, and Josh told the story.

"My family's Norwegian on my mom's side, German on my dad's. His family was German military. My grandfather fought Hitler but was pretty far right. That side is all Lutheran, though. I don't like the 'turn the other cheek' thing." He pointed at the poster. "The nine noble virtues are what speak to me."

Courage. Truth. Honor. Fidelity. Discipline. Hospitality. Self-reliance. Industriousness. Perseverance.

But all this nobility could end badly. He saw the body again in the moonlight.

Gus set an empty can beside the bed and started another.

"When I got to the university, Odin's Hunt had a few flyers up in the student union, so I checked them out. Bruni and I have had some good conversations."

"Tell me about them."

"You know, we were never all meant to live together. In other countries, people don't. Even in Europe, like in France."

That wasn't how Gus understood it. But he let Josh go on. The weed made him feel floaty and distant, open to the music and the angled rays of lamplight, not so much to close argument.

"Back in the Paleolithic, we were all tribes. Northerners stayed with northerners. Half the problem we have in America is all these people who shouldn't be here."

Gus guessed that he meant African-Americans.

"There's evidence to show that the Vikings settled here long before anyone else from Europe. We're the first Americans."

Part of Gus said, *This is stupid*, but part of him was willing to play with the idea. It appealed to his dark humor.

"What would you do with the Native Americans?"

"There's already reservations. But they came over the land bridge, right? Their ancestors are Siberian. Why not go back where they came from?"

Gus looked out the window. Across the street stood a small house. Someone there had left up Halloween decorations, a single string of orange lights around a window. Several had burned out, but most of the string remained.

So many people were struggling, and what Josh cared about was shoving everyone back to their ancestors' lands, except of course the Europeans. As if that were possible. And what about mixed-race people? It just made him sad.

"Sure," he said vaguely.

"Oh shit," said Josh. Gus heard it too: footsteps coming up the stairs.

"It's Pat. We've gotta get out of here."

Gus smiled. Paranoia from the weed.

"Where to?"

"There's a park a couple blocks down the street."

"Or my apartment."

"Let's start with the park. I feel like getting outside, anyway."

Josh took one more hit off the pipe, then offered it wordlessly to Gus, who shook his head. Josh stashed the pipe in the desk drawer and lurched to standing.

He couldn't be that drunk, could he?

Gus leaned down to investigate the beer. As Josh talked, he'd managed to kill four of the Rainiers.

Sighing inwardly, Gus slid the rest of the twelve-pack into the grocery bag and stood.

They pushed their way out Josh's door, Josh looking as if he was about to do battle. Pat glanced up from where he sat on the couch eating a bowl of cereal, a bearded stoop-shouldered guy with a skinny build.

Josh was afraid of this guy?

"We're going out."

Wide-eyed, Pat nodded.

Chapter 29

Н

Though it was a few days before Thanksgiving, it felt like early winter. Frost sparkled in the air. When Gus released a breath, it hung like smoke.

Josh headed down the block without looking behind him, and Gus ran a few steps to catch up.

Few people made their way down this side street. The buildings to either side were quiet, shades down.

"Hey, look!" At the corner, Josh pointed at a poster on a telephone pole. "All-ages show at the Leviathan! Let's do it!"

"Sure." Gus was in the mood for distraction. Close to the surface lay a sea of loss and abandonment. Alyssa had no time, and he had to be done with Max. He needed to find a lawyer, too, he needed to deal with the murder, but he didn't know how. What if he fucked it all up? "We still have six cans of beer, is all."

Josh brightened at that. "Chug them!"

Josh was a six-foot-tall child.

"Okay. You said there's a park near here?"

Maybe the park wasn't the best idea. It'd be safer to go to Gus's apartment. In the park, the cops would take one look at them and say public drunkenness and underage drinking.

"Yeah, the park's a block or two away."

That was much closer than Gus's apartment.

The park wasn't much, a block square, dotted with maple trees shorn of leaves. The leaves lay in wet brown piles below, the top layer edged with ice. A swing set sat toward the back of the space, a couple of benches up front.

One of the two benches was occupied by a bony young African-American man. He wore army fatigue pants, a black hoodie, and a stained white t-shirt. He sat in the center of the bench, arms extended to either side, head thrown back, eyes closed.

Josh and Gus took the other bench.

"How are we going to do this?" Josh asked, nervously.

"Be chill, to begin with. Hide it in your coat." Gus handed over a beer.

As if reading his mind, Josh said, "If we'd left it at the apartment, Pat would've drunk it."

Gus set to work on his beer, taking it in gulps. One down, he started another. They drank a few minutes in silence. The night hung overcast, the air heavy with damp.

Their companion of the next bench woke up. He sat up straighter, pulled his arms in, blew on his hands, and glanced over at them.

He saw the beer. He was going to come over.

They could clear out. Gus only had one beer left.

Josh was staring at the guy with a frown.

"I don't want that fucking nigger fucking with us."

"Can we just please—"

"Hey," said the man from the other bench. "Hey you. Is that beer you got? I'm pretty thirsty."

Gus looked at him closely for the first time.

The guy wasn't as out of it as all that. He had to know Gus and Josh could take him, if it came to that. He just didn't care.

"We could give him a beer," he said quietly.

"Don't do that. Fuckin' nigger. It's our beer."

The guy from the bench over levered to his feet, a bit shakily, walked a few steps to stand in front of them. "Who you callin' a fuckin' nigger?"

Josh leaped to his feet, standing face-to-face with the man, about a foot apart.

"I'm calling you a fucking nigger! Leave us alone."

The guy took a step back. "Y'all sittin' there drinking beer. That's not legal!"

"Fuck off!"

They were getting loud. Gus stood.

"Can we just not do this?" He leaned down to grab a beer from the bag. He was fine with getting rid of it. Especially since they were making a fuck-ton of noise.

Josh punched the guy.

The guy gasped out air, staggered backward, then righted himself.

"Fuck you, white boy!" He launched himself at Josh, pummeling with both fists.

Gus heaved a sigh and waded in, trying to grab Josh and

drag him away, getting his own head and shoulders pounded.

"Come on, Josh. This is stupid."

"Fuck no! I'm gonna beat this nigger's ass!" He landed a punch, and the black guy reeled backward. "Whyn'cha take your black ass back to Africa!"

"Fuck you! This is for me and my ancestors!" The guy pulled a knife out of his belt and brandished it.

Now someone was going to get hurt.

"We gotta go, Josh," Gus said, but Josh had drunk himself stupid.

"Fuck you, nigger!"

The black man lunged forward, knife pointed at Josh's midsection.

Closing on him, Gus brought his hand down in a karate chop and hit the man's arm. The knife fell to the ground. Gus kicked it away. Stupefied, the man followed it with his eyes.

"Josh, let's go!"

But Josh's blood was up. "Go back to Africa, you nigger!" He jumped onto his opponent, knocking him to the ground, and pounded the guy's head on the pavement.

"Josh, you're nuts!" Gus grabbed the young Viking around the waist, trying to heave him to his feet. At least he stopped him ramming the guy's head into the ground. "Get up, let's get out of here!"

He got Josh to his feet and took a quick look at Josh's opponent—out cold, face up on the sidewalk. There was blood in his hair, blood beginning to pool on the sidewalk.

"Josh, we've gotta go." He grabbed Josh and pointed him away from the body. "Now. Come with me."

Anyway Gus was getting out of there.

Letting go of Josh, he jogged away, across the street, down the sidewalk, headed for his own apartment. After a moment, Josh followed Gus.

Back at the apartment, Gus let Josh in and locked the door behind them. Going to the bathroom, he flicked on the fluorescent light and found alcohol, bandages, and antibiotic ointment in the medicine cabinet. Sitting Josh on the bed, he got him cleaned up—not too bad, some bruises and scrapes.

"Now we lie low and watch the news."

"What do you mean?"

"I mean, let's hope first that the guy doesn't die. Hitting someone's head like that can kill them. You know that, right?"

Josh shrugged. "I was pissed off."

"Whatever. I assume you don't want to go to jail for life. Second, let's hope no one IDed us."

Josh grunted, then grinned. "I still have a beer left." He pulled the last can out of his coat pocket. "You wanna go to the Leviathan?"

"No, I'm done for the night."

A wave of sympathy washed over him for young, blond Josh in his utter cluelessness. Josh couldn't help he was as dumb as a box of rocks. The racism went with it.

"I know you want to have fun. But there's an outside chance someone saw you beat up that black guy, and someone might see you at the Leviathan. You're pretty obvious, you know? People notice you."

"That's true."

"Mostly that's a good thing. Tonight, not so much. Tonight, you want to go home and sleep. If Pat asks you what you did this evening, say you came over to my house, drank some beer, and went home. That's our story."

Josh nodded sagely. "Okay, my friend. I understand."

He stumbled out.

For the next few days, Gus kept an eye on the police blotter notes in the neighborhood blog but saw nothing. He texted Josh, who was cheerful. Max was still out of town—his text got no reply.

Classes at least had people in them, the illusion of company. But having no real human contact depressed him. He tried to divert himself with video games, horror movies, and porn. The X-Acto knife looked attractive, but he avoided it.

He should find the lawyer now. But he had to study.

The Tuesday before Thanksgiving, he texted Alyssa again.

<What are you up to? How are classes?>

A blessing, she texted back: <I just got done with a big paper. Want to come over tonight?>

As the day died in twilight and cold drizzle, he got a bottle of cheap wine and took a bus over. The bus sighed as it juddered to a stop near her house.

Hannah's place was a small white bungalow, larger inside than it seemed on the street. By the door stood a trellis wound with a rose, green leaves glistening with raindrops. He rang the doorbell.

Alyssa opened the door, face flushed and shining. "Gus!" They fell into each other's arms.

"It seems like a century since I saw you."

"Come to my room."

Her room, at the far corner of the house, was tiny, barely enough to hold her double bed and a narrow desk. Shelves were built into the wall above the desk, one taken up by her personal altar. She lit two pale-pink candles in a saucer on the windowsill by her bed.

He fell with her onto the bed, kissing her.

She wriggled under him. He pulled her jeans and panties off, applying himself to mouthing, licking, biting her pussy. Fair close-trimmed hair glinted in candlelight.

After not much longer, he planted himself inside her.

The rocking, the waving movement of the candlelight on the white wall.

He tried to slow down. But they were both too close; she came, and then he did too, spilling himself into latex. He laid himself down on top of her, folding her into his arms, kissing her cheek. "I love you," he whispered.

She petted his hair with her hand. "I love you too."

After a few minutes, he pulled out, getting up to discard the condom in the trash.

"You know," she said, "you're the only one I'm seeing right now. You know my test results, and I know yours. We don't have to use condoms together, if you don't want to."

It wasn't a momentous change, more of a soft landing. "Okay."

He climbed back in bed and wrapped her in his arms.

"You're the best thing in my life," he said.

It was true. He'd loved subbing to Max. He loved Max. But that way lay danger. Grief. Murder.

"Tell me what's been going on," Alyssa said.

With a sigh, he did. As he finished, she sat up abruptly.

"You helped beat up some random guy?"

He sat up too. The candle flame bent double and righted itself.

"I didn't help beat him up. I did my best to keep Josh and him off each other."

"I thought you were going to find a lawyer. Why haven't you? The longer you wait, the longer they have to hide the evidence."

He put his head in his hands.

"You're right. I don't really know how. I looked on the internet, but I want someone who knows what they're doing."

"So ask for help! And now this thing. What if this guy at the park died?! You know for sure that Rob did. I guess I assumed you were dealing with all this." She pushed her hands through her hair in frustration. "If you don't tell the authorities, I will."

"I'm going to! But it's not like—I have classes and everything. Rob's already dead. Nothing I can do is going to fix that."

"Yeah, but the longer you wait, the harder it's going to be to get justice for him. Find a lawyer, okay?!"

"Okay, okay."

For dinner, Alyssa made pasta, and they split the bottle of wine. Gus drank most of it. At the end of the evening, she kicked him out. "I have an early class."

As he kissed her sweet, soft mouth, he felt her anger at him.

He caught a Lyft, splurging to avoid a half-hour wait in the rain.

Though he didn't have class till afternoon, he woke up early.

Someone was pounding on his door.

"Police. Open up."

Chapter 30

H

Gus stumbled out of bed, threw on a robe, and opened the door, his anxiety jetting through the roof.

Better cooperate. But not tell them anything. He needed to choose when and how to speak.

Two uniformed policemen stood there: a meaty, red-faced white guy, and an older black guy, grey at the temples. Something in their faces made it clear he looked unimpressive.

"Hi. Sorry, I just woke up."

"Are you Augustus Masterson?" the white guy asked.

"I am."

"May we see some ID?" the black policemen asked. Gus turned back into his apartment, found his wallet in the previous night's jeans, and showed his driver's license.

The policeman nodded. "We'd like to ask you some questions."

Another spurt of fear. He clenched his teeth.

"I'm sorry, I'd rather not talk without a lawyer here."

"Where were you the evening of November sixteenth?" the white guy asked.

The night he was out with Josh.

"I'd rather not talk without my lawyer."

The two policemen glanced at each other.

"Were you out in the company of Joshua Schmidt?"

They were persistent enough. "I'm sorry, I don't want to talk without a lawyer present."

"We'd like to take a look around your apartment," the older policeman said.

Guy shook his head, as if regretful. "I'm sorry, but not without a warrant, sir."

The policemen exchanged another glance. Then the older policeman retrieved a card out of his own wallet. "All right. Give me a call if you decide to talk to us. We may be back in touch soon."

Gus shut the door behind them. He threw himself on the bed and heaved a sigh of relief.

Then the terror returned, in a wave.

He fought it down. He wasn't arrested. Yet.

Maybe Josh had blamed him for the assault.

His stomach churned with fear, but his mind mainly registered anger.

Josh was an idiot. And stood out in a crowd. Someone had seen him.

Who knew what he would blurt if questioned?

~

Still feeling the wine from the past night, he managed to drift back to sleep. He woke to the alarm, to a grey morning, overcast but no rain.

He scrabbled for his phone, on the floor beside his bed. Still no text from Max, which was probably a good thing.

Wanting comfort, he texted Alyssa.

<Can I see you today?>

<Okay. I'm in class till 1:30. Late lunch?>

He agreed to meet her at the pho place. He was still broke, but he'd asked for and gotten more money from his mother. It meant an implicit bargain he'd come home for Thanksgiving and Christmas. Which meant dealing with Dad.

He knew at some point his father would say something homophobic, and he'd have to decide whether it was worth it to fight. If he didn't say anything, he'd feel like shit, and if they had a fight he'd also feel like shit. Dad would bluster and threaten, and Mom would cry.

He could ask his parents to spring for a lawyer. But, though his father would be not-so-secretly proud his son had been involved in violence, and the law-enforcement handshake might help, it would incur a debt he didn't want. And he'd have to put up with his father's racist bullshit.

Racist bullshit like that spewed by Odin's Hunt. Josh was only repeating what he heard from Bruni.

Gus had let Max sweep him away. But Max had to hold a worldview similar to Bruni's. He and Bruni co-led the group. Max had never used racist slurs or talked white separatism, but without thinking like that, why create Odin's Hunt with Bruni?

But Gus loved Max. He'd loved being swept away. For all his force, Max had a lot of gentleness. The currant scones. Gus had thought they might have a future.

Right now, it seemed like the best thing was to ghost him back.

At lunchtime, Gus pushed open the door to the tiny pho place, to brown-green walls and a scent of warm broth. The servers greeted him smiling, sat him under a photograph of a terraced valley, and brought him hot tea. He sipped. Warmth and scent and soothing colors brought him comfort.

He ordered, knowing Alyssa had an unpredictable bus ride. She came in as he sprinkled bean sprouts into his bowl, face pink with cold framed by a fuzzy pink hat and scarf.

She kissed him on the cheek and sat, pulling off her fuzzy pink gloves.

"You are ridiculously cute," he said, in satisfaction.

She grinned. The server appeared, and she ordered and quickly got pho and jasmine tea.

"Is there a particular reason you wanted to see me?" she asked.

"Because you're the best thing in my life." She blushed.

He told her about the police visit that morning.

"What are you going to do?" she asked.

"Clearly I need the lawyer right away. I thought about asking my parents for help. But that could be a mess."

Alyssa sipped her tea.

"You know who might be able to help, if I can talk them into it. Joanie and Hannah. They've both dealt with the law, and they have contacts."

He frowned. "Joanie doesn't like me, and I don't really know either of them."

"You need help from somewhere, Gus. The police just showed up."

"Okay. If you think you can get them to see my point of view."

"Why don't you have dinner over, and I'll invite Joanie and Hannah, and we can talk?"

They arranged dinner that night. Both Joanie and Hannah seemed eager to have the conversation, to Gus's surprise.

In the meantime, Gus checked in with his few Utah and Seattle friends who might understand the situation—the Josh part. He caught Chris on the phone, but Chris had no answers.

"Dude, I feel your pain. I know some of these right-wing nutjob heathen types. Your friend Josh sounds like a singularly stupid example. I don't have any leads on a lawyer myself, but I can ask around."

At least he was willing to try. Gus was afraid he'd end up falling back on his parents.

As quid pro quo, his father might insist on Gus's coming home for a semester, or changing his major from biology. It was hard to say what. Gus would again become part of his father's world, to be managed as his father chose.

After his afternoon class, he did further online research for criminal lawyers and found a few possibilities. Maybe Joanie and Hannah could help him filter them. He wondered what was up with Josh, but better not try talking to him.

Wanting to know what had happened to the guy from the park, he searched all the police blotter notes he could find, several local blogs, and the paper, but found nothing.

That night, he walked up to the white-painted door beside the rose trellis. The rose leaves dripped from earlier rain. He rang the bell, with a surge of anxiety. It was like going to her parents' for dinner.

"Come on in!" someone called. He recognized Hannah's voice.

He hung up his coat and entered the living room. Alyssa darted out, wearing an apron, hugged and kissed him. "I gotta go deal with the asparagus. Hannah's doing the main dish. I hope you like fried chicken!"

She disappeared. He realized there were two other people in the living room. Joanie gave him a strained smile. Her girlfriend was there, too, Cleo, her demi-afro wrapped in a chartreuse-and-purple scarf.

Stepping forward, Cleo said, "I think we've met." She flashed a grin that was all teeth. "I hear you've been beating up black guys and hanging out with white supremacists."

Joanie eyed her girlfriend. Cleo screwed up her face.

"So? It's on the table now."

Hannah came in, giving them all a quelling gaze. "What's on the table is dinner. Come eat."

The tiny dining room, painted wine red, sat at the far end of the railroad kitchen. Five wooden chairs squeezed around an oval table with a red-and-white checkered tablecloth.

Hannah and Alyssa had cooked Southern: fried chicken, mashed potatoes, gravy, and asparagus. There seemed to be an unspoken agreement no one would fight, or even discuss anything serious, over dinner. It was all small talk or "pass the mashed potatoes." The chicken was Hannah's signature dish, but everything else Alyssa had made.

"Heard anything from Clayton lately?" Hannah asked Joanie. Clayton, Joanie's other partner, was in California working on an engineering master's.

"I should see him at the holidays. Though he's finally dating."

"Do tell!"

Joanie laughed. "I mean he's had a date, with a girl. I'll let you know when I know more."

Gus took more gravy. "You made this?" he asked Alyssa. She nodded. "It's good! Gravy's hard. I've made some disastrous attempts last Thanksgiving, and I gave up."

"What are you doin' this year for Thanksgiving, Gus?" Hannah asked brightly, playing mom. She was old enough to be his mother, in her midfifties.

"Going to my parents'."

"Do y'all get along?"

He grimaced. "Sort of?"

She laughed. "My daddy had a habit of saying he'd throw me out every Thanksgiving. He used to call me a devil-worshipping whore. Always made my mamma cry." She shook her head. "Then he'd get drunk and fall asleep, and the rest of us would play cards."

"For money?" Cleo asked, interested.

"Yes, for money. What's the point otherwise?"

"Did you win?"

"Of course. I always wondered if it was my mamma's way of giving me a little extra spending money for the holidays."

Under a striped dishcloth lay a pan of apple cobbler. Dishing it up, the scent of cinnamon rising, they went into the living room with plates.

"Be careful, now. Don't get the furniture sticky!"

Cleo had a couple of forkfuls of cobbler and turned to Gus. "Tell me about this white supremacist bent of yours. Since you're hanging out with our girl Alyssa."

Hannah gave her a look, but Cleo said, "I have a right to say it like that."

She had a right not to be tone-policed. That was fair.

Gus told the story, starting from the first night at the Leviathan. Coming to the story of the hunt, he paused. "I'm going to skip forward here." He didn't want to drag them into the story of the killing, at least not before talking to a lawyer.

He told his version of the fight in the park. "I was trying to get Josh not to beat on the guy. I was fine with just giving him a beer."

"The great white hero," Cleo said.

"Give him a break, Cleo," Joanie said. Cleo gave her the side-eye.

Joanie turned back to Gus. "Where are you with Odin's Hunt? Alyssa says she thinks they're dangerous, and I have to agree. Are you on board with their white separatism?"

"No. I was drawn to the ritual and the community. Now, not so much."

Hannah looked from face to face. "I think we all can understand the call of ritual and community. And there's something there about connection to ancestors. You've said yourself, Cleo, that for you Inanna is a woman of color."

Cleo pursed her lips. "But I don't fall in with people who make up fantasies of the past to make their race special. Or beat up other people because of them. And I don't hold with fascism."

Joanie stared at Gus with her ink-spot eyes.

"If you don't hold with their beliefs, why did you join?"

"I became part of the Hunting Pack because of Max. He never said anything to me about sending people to Africa or Siberia."

"So you're loyal to your boyfriend."

"I don't expect to agree with everything everyone believes in, in a ritual group. But after this last bit, I can't see staying part of Odin's Hunt."

Joanie and Hannah glanced across him at each other.

Joanie gave a single nod.

"That's good news," she said. "Heathenry has an ongoing dance with white power. Clearly Odin's Hunt is on the wrong side of that."

Maybe she'd shifted her opinion about him. Gus let out a breath of relief.

Cleo set down her plate. "So, let me get this straight. You're giving up the white supremacists? For sure? Why the change of heart?"

"I never thought anyone should go back to Siberia, or Africa, or Germany, for that matter. I didn't know Odin's Hunt believed that. Now I know better."

"It's up to you to police your friends. You get that, right?"

"For Odin's Hunt, my plan is to just get out."

"That's not enough. You're on the inside, or you have been."

"It's not like I'm running the show!"

"You know enough, though. You have to speak out."

He met Cleo's eyes, the color of amber.

"Okay. You're right."

She stared at him another moment, then sat back.

Glancing at Cleo, Joanie said, "I came here to see where you stood, for Alyssa's sake. I know you're wanting a lawyer. I could give you general advice, but I think Hannah has more contacts."

He'd gotten her support, if barely.

Joanie rose to her feet. "I think it's time we go." The women traded hugs, and Cleo left with Joanie. Alyssa started gathering plates.

Hannah turned to Gus. "You understand why Cleo's got her knickers in a twist?"

"Yes, I do."

"I'm from the South; you probably got that. I grew up in Atlanta. We've got our share of white supremacists down there. My own path is to try to bring people round, but not by talkin' at them—by helpin' them. I understand you need a lawyer." Gus nodded. "I have a friend who's a lawyer, who can probably help you or get you some resources. Is that of interest to you?"

"Yes."

"I'm glad you're gettin' out of Odin's Hunt. I think that's the right thing to do. And I hope you speak up about their practices. But if they're like you say, there might be consequences."

"I know that."

"Be careful."

Chapter 31

Hannah's lawyer focused on family law but had some criminal law contacts. "I'd start with this one," he told Gus in email. "She'll do a free first consult."

Gus sat staring at the message, the weight of the whole thing hitting him. This could cost a lot of money. He'd have to get some kind of job. But what?

The earliest he could get an appointment for the criminal defense lawyer was eight a.m. the Tuesday before Thanksgiving. So soon, it felt like luck, and he took it.

He dressed randomly in near-dark and made his way to the bus. The weather was wet cold; he wore his peacoat over two hoodies and added his watch cap. The Utah boy still wasn't used to the wet, penetrating Seattle chill.

The office was downtown, the building's imposing facade all columns. The elevator interior had mahogany colored paneling, which he stared at dully as it began to climb floors. He was still three-quarters asleep.

After the elevator lobby, paved in marble and twelve feet tall, the law office proved human-scale, the waiting room pale green and hung with nature photographs. The receptionist said, "Ms. Atwater will see you in few a minutes." She pointed him to coffee.

The lawyer's small personal office faced outward through a floor-to-ceiling window toward Seattle downtown, tones of grey under an overcast sky. The lawyer stood from behind her desk.

In her thirties, wearing a coral-colored suit, she had long blunt-cut brown hair that swung naturally. She looked like a normal human, someone you could have a conversation with. It put him more at ease.

"What I tell you comes under client-attorney privilege, right?" he asked. She nodded. "So I can tell you whatever happened."

Gus started with the story of the assault in the park.

She sat behind her desk and searched a few things online. "Right now, I'm not seeing anything. It depends on how badly the victim was hurt, what charge your friend would get. My guess, and it's just a guess, is that someone saw your friend and identified him. He sounds pretty noticeable."

"He is."

"The police probably don't have you as a person of interest in the assault. They would have arrested you by now if they did. They probably wanted you to implicate your friend. Based on their not contacting you again, my guess is they have one or two eyewitnesses they can count on already. If those fall through, they'll come find you." She smiled, a little grimly.

"All right." He sat forward in his chair. "What if I wanted to talk to someone about Odin's Hunt overall? I mean—they've gotten up to some nasty stuff."

She looked at him under her eyebrows. "As you say, this conversation is covered by client-attorney privilege."

"What if someone died?" He met her eyes. "I didn't do it. I'm not sure who did. But that might have happened."

"As your attorney, I wouldn't suggest you do anything to incriminate or endanger yourself. If you report something like that to the police, there are obviously pros and cons. Your Odin's Hunt friends, there's a potential for danger from them. You'd want to have all my facts marshaled before you spoke, especially since you didn't tell the police about Josh. Which incidentally was absolutely the right move, or at least so I think."

She tapped her lips with her pen.

"One option is to go to the FBI, if what happened could be considered a hate crime. If it's not a hate crime, you could call in a tip to the police anonymously. If you're willing to go on the record but don't want to self-incriminate, you could prepare a police statement with my help."

He sat for a moment staring at his hands.

In the end, it was a question of right and wrong. The police could investigate better if he worked with them.

"It wasn't really a hate crime. I think I should tell the police. If I was going to put in a statement, what would I do next?"

"Make an appointment, and then we'd write the state-ment together. I would guess based on what you've said we could do that for five hundred to a thousand dollars, though that's just an estimate."

Maybe that was the right thing.

"Can you do it today?" If he had to, he could put it on his credit card and figure it out later.

"I'm afraid the rest of the day is booked, and I'm gone tomorrow. It'll have to be after Thanksgiving."

An anonymous tip might be better anyway—slightly less chance of repercussions from Odin's Hunt.

Maybe he could get Max to come forward. It was a long shot, but maybe worth a try. He had a hard time picturing it, though. Still stupefied by early-morning sleep deprivation, he couldn't think of anything else to say.

"Give it some thought. The receptionist can set you up with an appointment."

The lawyer stood up, came around the desk, and shook his hand.

"A word of advice, just on a personal level. Whatever you decide, get away from these Odin's Hunt guys. If you have a habit of criminal activity, eventually you get caught."

He caught a bus back to the University District. Already holiday ornaments drenched the neighborhood, blinking red, gold, and green. The pho place had dressed itself in tinsel. After his morning class, he stopped by Alyssa's coffee shop, but neither Joanie nor Alyssa were there. Recaffeinated, he rolled out, hunched into his coat, blinking as the rain blew into his face.

He nearly ran into a guy on the sidewalk, a skinny pale guy with bright-red, close-cropped hair and a black puffy jacket over a black hoodie. The guy dropped back half a step.

"Hey, look where you're going."

"Sorry."

Gus was about to go on, when he saw the guy looking at him funny.

"Do I know you from somewhere?" he asked. Then it struck him.

It was Pete, the Antifa guy that Max had punched beside his building.

At the same time, the Antifa guy recognized him.

"I know where I know you from. You're the guy who was with Max Dwyer that night we went to see him, after he gave Rob that fucking goat head." He glanced over Gus. "How come you're not all patched up with Odin's Hunt shit? I thought you guys always wore your colors."

Above the University District sidewalk, the sky was still spitting rain. Gus was pulled strongly in several directions.

He didn't owe this Pete guy anything. Pete and his Antifa friends had been about to kick the shit out of him when Max drove them off.

Fuck you, Pete Antifa Boy.

On the other hand—he saw the pale body in moonlight, the pool of black blood under it.

"I'm not a member of Odin's Hunt. I've been a member of the Hunting Pack. As far as that goes."

"That goat head thing was some fucked up shit." Red-headed Pete watched his face closely.

Heat rose, a tingling in his knuckles, a desire to strike. But Gus kept himself in check.

"Max punched me pretty good that night," Pete went on. "Pretty sure he broke my nose." It had set crooked. "But Jonathan was all set to kick you, which set him off. Jonathan was out of line. That's not what Antifa is about—Antifa's about protecting people. It's why I went along, to remind them." Pete stared at Gus frowning. "I feel like I owe you a beer, after all that."

Gus had finals to study for, and he didn't care if this guy Pete felt guilty.

But again, he saw the pale body in moonlight, the pool of black blood under it.

"Okay. I'll take it."

"I know just the place."

They walked two blocks against the drizzle flipping cold water in their faces. Pete pushed open a door, and they were inside. Dark, wood-paneled, full of beer signs, with an unoccupied nook for pool. Pete claimed a sticky vinyl-clad table, and after a minute a waitress showed up. Gus ordered, and quickly got, an amber ale.

Drinking midday before a day of studying was obviously a great idea.

He stopped his fingers from drumming on the table, which would show his tension.

Now they needed something to talk about. Besides the fact that Max and his buddies had killed Pete's friend.

"Are you in school?" he asked Pete.

"Grad school, political science, taking a semester off." Pete also had ordered a beer, drank a few mouthfuls, wiped his mouth. "You?"

"Biology undergrad."

"Going to medical school?"

"Thinking about it."

"Where're you from?"

It was a lot of rapid-fire questions. Was this guy working up some kind of dossier? Gus had read that all the leftist groups were infiltrated.

"Utah originally. And you?"

"New York. Though it's been a while since I've been there."

"Do you know Max from there?"

It was a stab in the dark. Though Pete didn't seem like one of Max's gay friends.

Pete stared at him a moment. "No, I don't. But Rob does."

Information was exchanged, gaze to gaze.

Rob had been an ex of Max's.

Cold fingers touched his spine.

"Actually, Rob is missing right now," Pete said. "A couple folks thought he went back to New York. He has family there. But that seemed weird to me. I thought he was estranged from them." The door opened, and Pete glanced over, then away. "Do you happen to know anything about that?"

"About what?"

"Rob being missing."

They exchanged another stare.

"I don't know why you think I would. Even if Odin's Hunt had anything to do with it, they wouldn't tell me."

A sardonic look crossed Pete's face, but whatever he was going to say, he let it go. "Okay."

Gus swallowed the rest of his ale and stood. "Thanks for the beer, but I'd better be taking off. I have a lot of studying to do."

Pete put out his hand. After a moment, Gus shook it.

"If you do hear anything about Rob, I'd appreciate knowing about it."

Gus shrugged. "Sure." He dove into his backpack, grabbed a pen and a random sheet of paper. Pete scrawled his name and number on it. Gus stuffed it in his pocket and headed out into the rain.

Next morning, he skipped his last class and took the bus home. It was a twenty-hour trip, and he hated it. Besides a pocket flask of whiskey, some games and music, and a biography of Lincoln, he'd brought homework. He ignored it, staring out the window. The bus toiled up through the Cascade Mountains, snow halfway down their flanks.

If he understood the lawyer, it'd be good to have as much information as possible. He knew some of the guys' names, though not all of them. Maybe he should talk to some of them. He wasn't the only one shocked by the death.

Maybe not. They might run to Bruni. He knew a lot already—the location of Odinshof, and where Rob fell.

Max would never tell him what he did with the body. In fact, right now, the silence from Max was complete.

He slept fitfully overnight, leaning on the cold glass of the window, and woke at dawn in Box Elder County, flat and cold. A faint light glowing at the horizon was the only evidence of sun. A cold front had blown in; a thin snow had started.

The bus came into the station an hour or so later. His mother picked him up. He was happy to see her, which half-surprised him. He'd missed her more than he'd realized. They awkwardly hugged across the car's front seat. As she drove toward the house, the town lay empty and pure, like a neutral-toned holiday card edged with snow.

Thanksgiving passed like an anxiety dream. During the day, his mother having refused all help in the kitchen, he borrowed her car and escaped to a park at the edge of town for a long walk. His goal was to let go of all thought. A lot of other people had done the same thing, though, and he found himself tense even here, deciding how and when to nod to walkers as they passed.

At dinner, he bit his tongue to avoid a fight. Afterward, he sidestepped his father by texting some high school friends and going out to get drunk. His ride stayed sober and dropped him back home at two a.m. with no incident.

In his childhood room, in darkness, he lay staring at the ceiling, which slowly whirled. He'd already puked in his friend's backyard so he expected to sleep now. But he couldn't.

His mind returned to the tangle with Odin's Hunt.

Everything was pointing one direction—morality, pragmatism, sanity.

But he needed to see Max again before he could be certain.

Part of him still hoped for some magic that would give him Max back.

His mom dropped him off at the bus station late the next morning. The green glass of the station windows reflected wan sunlight. She got out of the car to hug him good-bye. "This bus ride is just too crazy. For Christmas, let me buy you a plane ticket, okay?"

"Sure, Mom. Thanks!"

For all values of "sure, thanks" that meant the opposite.

But he needed her as fallback for paying a lawyer.

He wanted to do it without them, if he could. He wanted to go forward with his life, not slide back into being his parents' son. But right now he still needed them.

The same bus ride unrolled in reverse, but at least he was going back where he wanted to be, sort of.

He'd been home barely fifteen minutes when he got a text from Max.

<Back in town. You free this evening?>

A jolt of anxiety, so hard he almost dropped the phone.

A million thoughts went through his head.

But he'd wanted to see Max.

<Yes>

<Come over at 8>

He walked to Max's apartment through a chilly night, over-cast, no rain but with mist haunting hollows and low places. Christmas lights had gone up around windows and trees even in his student neighborhood. The beginning of the festive season was in the air. About the holidays, he just felt numb.

On the stairs to Max's apartment, the shadow of the bannister had never been so film noir. The dense shadows whispered about killing. Someone *had* been killed.

He paused on the steps, and darkness engulfed him—fever dreams, whispers of danger, poison romance. Nothing was like being thrown onto the bed as if he weighed nothing, held down by the man on top of him and fucked. Sex that consumed like fire, better than whiskey, twisted life in it rising, entwining him, filling him. Bruising sex that was love. A violet-black cord pulled him toward Max.

At the end of the apartment house hallway, by Max's door, he knocked. Max opened. They stared at each other, checking for subtle signs. Max looked unchanged.

"Come in," he said.

He stood silhouetted for a moment against the torchiere glow, a solid presence. As they moved into the light of the apartment, he came into three dimensions. Light gleamed from his shaved head. His shirt strained on his broad shoul-ders; the collar showed the edge of the tattoo that curved from his neck down his back, a wolf and a waterfall of runes.

Gus's body felt heavy with doom, but a haze of physical attraction filled him.

"I've been running around and haven't had time to make dinner. Want some pasta and red sauce? The sauce is store-bought, but I can put some hamburger in it."

"Sure."

"I have some wine if you want it."

Gus seated himself on a stool at the kitchen counter, accepted a glass of syrah, and watched Max cook.

The fog from the hallway backed off.

Max still hadn't touched him. Part of him still longed for him, even while so much argued the other way.

"I heard about Josh and you fighting the guy in the park," Max said, stirring the sauce in the pan. He glanced at Gus, inviting a response.

Gus told his version of the story. "I wasn't interested in fighting. I just wanted to get us out of there."

"Smart of you. I gather Josh was questioned by the police."

"They came to my door too. I told them I didn't want to talk without a lawyer. They pushed me a little, but then they left. I haven't heard back. I talked to a lawyer, though."

"Good idea."

He stared at Max, who reached for some oregano.

The fear returned, knotting his stomach.

Looking at the pan, Max said, "I think you're probably safe. Josh has been talking to Bruni. Bruni was able to find out that the guy survived. So Josh is up for assault, not manslaughter. I hooked him up with my legal contact. He'll get taken care of." He eyed Gus. "You definitely want a different lawyer, from the purely legal point of view."

Max could be so sane. So pragmatic. Sometimes.

Part of him wanted to walk over, put his arms around Max, be in his space, his smell, bay rum and sweat and the indefinable scent that was Max.

Part of him was heavy with fear.

How could Max justify killing?

"Josh thinks blacks should go back to Africa," he said. "Bruni is interested in white heritage. What do you believe?"

Max kept poking at the pan with a wooden spoon. "Let's talk over dinner."

He served the pasta at the kitchen counter, lighting the orange candle with three wicks. After a time, face in shadow, he began.

"For me, it's not about fascism. I'd call myself an esoteric traditionalist. It's about going back to an earlier world, to the Paleolithic. To tribe. A word that doesn't just belong to Native Americans. The ideal tribe, the form that lies beyond the forms of men. In that and through that deeply knowing the self. Being a warrior, a warrior with spiritual power. Taking oneself out of the modern world and returning to the world of transcendence. Struggling toward enlightenment through the most traditional forms, seeing through and past and deeper at every step. To the heights and depths of the warrior spirit. A man in the deepest sense, a man among his tribe."

Gus saw the image that glimmered there, moving in the air above the candle like a dark flame.

"It's a utopian idea, I know."

"But Bruni talks about white heritage. What does your utopia have to do with that?"

"I work with those I feel a kinship with, and Bruni is one of them. He is a true priest. As is Ganefard." The Hunt name of Jake, the gothi. "We don't agree on every point, and that doesn't matter."

He gestured with the wine bottle, and raised an eyebrow—more wine? Gus nodded. Max filled his glass.

"I agree with Bruni in that I'm not an egalitarian. I don't believe all men are equal. I believe some men retain the god-spirit, and some men don't. Some men have the passion to seek the deep and primal, the world of original form, which is the true tradition. In a way it doesn't matter what tradition you start from, but we start from the Northern one."

There was something here, beautiful if dark.

But he saw again the pale body in moonlight, the pool of black under it.

"Someone died, Max. Someone who I think was your friend, at one point."

Max sighed and took a mouthful of wine.

"I regret the death, but I also don't think of it as the worst thing possible. Rob died well, and he's out of this sorry, fucked-up world now. Arguably a good thing."

Gus thought of his own X-Acto knife, the cuts along his legs, which he knew were only one step before cuts along his wrists.

"I did not choose it. Odin chose it. I respect Odin's choice. I was in a place to let Rob go free. But that wasn't what happened. I see no need to explain what happened to the gatekeepers of the current state."

Max was hypnotic in his utter certainty. His connection with his own spirit—higher self, shadow, hard to say—gave him clarity. He showed no doubt.

He was watching Gus's face. He reached out, grabbed the hair at the back of Gus's head, drawing him forward kissed him, biting him, so Gus's lip bled. Max sat back with blood on his mouth.

"I want to fuck you."

This might be the last time.

The gunmetal coverlet lay folded back. The room filled with cast shadows, from the black candle on the bedside table. Max laid him face-down, and touching his cock entered him, at first slowly, letting Gus adjust, and then ramming. Gus did his best to let go, and as Max fondled him came into his hand.

The energy flowed, a taste of fire and wine, but far away. The deep release, the utter giving up of spirit didn't come. Too much of Gus was ambivalent.

He didn't ask what Max did with the body. Max didn't volunteer it.

Max seemed to fully believe Odin had wanted it.

But letting a god talk you into murder was insane.

~

Puabi-Ekur drew closer, carefully. They didn't want to be perceived.

They knew who the djinni was now.

Djinn had a particular flavor. A little insane. They thought themselves gods, and they were gods, or had been millennia ago.

Max.

Chapter 32

At midday, Daegal and his men neared the farthest outpost of Ealdorman Adel's holding, a village barely big enough to have a hall. It was a hot day—he'd stripped to his tunic. A brilliant sun sparkled in a fair sky; the scent of flowers floated everywhere.

Flanked by oak trees in new leaf, the road widened as they approached the village. The horses were tired after the long trek, or he'd have ridden in.

It hardly mattered if he entered in state.

"Boy," he called, to a barefoot young man who'd stopped hoeing a rocky field to watch them pass, "is this Lord Wihtred's holding?"

"'Tis. You will come to the hall soon, if that is where you are heading."

The hall produced no one of more rank than the house-keeper, but in short order she got Daegal and his men quartered. They would sleep in the main hall.

The cook gave them a lunch of barley soup and beer in the kitchen annex. Afterward, the master of arms met them in the practice field, a long slope down from the hall.

"I am glad I stayed," he told Daegal. "Most of the rest of the force are off hunting."

"With dogs?"

"No, they dare not take the lord's hounds. The lord goes only once or twice a year. The men go in handfuls, deer stalking, several spots around here. It is a rare wood for deer." He grinned and sized Daegal up. "Let us spar a little."

After he knocked down the master of arms with a practice sword, then bruised him with a practice spear, Daegal said he was getting tired.

It was clear the hearth-guard here had no real captain. The master of arms provided training and some governance, but not much more.

They had to be trying him out for captain of arms. At least Lord Wihtred was unlikely to try to seduce him. Wihtred had been married nearly fifty years to the same woman and had fathered two sons, each with their own nearby holding.

That evening, Daegal attended supper in the main hall. If Adel's hall was the grandest he'd ever been in, this was the smallest, not even as large as his father's.

The hall's pine rafters held up an arched ceiling above a middle aisle. Along the walls draped woven and embroidered hangings, deep greens and blues. Everything was doll-sized compared to Adel's hall. Daegal sat at the head table, his seat to the left of the lord's, but serving began without lord or lady in attendance.

"Where are Lord Wihtred and his lady?" he asked the serving woman, a broad-faced villager in her middle years.

"My lord, it can take them time to make ready. We are asked not to wait."

The cook provided mutton stew, and the serving woman poured a decent ale. Daegal's party, at a nearby table, got the same provender. There was nothing to complain about.

He glanced across the hall, buttery in the light of the hanging lamps, the gathering of people eating, talking, laughing.

Why did he feel wistful?

A pang crossed his heart. His life had flowed through his hands like water; he had nothing left to show for it.

His marriage was over, Ethelreda gone, her wave of dark hair and slightly acid sweetness lost forever. He was too angry to miss her, but they'd had happiness sometimes. His children were dead. Long-ago laughter, voices calling in a meadow, the buttercup color of his daughter's hair—all his memories were so threaded with sorrow he couldn't touch them.

He was young yet. He could marry again. He could have children.

He turned back to his ale.

Halfway through the meal, each on the arm of a servant, Lord Wihtred and Lady Gunhild entered. She was tiny, white hair wisping from a headband. Her shut eyes, her timid movements, her hand clamped on the arm of her serving-maid told him she was blind.

Lord Wihtred was much taller, with a drooping salt-and-pepper mustache, and Daegal could imagine him as a fearsome fighter once. Even now, the bristling brow could strike fear into underlings. But his gaze was vague, and he seemed brittle if well-tended, leaning heavily on his serving man. Daegal rose and bowed as Wihtred came to the table.

Wihtred stared at the younger man blearily. "You must be Lord Daegal, come from Ealdorman Adel in the east."

"I am, my lord."

"Welcome to my service. We shall do the swearing-in tomorrow, when we can locate the priest."

Wihtred turned himself to his food, muttering and chomping, occasionally reaching out to take his wife's hand. She was fed by her maid, although she was allowed to take bread on her own.

It was a very different court than Adel's. Daegal didn't miss the recent past, but here he was alone entirely.

He cast his eye along the hall, half-empty though it was tiny. The master of arms had said most of the men were hunting. They hadn't returned for supper. That seemed an unwise call.

They held this place against the Britons. He could have taken it with twenty men. His work was cut out for him, training them.

Besides the few who'd come with him—nominally his men, though he didn't know them well—there were perhaps twenty more people. Dessert was served, milk pudding, and soon after Wihtred and his lady left. The master at arms gestured Daegal to his table and introduced him to the men present.

Daegal made his excuses as soon as he could, giving his men leave to stay. They were happy to be sitting still and drinking ale. Outside lay a spring night, only a few stars visible, haze lit by a half-moon.

Next morning, high-flying larks calling, he began gently to nudge the master of arms to more rigor.

They sparred on the trampled grass of the practice field. Between two bouts, breathing hard, the master of arms offered: "We keep a pretty good eye on where the Britons are ranging. The traditional time of raids is early winter. It is true they could strike so early. But it would be very rare."

Daegal satisfied himself with knocking the man down a few times. When the hearth-guard came back, he took their measure. One or two neared his own level of skill, and he began to train with them.

He was the best of them.

He hadn't expected that.

He'd focused for months on his own training. It had been his only outlet. He'd had few friends and little society at Adel's hall, marked as he was by his friendship with the ealdorman.

The master of arms didn't care he'd been bested. "I am glad the ealdorman sent you! We have need of a good fighting man around here. Someone to help train these green young boys, who think they know what they are doing."

A couple men were Daegal's age, late twenties. After a time, finding him easy of conversation and not condescending, they struck up friendships.

Over ale one supper, one of them, Eadwine, defended the hearth-guard's hunting.

"We are not as careless as you think. It is unknown for the Britons to come so early. They are tending the fields, as most of our folk are. Hunting, mayhap. Not fighting. It is not the season for raiding." He drained his ale and gestured for more. "But you have the right of it. We shall not leave the holding so unattended again." He leaned in and spoke more quietly. "You must come hunting with us, though. The roe deer, in the woods here, give excellent chase."

A last sickle of waning moon, a thin remainder like a rind of cheese, hung in the sky as he, Eadwine, and a couple other men-at-arms left the village. They camped at the forest's edge and woke in the forest before dawn, in the blue dark where he could barely distinguish tree from tree. Fog lay in the hollows, wisping between trunks, a veil upon the blackthorn.

Between dark treetops, the sky lightened to pale blue. The dawn calls of birds came, a thrush nearby singing, whistling, talking. The men rustled in their bedding. They had no fire, nothing to warn the deer. The scent of crushed greenery rose, and a wave of flower-scent from a dell between trees that brimmed with bluebells.

He was awake, his bedding rolled up, eating a heel of bread he'd brought, when Eadwine hunkered down beside him.

"There is a path the deer take in this part of the forest.

They frequent a line of glades, further on, and the path is their way there. It narrows; there is a cutoff. We thought to wait there. A few days ago, a couple of us made a blind."

Daegal got up and stretched, and silently the men made their way there.

The thrush continued, like half of a conversation in bird song. A breeze jostled the brush.

He recalled when he was a boy and he hunted the stag alone. The beginning of his life, that had been, in its way, his life as a man.

What had he done since then? Many things, but they amounted to little.

And here he was again.

A memory rose of deer-stalking with Maelan. Summer days, golden-green meadows shimmering under the sun, dark forest bowers. A breath of crushed greenery, the liquid of Maelan's mouth.

His thoughts glanced aside, to the deer itself.

That moment when a deer's dark-brown eyes caught his. Another life, different, wild, unknowable, gazed into his.

Whether or not they caught prey today, he was in the forest doing what he loved.

He was starting over. The thread went back into the weft, a new beginning.

As the last of rose color left the dawn sky, they found their places for the long wait.

Two of the men climbed trees; Daegal and Eadwine hid

in the blind. They'd made it of woven blackthorn, impenetrable, brushed in completely, invisible to a passing deer. Eadwine had brought a kind of vegetable mash he'd concocted, boiled leaves, pine needles, and dirt, which he swore tricked the deer's noses, and smeared it all over himself. He had plenty to share. For something to do, Daegal got a double handful and applied it.

"I have my eye out for this one buck," Eadwine said quietly. "Six tines, one broken off. He must have been fighting early."

They settled into a green meditation as the woods came fully into day. Birds disputed. Rabbits crossed the path. Daegal had brought a packet of bread and dried apples, and he brought some out when his stomach growled.

Then Eadwine tensed, and Daegal knew.

Away in the trees, the buck ambled slowly, big for a roe deer, his antlers six-tined with one broken. Among the crossing trunks and branches, a brownness browsing in the brush.

It would have to be Eadwine's shot. Daegal let himself go back into stillness.

The buck closed on them, nonchalant, clearly feeling unobserved. Eadwine nocked an arrow and shot.

A good shot, it landed in the buck's shoulder.

In a flurry of motion, the buck leaped. Eadwine grabbed another arrow and shot, hitting the disappearing hindquarters. A third arrow missed.

The men dropped out of their tree perches.

A trail of blood spattered the path.

"I have to go after him!" Eadwine cried. "He is wounded."

"You will not catch him," Daegal said. "You are on foot. He is a roebuck."

"I need to try. My arrow is in him. It is the right thing."

"Very well. You do not need me."

"No." The other two men followed Eadwine, wordlessly. They'd help fell and butcher the deer, if it came to that. Grabbing their remaining arrows, the three men left along the narrow trail, jogging.

Daegal heard their footsteps a while, then they grew quiet.

He found himself frowning and tense, angry, but he didn't know why.

He'd seen himself in the buck.

Men chased the deer. Wolves chased the deer. The deer ate grasses, trees, berries, mosses—they ate the forest. All beings were food.

And yet, on a spring morning, couldn't a lord of the forest be left alone?

He sat a long time in the ruined blind, kicked apart as Eadwine leaped up to shoot.

After a time, he came to himself. The forest returned to its noisy peace. The thrush called, and another answered, trading bits of song, talking about territory or flirting. Finch and redwing darted in and out. Above the tree canopy, the wide sky arched, deep clear blue. A wind shook the trees, and the branches danced.

He let go of the passion that had swept him, which he still didn't fully understand.

Then he saw her.

Between the boles of two big oaks, her ears twitching, cropping a tuft of grass, sniffing further, stood a doe.

Reflexively, he grabbed for an arrow, and then he dropped it.

She hadn't seen him, and he sat quiet in the remains of the blind, his scent still covered by Eadwine's glop.

She was a being like he was, and he was visiting her house. He had no strong need of meat, as he would in winter. He could let her go.

He was content to watch her, delicate, discerning as she nosed along the ground, choosing her food thoughtfully. This was deer nature, but it put him in mind of a woman, a maker of careful choices, and you would never know why she chose one thing over another, even if she told you. A conversation he'd had with Reda: "Of course I could not wear the green kirtle. There is a green kirtle here already; it belongs to my sister!" Never mind it wasn't the same green, nor even close.

He had prayed to Woden for the hunting, but this doe didn't belong to him. A fairy, perhaps, or one of the fairy cattle herded by the uncanny glaistig.

"O lady of the greenwood," he said to the deer-girl in his mind, and stopped.

There was a peace to be made, and he didn't understand what.

So often he'd hunted—as a boy, with Maelan, as Reda's husband, and now. There had been a break, after Reda. In Adel's household, he hadn't spent much time in the greenwood.

This was his peace, and he had not had it.

He sat and watched the doe, minute after minute, in a trance. After a time, she looked up and caught his eye, as he knew she would. But she sensed he had no ill will toward her and went back to nosing and cropping.

He would never have a fairy lover. But he loved the wood with all his heart. Perhaps it returned his love, in its fashion.

After a time, she bounded away.

Chapter 33

*I*n the morning, Gus woke to a chilly room, shadow spread across the white ceiling. Max was gone.

He pulled on his shirt and jeans. On the kitchen counter, Max had left a cardboard box that held a couple of croissants. From under this poked a note, written in Max's square hand in thick, black ink:

Had to run an errand. Back in an hour or so.

Gus heated the croissants and made coffee, in no huge hurry to start the day. He preferred Max's apartment to his own, though he wanted to be out before Max returned.

It was the Saturday after Thanksgiving; he should study for finals, and he would eventually, but not yet. He inhaled the coffee as he scrolled through social media on his phone.

After a while he sat back, let his gaze fall out the window to black empty branches, beyond them a concrete sidewalk and a spray of green grass.

In his body lingered the deliciousness of their last fuck.

Did he really have to give this up? Maybe he could talk Max around. Max was an intelligent man, after all.

He hadn't told the police anything yet. What if he could change Max's mind? After all, it wasn't actually Max who did the killing. You could argue it was all a huge accident.

He heard the apartment door open, and after a moment Max came into the tiny living room.

"That went faster than I expected. Do you ski, or snowboard?"

"I have snowboarded."

"We should go up to the snow. My friend has a cabin."

Maybe this was Max's way of asking for a truce.

∼

Max dropped him off at his apartment. "I'll go to the grocery, get some things for the weekend. It won't take me long."

Upstairs, Gus packed his duffel bag with overnight things, thinking of the snow: long underwear, a second pair of jeans, extra wool socks.

Maybe it made sense that Max acted like nothing had happened.

From Odin's Hunt's point of view, Gus had sworn a blood-oath. He'd told both Max and Bruni he thought it was dangerous to go outside the law. But Max felt protected by having a good lawyer. Max knew Gus had seen his own lawyer, but he approved.

Maybe Max assumed that, whatever Gus's misgivings, it would sort out.

Gus owed him a conversation to break things off, anyway.

He threw on his puffer coat—a heavy parka, for winters in Utah—and ran downstairs with his bag.

But foreboding sat in his gut, and when he saw Max's big white truck at the curb he stopped short.

As he stood on the sidewalk, rain spat in his face. At the pass, the weather app said, there was snow.

Maybe this was crazy. Max was dangerous.

But Rob had written an article naming Max in a crime. Gus had done nothing, at least not yet.

Part of him just wanted a vacation. He'd been studying for finals. Christmas at his parents wasn't going to be any fun. Just to get away and snowboard and eat and drink and fuck and not think about things—couldn't he have a vacation like that?

Max leaned across the seat and popped open the passenger door.

"You getting in?"

People passing on the street were eying him, like he should get in.

Simple courtesy pushed him over the edge. He got in.

They took the drive up to the snow, up to the pass.

Coming out of the city, stop and go traffic clogged the

highway. Some tiny red convertible cut Max off, which he took in stoic silence, knuckles clenched.

They drove in silence—fifteen minutes, a half-hour.

Along the way, the rain turned to sleet, and then to snow. First, the verge beside the road began to show a dusting from earlier, then the thick firs, like green bears hunkered in for winter, each wore a shawl of snow. Then the road itself showed snow-dust, a thin skin with tire tracks through it, then thicker.

All this time, Max had been silent beside him. It didn't feel like the companionable silence they'd driven in, his first visit to Odinshof.

They weren't in the first flush of sex. But that wasn't it.

In the space behind the bench seat, Gus noticed grocery bags. He poked through them: steaks, broccoli, potatoes for dinner; breakfast things. In a separate bag sat a fifth of bourbon.

"I can help pay for the groceries."

"Don't worry about it. You're a starving student."

"Not literally starving. You were saying about snow-boarding?" He was desperate to keep the conversation going.

"There're some snowboards and boots up there, at the cabin. You may fit them. We could do a rental, too."

"Let's check out what's at the cabin first."

Max nodded and kept driving, eyes on the road.

The road though slick was still wet, not icy, with snow that melted under the tires. Max had studded tires on the truck, so there'd be no need to stop and switch to chains.

The driving didn't take that much focus.

"Maybe this isn't the right time to talk, but we do need to," Gus said.

"I don't want to talk right now."

"Okay." There was never any use pushing Max. Besides, a big part of Gus didn't want to talk either.

"I was thinking we'd go to the cabin first, then boarding, if you like."

"Sure. I haven't been for a while, so I should start out slow."

The silence didn't ease.

The mountains loomed, slate blue where snow found no purchase. Huge curtains of icicle, frozen waterfalls, fell across walls of basalt. The plowed snow stood six feet tall, then ten feet tall.

Max crossed the pass and after a while took a side-road, deep in snow. Even with studded tires and all-wheel drive, at one turn the truck began to fishtail, a sideways wiggle as if it had its own life. It began to fully slide in deep snow. But Max straightened the truck and drove on.

Up a short, steep, unplowed driveway, with a quick turn and a burst of momentum they were there. Max killed the engine.

The small house had a stone-built foundation, shingles above blackened wood that had never been painted, above those a roof alpine-steep. Snow filled a couple gabled corners. In its way, it was perfect, in the blue-shadowed snow of afternoon.

He wished he could keep Max as a boyfriend. That couldn't happen, but he wanted to make it an excellent good-bye.

Gus climbed out, duffel bag over his shoulder, and crunched through the knee-deep snow. Max strode up spindly-looking stairs and plugged the combination into the electronic lock. Inside, they loaded the groceries into the fridge.

"I brought wood for the woodstove." Max returned with a couple bundles. From the clock in the kitchen, Gus registered it was nearly two.

Max followed his gaze. "Do you want to try getting a few runs in today, before it gets dark? We can snowboard in the dark, too, I'm okay with that."

Gus shook his head. "Going at night seems dumb. It's been a few years since I've been on a snowboard."

"Let's check out the stuff here."

One pair of boots was close, but not close enough. "Let's just rent," Gus said, leaning back, sitting on the floor of the mudroom. "It's not that big a deal. I don't want to break a leg because my boots don't fit." He grinned at Max. "If I break a leg, I want to do it out of my own personal stupidity."

Max grinned back.

Maybe he was finally chilling out.

But it was two-thirty now. They had only an hour and a half of sun left, minus time to do the rental.

"Let's bag it for today, for the snowboarding," Gus said. Now he wished they'd come up Friday and taken two days.

"There are some trails," Max said. "We could snow-shoe." Max had brought all his own winter gear, and several pairs of snowshoes hung on the mudroom wall, easier to fit than snowboarding boots. "We just need to avoid breaking up the cross-country runs. I'll start the fire before we go out."

Gus found some snowshoes that worked. Max built and lit the fire. They threw their parkas back on. Past the deck behind the house rose slate-colored peaks capped with snow, below them a solid bank of fir. The sky, ice blue at zenith, held a hint of peach near the horizon. The air smelled of woodsmoke.

Already the sun was falling behind the mountains, which cast long shadows on the untouched snowfield behind the house. "If I break trail for a little, there's a path we can catch up with, behind those trees."

They crunched and squeaked, walking through new powder. A cold sifting made its way into Gus's left boot. Gus was satisfied to let Max break trail, taller and bigger as he was, making a path maybe six inches deep; it would have been thigh-height if they'd tried to walk. The main path was twin, a left lane for snowshoes, a wider right lane for skis. Over the pale blue snow indented with shadow, dark green almost black firs leaned, among them a sprinkling of pale-trunked alder.

His body dropped into hiking mode, and happiness settled on him. The trail climbed from lookout to lookout. At one, over a sheer drop, across the sky a peak gleamed with the last orange sunlight on it. He breathed in deep, bringing the cold air into his lungs.

It had been a while since he'd been in the mountains. He'd missed it.

From behind, Max grabbed him in a bear hug. He relaxed into Max's arms.

"You have a feel for the outdoors," Max said. "I don't get —never mind."

"What is it?" Gus felt at last they might be getting somewhere.

"Never mind." There was a full stop in Max's voice, and Gus dropped the subject.

After that, though, the tension eased. At a further lookout, Max checked his phone for the time.

"We should head back. Though, with the snow, there'll be light to see."

"Maybe we can walk again tonight."

Max eyed him. "Maybe."

In the cabin, Gus grabbed the bourbon and two glasses, poured a finger into both, opened the woodstove, and threw himself on the braided rag rug in front of it—ancient, obviously a fire rug, burnt in places.

In the flames, red caverns opened below minarets of gold. The bourbon warmed his throat and belly.

Max was messing in the kitchen. Gus said, "Come sit with me."

Max turned a stare on him, almost hostile, but came to sit.

Gus took another sip of bourbon—flaming all the way down—and began to snuggle Max, playful, biting his arm through the thick flannel.

Taking both Gus's shoulders, Max pushed him to the floor. His head knocked the wood, hard, but he didn't react.

Max lay on top of Gus, kissing him, biting him as if he'd eat him.

Gus responded, rising from the floor enough to lift Max, crotch against crotch. Max bit him, hard, on the neck, on the jawbone, shoved Gus down again, kissed him forcing his mouth open, pinning his wrists to the floor.

Then he stood and hoisted Gus standing, by the arm, unbuckling his belt.

Gus snagged his glass and tossed down the rest of his bourbon, letting Max do what he wanted.

Max ripped down Gus's jeans; they fell at his ankles, trapped by his boots. Max grabbed Gus's cock, flipped him, and bent him over the back of the couch by the woodstove, fondling his ass and balls, sticking an unlubed finger in his ass. Stepping away, backward, to his backpack, he pulled a condom and lube from the front pocket, ripped open the shiny packet, slicked himself.

Planting himself in Gus, he again grabbed Gus's cock.

His body wanted to jet immediately. Sensing this, Max held off, taking his hand away, grabbing Gus's hips and pounding himself into Gus, hard, harder. Then his hand returned.

Like the fire, it was magic, stories from the Otherland, pleasure, yearning. Max's energy was like living fire. Again, again, again; the rhythm built. Gus came into Max's hand. Max groaned and emptied himself.

A moment of stillness fell, a moment of connection; Gus released his energy into the space between them.

Whatever this was, it wasn't over yet. There was something here.

He could tell Max felt it, too.

Max kissed the back of his neck and levered himself off. Peeling off the condom, he tossed it in the trash.

Gus found the bathroom and cleaned himself up. He showered briefly, letting the hot water wash away confusion and a feeling of somehow being trapped.

As the sex ebbed, his uneasiness returned.

What did Max have in mind?

He threw on the same clothes, and found Max prepping the steaks in the kitchen. Scent told him the potatoes were in the oven.

He settled himself, leaning against the kitchen counter, next to Max.

"We need to talk," he said.

"After dinner."

Full night had fallen. In the small living room, Gus lit candles. He handed Max his glass of bourbon; Max took a swig. "These can sit for a few," he said, setting the steaks aside.

"Come sit with me," Gus said, patting the couch next to him, and Max did. Gus put his arms around him. Despite his hovering unease, he felt release in Max's aura.

After a minute, Max said, "I was going to do this later, but now seems like the time." He stood. Gus moved to follow, but Max said, "Stay here."

He went and rummaged in his duffel, still in the mudroom. Coming back, he tossed a cobalt-blue velvet bag onto the low table in front of the couch. Gus raised his eyebrows.

"My runes. Ground yourself and pick one."

"For what?"

"For the weekend."

Gus did as he was told, grounding himself and throwing a cord upward to the sky, to the universe, as he'd been taught and as Alyssa's coven did. The idea of Alyssa flared, a bright star in his firmament.

Max might be going, but he still had her.

Letting the thought go, he felt his connection with earth and sky.

An image crossed his mind, of the Hekate wheel stone. He touched it in his jeans pocket.

Lady, you offered protection. Please, now, just in case, I ask for your help. I may need it.

Hearing this call, Puabi-Ekur was pulled out of the ether. They knew that the Lady had deputized them in this conflict.

They accepted her choice.

Chapter 34

*E*adwine lost the buck and returned in a foul temper. Daegal commiserated with him, but he wanted to be left alone.

As spring advanced, fawns appeared in the woodlands, lambs in the village yards. Wood anemones bloomed in the forest valleys, shaded by the canopy; shy dog roses heralded the start of summer. Daegal continued training the hearth-guard, settling into it.

One summer day, after a rainstorm had left the yard around the hall all puddles, Daegal crossed it, whistling on his way to the practice field. He saw out of his peripheral vision Lady Gunhild and her handmaiden, crossing the other direction, tentative and slow. Despite her handmaiden's help, Lady Gunhild slipped and fell.

He was there almost immediately.

"My lady! Let me help you up!" Between him and the maid, they had her upright quickly. She weighed nothing, like a twig dressed in linen, her hair white down-fluff. "Are you hurt?"

"Oh, oh! Oh no! My ankle! Let me sit."

They supported her into her chamber. With her lord, she shared a nearby smaller hall, lime-washed wattle and daub. Indoors, one simple room, it had permanent benches and a broad bed with a linen coverlet whose muted reds and purples matched the walls' woven and embroidered hangings. As she had for the main hall, the lady had created these with her women before she lost her sight.

The girl knelt before Lady Gunhild, put her foot in her lap and pulled down the stocking with care. The ankle looked pink and puffy, beginning to swell.

"How is it, Louana?" the old woman asked the girl, her voice quavering.

"My lady, it may be sprained."

"Oh, no, no, no." The lady clutched herself, beginning to rock back and forth. The girl moved the foot carefully, watching her lady's face.

"My lady, I think it is not broken, though I am no expert."

"Who should I call in?" Daegal asked the girl. "Have you an herb-woman or bone-setter or such?"

They needed to deal with this, and best before the lady was too distraught. Worst case, she could hurt herself further; otherwise, with care it would likely pass off in a week or so.

Louana met his gaze. Her eyes were cornflower blue. He'd never noticed that.

"There is a healer in the village, my lord. I can wrap this

in a flax and hemp seed poultice while I send one of the boys for him."

"If you think so."

"I can go get the things, my lord." She hesitated, then said in a rush, "My lord, please can you sit with my lady, for a few moments? I fear she will be afraid otherwise."

"Oh, stay with me," the old lady cried.

"I shall do so, my lady." To Louana he said, "Be you quick!"

He didn't want the old lady frightened; he wanted her ankle to mend. But he also didn't want to be tied up with this all day. He'd been on his way to spar with the men.

"I shall, my lord." The girl dropped him a quick curtsey —he far outranked her—and scrambled out the door to find poultice materials.

The old lady took his hand. He squeezed hers.

"You are a kind man, Lord Daegal. Thank you for troubling yourself with an old woman. I hear good things about you! I believe my lord husband will make you captain of arms soon."

That was good news. Though who knew how true.

"Thank you, my lady. I would like to be of service. I am admiring your hangings."

"Those are from the first years of my marriage."

She told him some history of the holding. The door opened to a ray of rain-washed sunlight; Louana stood there with a wet cloth bag and strips of linen. She cleared her throat.

"Ah, Louana. I will tell my lord of your kindness, Lord Daegal."

Curtseying, the girl met his gaze a moment.

Eyes like scraps of summer sky. Of course, she usually kept them cast down.

The Briton girl was a slave belonging to the lord. There'd been few in his father's house, more here because of the closeness to the disputed border; captives often became slaves.

In a glance, he checked her over. She couldn't be older than late teens. Her bronze-colored hair hung in a long braid, wisps framing her face. A sweet form in her long kirtle, plump breasts and thighs like a pullet's.

No time for such thoughts.

"Have you sent a boy to the village?"

"I have, my lord."

He turned to Lady Gunhild.

"My lady." He bowed to the lady—she couldn't see it, but it was second nature. "I will take my leave."

After that, Lady Gunhild sometimes asked him to sit with her in her chamber, or beside her at supper. The girl Louana stayed by her, helping her walk and eat and running small errands for her. She was shy with Daegal at first, but warmed up over time. He found himself looking forward to seeing her, trying to get her to talk.

Trying to get a side glance from the blue eyes. Thinking about how she would cry out underneath him.

He needed to take care. She was unmarried, far below him in rank, and the main help of Lady Gunhild. Also skittish. Not like his goose-girl.

A pang shot through him, for the girl who'd first taken

him into her bed, for the pleasure of it. But Louana wasn't her.

He kept it to the lightest of flirting—glances, nods, a tone of voice. He did not touch her.

Summer reached its height and began to wane. Lord Wihtred formally made him captain of arms, and for the appointment threw a feast.

Midday, on the practice field, the priest and lord led a small ceremony, banners whipping in the wind. The men offered him allegiance, as he had done to the lord. That night, local gentry and much of the village crowded into the Lord Wihtred's hall, torch-lit, tall yellow flames showing off still-bright hangings.

The cooks and bakers had worked for a week ahead. The meal came out in courses: pigeon with hazelnuts, rabbit stew with herbs, mint-flavored young mutton, venison with bacon, pork with apples, and with them broad beans and peas, mushrooms, cooked turnips and carrots, and salads of greens. Alongside were breads of many kinds, including a shortbread that was a specialty of the local bakers. The meal ended with cheeses soft and hard, and honey tarts. Throughout, three maids served ale and mead, and to the high table imported wine.

A scop, a poet who sang to the harp, performed traditional lays and songs of his own creation. Toward the feast's end, with the honey tarts and a light, sweet white wine from the south, Lady Gunhild called him to sit by her side.

"My lady, you shall make me jealous!" Wihtred said, grinning at Daegal. After numerous cups of wine, Wihtred was expansive.

"Jealous, my lord? I think not. But speaking of love—come sit by me, Lord Daegal—we should discuss these things."

He settled beside her on the bench, frowning in unease.

"Now that you are captain of arms, we must get you a wife, Lord Daegal!"

"My lady, I had a wife before. We are divorced."

She waved her hand airily. "No matter. I knew of it. There was no dishonor to you in it." She leaned toward her husband. "My lord—my lord, do you hear me? We need to have more feasts such as this, and invite landed war-companions and ealdormen, and their daughters!"

Wihtred chuckled. "If you so desire, wife."

She turned back to Daegal. "We shall get you a good-looking one. But there is a measure in these things." Over her shoulder, toward Louana, she said, "Tell me, Louana. Would he turn the eye of a good-looking woman?"

Louana gasped. He glanced at her out of the corner of his eye; her face was a heated pink.

"Oh, my lady—I cannot answer that!"

"Yes, you can, silly girl. Or, if you cannot, describe him to me."

He caught her eye. She bit her lips, trying not to laugh.

"He is of middle height, with sandy blond hair and a pleasing countenance. He is very fit. He has a warm smile. He... my lady, even the prettiest woman would have some interest!" He laughed and mouthed a kiss at her. "He is, after all, our strongest fighter and our captain."

"Very well," said the lady. "You have told me what I need to know. We shall find him a pretty lady."

Maybe Gunhild didn't notice the atmosphere; maybe she didn't care. She herself had drunk several cups of wine. Even the Briton girl had had a cup or two; the lady made sure she'd tried it. Daegal had drunk many.

Louana wore a long pale-blue tunic, trimmed in blue ribbon. The torches struck gold from her bronze hair. He wanted to see the blue in those eyes as they opened wide, and wider. In surprise, he hoped in pleasure. He'd had his share of women; he understood a bit about their desires. Though part of him simply wanted to trap her and have her, as a male cat does a female, climb on her and thrust himself between her thighs.

Better not. All the rules still applied.

A few minutes later, he stepped out to relieve himself.

The hall's exterior was also ringed in torches; above their light, the moon stood just past full in a clear black sky like water, at its edges stars. He walked a little, toward one of the annexes. He felt the turning of the season in the air, a hint of chill. Among the far trees, a stand of birch had begun to shake free of its leaves. The branches whispered in light wind.

Shortly the villagers would be needed for harvest. He'd need to drill them and the hearth-guard harder. They needed to be ready for the Briton raids.

Done, he paused a moment behind the annex building. The breeze cooled his forehead and arms. Between the torches and assembled bodies, even with the door open the hall had heated up. He stood letting the night wash over him.

He'd turned the corner to walk back to the feast when

he saw her. Quickly he retreated behind the annex. Louana came forward with head lowered, looking at the muddy straw-stuck track through the grass as if she sought something she'd dropped.

He should avoid her. She was young and had drunk strong wine. Perhaps the words of Lady Gunhild had fanned her ardor.

If the lady wanted to get him a wife, this was no time to take a concubine. If he needed release, there was a house in the village he could visit.

The girl passed the smaller hall's corner and stood looking all directions.

He realized she was looking for him.

The moonlight made sight tricky. He stood clear of the building, to be in plain view. When she saw him, she ran to him.

"What is your trouble, Louana?"

"Oh, my lord, I am so shamed. I spoke too freely."

She stopped a yard away from him. The blue of her kirtle shone, intense in the bluish moonlight.

"You mean, in describing me?"

"Yes, my lord. I am very sorry for it."

"It is no matter. I did not mind."

"You must think me a hoyden, a trollop." She advanced a few steps and stood biting her lip.

"No, I do not."

He was perhaps ten years older than she, and it felt like a century.

"You need to return to the hall, and before I do."

She peered at him in the uncertain moonlight.

"Do I?" she breathed.

Very young, and drunk.

"Yes."

She stepped forward, one step, two, till he felt the heat of her body. She smelled of honey, and below that female.

"Are you sure about this, Louana?"

She said nothing, only grabbed his hand and kissed it.

"Look you," he said, "this is not the time or place. It is my feast, I cannot disappear from it. And I would have you be sure of what you do. But do not feel ashamed."

He quickly scanned the area. No one was about, but he knew he only had a minute. Quickly, all in one movement, he grabbed her and pulled her against him, planting his hands on her firm young ass, and kissed her, deeply, plunging his tongue into her mouth. She tasted like honey and wine. Her slender tongue met his, and her pelvis pushed against him.

Using all his force of will, he put his hands on her hips and set her away from him.

"Think what you would do. But I will not take you now. Go back inside."

He wanted her gone before he changed his mind.

In the watery moonlight, she gave him one last, long look, then turned and hurried away. He stood for a minute, breathing heavily.

Chapter 35

*P*uabi-Ekur found themselves suddenly before the throne of Hekate Soteira.

"...my lady?"

The throne sat empty. Beside it, two torches flared, and red flames flickered below it.

They were supposed to figure this out without help.

Which meant that it was obvious.

Puabi-Ekur had poked a while at the story they shared with Gus. They hadn't seen the end of the fight, but they had a strong suspicion.

An empty throne, in the nonair the torch flames crackled.

Gus had called on them.

They had signed up for this.

Gus picked up the velvet bag and stuck his hand inside. Max's runes were ceramic or glass, he guessed glass, cool to the touch.

This weekend. Let it be all for the best.

He let his fingers choose a rune and pulled it out.

It was clear, thick glass, like ice.

Inguz.

He put it on the coffee table.

"Hmm," said Max, giving it a glance. "Fertility, particularly male fertility. A time of waiting, preparing for birth. Sometimes, endings before new beginnings, the finish of something. Some readers call it a portal to the Otherworld."

Gus had his own interpretations, similar enough, but an old annoyance rose inside him. Max always had to know everything.

"Yes," Gus said. He looked up, into Max's face. Max's hazel eyes met his.

"What does it mean to you?" he asked Max.

Max stared back, unblinking.

"I'm not sure yet."

"Okay."

He knew Max liked to play the big man, the strong, silent type. But he got sick of Max's need to always be in control. The only time he let go was when he came.

But it was a moot point.

"Time for me to cook."

He needed to talk to Max.

After dinner, Max had said.

~

After dinner, Max poured them each more bourbon. He gave the fire more wood, and they sat again by the woodstove, Max on the couch, Gus directly in front of the stove. Wanting to see the fire, he opened the glassed-in front door—the glass was smeared with soot.

"It'll make the room smoky," Max said.

"I'll close it in a minute."

Max breathed out, hard, as if he were angry, but Gus ignored him.

But feeling the heavy atmosphere behind him, he took no joy from the waving flames. He closed the stove door.

"What?" he said, without turning.

"Come sit beside me," Max said.

Gus almost said no. But he stood and went to the couch—an old caramel-colored leather one, with a tartan blanket thrown over its back.

He sat down, cross-legged on the couch, and turned toward Max. Max shifted so they faced each other.

"Tell me about talking to Pete, the Antifa guy," Max said.

Pure fear spiked in Gus. How did Max know about that?

"I ran into him on the street. He said he owed me a beer. I will generally take a free beer, and I did."

"What did you tell him?"

"He seemed curious about my life. I told him I was considering going to med school. I didn't tell him much."

"And?"

"And what? He asked if I knew where Rob was. I said, how should I know? He said, if you hear anything tell me, and he gave me his number. I said sure. We were both pretty clear I'd never call him."

A half-foot away from each other on the couch, he and Max stared into each other's eyes.

"You expect me to believe that," Max said.

"I do. Because it's true."

The fire flared and roared.

What was Max planning?

"Okay," Max said.

He stood.

"You wanted to take a walk. Let's go now."

Putting on their snowshoes, they followed the same path they had before. Max wanted to go farther. A waning half-moon had risen, which reflected from the snow made it bright enough to walk without a flashlight.

The cross-country ski trail disappeared, but a dent in the snow showed a lightly used hiking trail going up the side of the mountain. They took it.

Gus didn't know why they were out here. What did Max have in mind?

Unease settled in his gut.

A turn and then another brought black trees draped in blue, the hush of the snowy night. But he didn't trust this walk.

He stopped in his tracks. "I'd like to go back."

"Just a little way more. There's a lookout I'd like to show you."

Maybe it was a romantic gesture. Or mystical. Or something. Then they could be done with this walk.

He continued tramping behind Max.

Pushing past two big firs, which shook snow down upon them, they reached the outlook. A shoulder of white snow curved atop a cliff, a drop-off, basalt boulders far below. They crunched over to the edge.

Even with the moonlight, the stars shone like a scattering of jewels. Around stood a hundred-eighty degrees of mountains, a jagged rim with teeth of snow.

"If you cry out, you can hear an echo. But don't."

No. He could start an avalanche.

"I wanted you to see this view. It's one of my favorite places on earth."

He drew Gus close, puffy coat to puffy coat, and kissed him, warm liquid mouth yearning.

Gus's whole body relaxed. Max still loved him.

Max shoved him off the cliff.

Chapter 36

The day after Daegal's captaincy feast, he started the hearth-guard's drills at midmorning, not dawn. The whole day his mind was on Louana.

Eadwine laughed at him. It was summer still, with a hot sun—he found himself lying on the grass staring up at it, after Eadwine butted him with a thrust from a practice spear.

"Too much of that fine southern wine last night!" Eadwine cried. "You are slow!"

In the evening, Daegal sat by Lord Wihtred at the high table. Louana wouldn't meet his eyes, looked anywhere but at him, assiduously helping Lady Gunhild.

He let her be.

Who knew? He had to give her time. He wasn't in a hurry.

At the end of summer, in Lord Wihtred's holding, everyone worked together to bring in the harvest. With much work to do in a short amount of time, racing the weather, the social hierarchy broke down. All the villagers helped their lord, and in turn the lord's people helped the village—none was so high-ranked as to refuse. The priest and household performed a small first-fruits blessing on loaves from the first grain. Then came grain harvest and fruit harvest. Throughout, the women gleaned their kitchen gardens, pickling and drying vegetables and herbs.

Daegal kept a short guard for some semblance of order. For the grain, scything was the first task. Village laborers did most, but it was good, hard, thoughtless work, and Daegal was happy to help. He missed his own land, but he set that aside.

He was captain of the hearth-guard, Lord Daegal, rising here. That other life was a world away.

When they'd gotten the grain into the barns, they turned to other harvests. The village had several apple orchards, and it had been a good year. It was an all-day task for several days to pull the ripe fruit down and collect windfall for the pigs.

He spent these days training, but early evening of the second day, he came down the hill to see how the apple harvest went. He was late; most of the village was gone to the communal harvesters dinner.

In the blue dusk, gnarled trees stood in a haze of mist and shadow. He walked into the orchard, for pleasure.

At the far side, where long pale grass lay fallen among the trees, Louana sat up in a tree, barefoot.

Her skirts tied up, she'd climbed to gather the last

apples. Her basket sat at her tree's base in the gloom, her shoes and an unlit lantern beside it.

A swarm of midges rose, wings catching the last peach-colored light. Stretching for an apple, she didn't notice him.

He stepped on a twig.

"My lord!" she said, and stopped, clutching the apple to her chest.

"Hello, Louana." He leaned in among the branches. A scent of apples rose. He was close enough to touch her bare foot, but he didn't. "I have you treed, my dear."

She looked out the other direction, the trees looming from the blue haze. Far above, in a clear sky shading to indigo, one star shone.

"I could jump down, my lord, and run away."

"I might chase you."

She smiled. "I might turn to a rabbit and elude you, my lord."

"I might turn to a dog and catch you."

"I might turn to a fish and leap in the river."

"Would you run, though?" He reached up and stroked the sole of her foot. "In truth?"

She closed her eyes. So close, he could smell her, warm scent of girl. He clasped her foot, like clasping a hand: dusty, pink at toe and heel. Pretty, all of a piece with her fair skin, pink cheeks, bronze hair.

"I might not run," she whispered.

"I will wait tonight in the birch grove," he said, "the one you see from the main hall."

Her mouth fell half-open, lips like a promise.

"I do not know if I can get away."

"I know." He dropped a kiss on the top of her foot.

"I must get down now, my lord." He stood back, and she leaped down in a flounce of skirts, in a flurry untied her kirtle, let it fall.

In the half-dark, he felt her watching him.

Stepping up, she kissed him full on the mouth. He put his arms around her waist and drew her close, finishing the kiss. The smell of her, the feel of her, a double armful of girl. She broke away and searched his face in the dusk. Then, grabbing her basket and shoes, she turned her back and walked away, winding through the apple orchard to the long path. A couple other folk walked there, going toward the later hall supper.

After a time, he let himself catch up.

At dinner, Louana attended her lady, all circumspection; it was he who urged the Lady Gunhild to drink more than usual. Her husband wanted her to try the new imported wine. Generally, Louana slept at the foot of her lady's bed, in case her lady needed help in the night, but with a little help from wine, the lady might sleep the night through. No one cared if a man absented himself from the main hall at night unless he was part of the night watch.

After supper, knowing he might be there all night, alone or with company, he made his way to the wood. White birches shone against the darker line of trees.

The fingernail moon had long set when Louana came out carrying a covered lantern. The broad grass swale between the hall and the wood's edge rolled evenly enough for a walk by starlight.

She paused at the edge of the birches.

"Louana."

He stepped forward, and she came into his arms. He kissed her: thoughtful lips, a little chilly. Her body was tense.

"Come further into the forest. Here we may be seen."

She followed him like a lamb on a lead.

What was he doing?

He had little stomach to pursue a woman like Ethelreda —a potential wife. At least the harvest had precluded feast invitations to ealdormen's daughters. For a Briton slave, it would be no fall from grace to be his lover.

They passed through the silent, pitch-dark forest, their path broad enough they needed no light. Wind ruffled the branches with a sea-sound. An owl hooted.

At the base of an oak tree, he threw down his cloak. "Come, sit."

Feeling her fear, he set his back against the tree and took her in his arms, drawing her to lean against him. He stroked her hair.

"You are a beautiful girl. I am sure you have had many men pursue you."

"No, my lord. None at all. I have been dedicated to helping the lady since I was barely twelve summers."

"Mmm. No encounters, nothing?"

She shook her head. She shifted to face him, picking up the tiny leather-strung deer skull from his neck.

"What is this?"

"A hunting charm. My foster-brother gave it to me, years ago."

"Does it bring you luck?"

"It does. But you heard me say to Lady Gunhild I had been divorced. I had a wife named Ethelreda. We were married five years. We had three children. But the children died of fever, and she left me for her cousin."

She muttered something.

"What is that?"

"She was foolish, your Ethelreda. My lord."

"You need not 'my lord' me if we are alone."

She peered at him in the dark. "Please, do not talk. I have made up my mind, and I am here."

He kissed her then, gently, along her hairline and her nose and cheeks, then her mouth: sweet, she'd been chewing mint. Pulling up her skirts, he stroked her thighs, touched her warm, wet pussy.

Sitting up on his knees, he pulled her kirtle over her head, leaving her in her linen shift. He kissed and bit and licked her throat, neck, and shoulders, playing with her, tasting her, a little salt from sweat. Through the thin linen he squeezed and bit her plump breasts. She was moaning before he returned his fingers to her pussy.

Standing, he shucked his trousers. She stared at him in the black dark.

"Lie back, my sweet."

He thrust himself into her. It had been too long since he'd been with a woman; for all his caution, he spent himself quickly, groaning as he let go his seed. She patted his back, at random.

"I can do better by you, darling. Give me a little time."

In the meantime, he stroked her wetness with his fingers, again and again over the soft-hard nub; she began to pant and wriggle. He continued, teasing. The touch of her wet folds made him hard again, and he mounted her, feeling for the rhythm of her energy, waves growing stronger as the storm rose. She came, all of a sudden, crying out, and he let himself go into her, full release.

She clutched him and burst out crying.

"Louana!" He rolled to his side and gathered her to him. "Why do you cry?"

"I want this, I want you, my lord, but... ah, my lord, I do love you."

Love, love, what was love?

"No shame. Love is a goodness." He kissed her face. "Louana, do not cry. Look you, there is nothing wrong."

Chapter 37

Falling, helpless, out of control, he tumbled head over heels. He hit rock, again hit rock, then slid on snow.

Off a lip of snow, he slipped; he was falling through the air now. Winter night and stars flew past.

He hit with a hard thump.

Darkness.

From a half-dimension away, Puabi-Ekur watched him.

Their task was clear. They had to keep this one alive.

Gus drifted by degrees further and further away from his body. Around him, shadows twisted, dark like those in Max's stairwell, long crooked fingers plucking, sibilant voices whispering.

And there he went. The spirit exited the body. New to

the astral in this form, he bumped around, blind as a bat. The experience, Puabi-Ekur knew, was something like blundering into a dark closet full of black wool coats.

The shadows darted in. Lunging forward, Puabi-Ekur shot energy at them. A blue wash of flame cracked like lightning.

The djinn hadn't expected that. They disappeared, apporting to some other dimension.

This time, theirs wasn't a full-on assault, but instead a guerrilla war. Why waste your strength, if stepping in at a key point had the same effect?

On the astral, Gus was still fumbling. Puabi-Ekur appeared, fuzzily, as a shining human-shaped form shot with rays of light.

"What?! Who are you?" Gus cried. "Where am I?"

"You're temporarily dead, and you need not to be."

"I want to be dead. Everything back there is pain."

"Your boyfriend threw you off a cliff. Remember that—it will come in handy."

"If my boyfriend threw me off a cliff, why do I want to be alive?"

He really loved this Max, the djinni.

"There are other boyfriends. You have a girlfriend. Stay alive for her."

"But I wanted him too. I love him!"

The spirit balled itself up, on what it perceived as floor, and emoted pure sorrow. If Gus had been alive, he'd have cried.

"I understand that. He's still a bad boyfriend. Like you say, he tried to kill you."

"Is this heaven? Or the Summerland? Or Valhalla? Are helping spirits supposed to argue with you?"

"This is a bardo. And you need to go back."

"Why?"

"There are fates that depend on you that are better fates if you're there. Among them yours." Otherwise, Hekate wouldn't have pointed Puabi-Ekur to look after Gus.

"I want to sleep forever."

"That's not what death is. You'll be reborn. If I were you, I'd stick with your current life and try again." Gus made no answer, just projected sorrow. "You asked for protection and help. This is what it looks like."

"I don't want to go back. I'll probably never be able to walk again. At least."

"You'll be able to walk. Gus, you have a special fate. You're important." This was true for all souls, but also Hekate had indicated by her actions that Gus and Joanie and their community were special. Perhaps they had potential to create a tipping point. "And Alyssa truly loves you. That is a gem worth keeping."

"The current world is a shit-show. You can't blame me for wanting out of it."

"You signed up to help fix it, or you wouldn't be in it. Are you going back?"

"You never answered my other question. Who are you? Are you an angel?"

Yes and no, but not by Gus's definition. "I'm one of the spirits trying to help you." They gave a deep inward sigh. They hated to do this, but it seemed required. "My name is Puabi-Ekur, if you need to call me."

A long time ago, they thought, *I was your boyfriend Maelan.*

They'd been a better boyfriend than Max. Or Gus.

Gus heard a hollow booming. He realized it was his heart.

If he wanted to, he could stop it. He was that close.

But a gust of anger kicked up.

So cold, ice-cold, and so much pain.

Beyond everything, he wanted to sleep.

But his phone kept ringing. It wouldn't stop.

Ring. Ring, ring.

Experimentally, he shifted his arm. It hurt, but it moved.

He rolled slightly—it was excruciating, shooting pains all directions—and found his phone in his pocket, somehow uncrushed.

"Hello?"

"Hello? Gus? Is that you?" It was Alyssa.

"Yes."

"Are you okay? Your voice sounds funny."

"No, not really. I fell off a cliff."

He'd been pushed off a cliff.

Some odd superstition, as if Max could hear him, prevented him from saying it.

In the snow-light, black basalt boulders hunkered

among drifts of snow. He lay next to a snowbank, but on rock, dusted with powder snow.

"Are you with Max?"

"No."

"Is he looking for you?"

If he was, it was to finish him off. His feelings were numb; he couldn't make it mean anything.

"I don't know."

"Where are you?"

"I don't know."

"Okay, let's get the phone location. I can tell you how real quick... give me a second."

She read him instructions. Painfully, patiently, he did what she said.

"Can you see my phone now?" he asked.

"Yes! You're way the hell out in nowhere. Near Little Kachess Lake. Does that make sense?"

"Yes." Something nudged him to say, "Write down the phone location. I'm going to lose signal eventually."

"You're right. I'll do the best I can. I'm going to get someone out there to get you. Stay alive, Gus! You sound bad. I love you!"

"I will. I'll try. I love you too. Right now I'm going back to sleep."

Darkness. Black rock, white snow. The waning moon had left the canyon. A cold wind blew.

Puabi-Ekur nudged the boy into as warm and safe a

position as possible, encircling him with protection and healing.

They could only do so much, without help in the mundane world.

Hurry, Alyssa.

Chapter 38

Harvest in, threshing done, herd culled, three oxen sacrificed to the gods—before the roads got too bad, it came time for the feasts Lady Gunhild wanted, for Daegal to meet the local women of rank.

Before the first feast, he spoke to Lady Gunhild at supper.

"My lady, I wish you would not do this. Surely there is the chance of a raid?"

"Pish, there is not. You still mourn your Ethelreda! For all her casting you aside."

"No, my lady, I just—"

"If you are seeing some lesser woman, that is no matter! You are like a son to me. I will see you well-wed."

Behind her, back to the moss-green hanging, Louana stared into the distance. The fire inlaid gold in her bronze hair, but her face was dead, a replica in fired clay.

As a slave, she had no right to free time. Also he had

much work now, mustering the hearth-guard and the village force to be ready for early-winter raids. Yet Louana was on his mind.

At the edge of the main hall yard stood a small group of buildings, several of them storehouses for the priest's ritual goods, one holding beautiful plate, gilt and edged with runes, another one ox-skulls kept after sacrifice. One formed a small permanent chapel to Woden and Frige, though the most important ritual location was the gods' grove outside the village.

Up to late summer, Daegal had been on a nodding basis with the priest—he had never been pious. Now he was guard captain. Because of the beautiful plate, a guard was set at the central storehouse overnight, sleeping on a pallet by the door.

At the end of one supper, Daegal sat down beside the priest, who sat at the opposite corner of the high table.

"I was impressed, at the oxen sacrifice, at the beautiful things we have here for the gods." The priest, a little surprised, mumbled thanks. "I know we set a guard at the storehouse, but I understand you are still nervous. Would you feel better if I guarded the storehouse myself?"

"Oh, my lord, I could not ask that. That would not be comfortable or fitting for you."

"Think of it as an offering to the gods."

By the end of supper, the priest was persuaded.

If Daegal wasn't on active guard duty for hall or village, that early winter he slept inside the storehouse.

A slave could get up and relieve herself outside, if she so desired, even if there was a chamber pot. Louana had a small lantern with wire-work sides. He taught her a whistle like the cry of a plover.

The first night, he waited in the storeroom doorway, the last of a goblet of mead beside him. Not long after supper's end and Lady Gunhild's bedtime, the wire-work lantern shone out. Recognizing it, he whistled; a call answered. A few moments later, she was there.

In the chilly room, the lantern flame flared. On the floor lay the straw pallet, covered in wool blankets and a sheep-skin throw.

"Get in!" Dropping her clothes, she slid in. "My gods, the feel of you."

"Quick! Ah, your hands are so cold!"

"So are yours!"

A pause, a hush at the moment he entered her warm body, sensation pouring over him. She gasped and moving below him moaned. He covered her mouth with his hand.

"Hush, you cannot cry out."

"I do not do it by design."

Afterward, wrapped in his arms, she was silent. Passing his hand over her face, he felt her tears.

"What is it, love?"

"It is nothing. I am simply bound to lose you."

"It is not so."

"The lady will marry you off, and it will be as if we never met."

"That need not be. I will think of a plan."

"If you say so." She sat up, began searching among the clothes on the floor. Shaking out her shift, she stood up and pulled that and her kirtle on. "I must go."

He grabbed her, kissed her, then let her leave. The door shut behind her. He stared at it in the darkness.

He should never have started this.

But a wife wasn't what he'd wanted. He'd wanted her, hot and sweet, and a connection that seemed simple.

To call Lady Gunhild off, he consulted the younger of her and Lord Wihtred's sons—the older held himself aloof—taking his horse from the stable and traveling half a day to Lord Osric's holding, to a cold welcome. He was feasted, but Osric's wife would not sit at the table with him.

Much the size of Lord Wihtred's, Osric's hall had newer hangings, in crisp blues, by his lady and her women. Osric, seeing him gaze at these, cleared his throat.

"My wife thinks I should not talk to you, that you will take whatever portion my father has left when he dies."

"I serve your father as a guardsman and war-companion, Lord Osric, but in due time I shall return to my own land. Indeed, it is in your own interest to help me with your mother."

"I wish there were help. She were ever stubborn. I can tell you, if you like, how to offend each woman she presents. But—with respect—why not wed one of these women? Several come with land in their own right, did you choose to stay, or you could take your wife east."

"I have no stomach for it."

"You have a woman, then. Or, mayhap, a man?"

"Not a man."

"Someone you love well who will make your life hell if you marry. You need not answer. I see it."

"My lady also understood that might be. It has not stopped her."

"Lord Daegal, there is no stopping my mother. Mayhap if you are willing to threaten, like my brother. This does not seem to be your approach. I say stall and give offense."

In the morning, Daegal rode away, still with no clear plan.

Lady Gunhild couldn't marry him off against his will. Even a woman had a right not to wed against her wish.

Setting the matter aside, he focused on planning the defense of hall and village, and on training.

Eadwine, with Daegal's tutelage, had become a strong second-in-command. Daegal made him leader of the fyrd, the village war-band. With the master of arms' advice, and that of the lord, Daegal oversaw the general strategy.

They met in the great hall, staying after midday meal—Lord Wihtred, Daegal, Eadwine, the master of arms, and two other men from the hearth-guard. Commandeering a table, they took bits of wood from the central firepit and ivory game pieces from a set of the lord's. Eadwine made a rough map of hall and village using sticks and coal.

The lord stared at it, stroking his long mustaches.

"The Britons will have heard of you now, Lord Daegal," he said. "They will want to test you."

"Tell me again how they usually approach," Daegal said.

"Through the village," the master of arms said, laying out a line of game pieces to indicate the Britons. "Our hope is that they will not burn the houses."

"It will not be a large group," Eadwine said. "Also, as

much as anything they want to steal cattle, which is why we keep our herd in the enclosure by the hall."

"We can take the villagers' cattle there as well," Daegal said.

"The Britons may steal anything else of worth in the village," Eadwine said. "But it is a cattle raid mostly. Unless they think we are weak. I suspect news of you and your constant training will provoke the other response."

"What is that?"

"Some kind of test, as the lord says. Nothing like a full battle—they have not the men. But they want to see who you are."

Around the village, they bunched the village fyrd, strengthened by a number of the hearth-guard. "The men will have the motive to preserve their homes," Eadwine said. The remaining hearth-guard would keep the hall stronghold.

Over the next days, the villagers brought their cattle to the hall's enclosure, keeping the goats and chickens, needful for day to day, and which raiders were less likely to go away with.

At supper, Daegal broached the subject once more. "Perhaps now is not the time to invite women of rank, my lady. Your lord tells me we are in danger of attack."

"He is right, Gunhild, my love."

"Very well," the lady said petulantly. "In springtime then."

Louana stood behind her lady, her green dress vanishing into the moss-green hanging behind her. She gave Daegal half a smile.

At dawn on a winter morning, frost glazed the hillside below the hall. Red as cherry iron at a forge, a rim of first sunlight lined the horizon.

In the silence came the croak of a raven—Woden's wisdom, or the Briton war-goddess's threat.

They would come today.

In the cold stillness, a rumble rose from the valley.

This was it.

A single war-horn blew, the Britons'. His men's war-cry followed.

The war-plan placed Daegal with the hall defenders, but he knew how it would be. The village fyrd would be lined up athwart the road a half-mile from the village. The line of a double-handful of men would be reinforced as soon as word went out. The whole force was only several dozen men, but the Britons would not bring more.

The Britons might start with a volley of arrows. The Angles' leather-covered wooden shields would hold these off if all went well. Then both sides might throw javelins. The Britons' were lighter and more numerous. Then maybe the lines would advance and clash with short thrusting spears.

But the rumble didn't sound like that, and next came the pound of running feet.

Up the long path from the village, a young boy ran, perhaps twelve, in a ripped tunic and no cloak, his breath a fog behind him.

Daegal strode forward from where he stood before the hall.

"Lord Daegal!"

"Yes, my lad?"

"You are challenged to single combat by the Britons' champion, Maelan son of Ronec!"

Chapter 39

The whizzing thud-thud-thud-thud of helicopter blades woke Gus. Above him, the sky showed a brilliant sun.

A couple men in navy coveralls with red rope strapped to them dropped to the ground near him, with a crunch, into the snow. "Here he is."

One of the men approached. "He's awake! Hi, I'm Tyler. I'm an EMT. You must be Gus."

"I am."

"You're a pretty lucky guy! Let me check you out, see how you're doing here." The EMT shone a light into his eyes, moved his limbs gently. "That hurt?"

"Ow!"

"But you can feel it! That's good."

After a bit, one of them gestured at the sky, and a bag was lowered, then a couple other pieces of equipment, including a stretcher. They got him in the stretcher, strapped him in, and he rose through the blue-white air to the helicopter. As they lifted the stretcher inside, everything went black again.

Alyssa leaned over the bar of his hospital bed, staring at him.

"You shithead. They say it's a miracle you're alive, let alone as undamaged as you are."

They'd flown him to the hospital and checked him quickly, but it was evening before he was out of the attendants' hands. Now it was the following morning.

He'd come away with a couple of broken neck vertebrae, a concussion, a broken shoulder blade, and a couple huge gashes to his head—and that was it. His spine hadn't been severed; his skull wasn't cracked. He'd have to wear a neck brace and a sling for a while and be careful about the concussion. But he should heal fine after about a year of physical therapy, if he didn't do something stupid.

He also hadn't frozen to death. Two of his toes were frostbitten, and the nails had come off. A layer of skin had come off his face, wind-burned. But that was all the weather had done.

Alyssa and his parka had saved him, the doctor told him.

(And Puabi-Ekur. For some reason he remembered the name of the spirit who had stopped by—there had been something oddly familiar about them. Something to look at later.)

They planned to discharge him tomorrow, after making sure he was sewn up, hydrated, fed, and had no other negative repercussions from his head injuries.

Alyssa shifted to perch on the edge of the bed. "So tell me what happened!"

It was the first chance they'd had to talk alone.

"First, you tell me—why were you calling me, anyway? You had a feeling, didn't you?"

"Yeah," She bit her pink-polished thumbnail. "That night, it was like something was poking me with needles. So what happened?"

"Max pushed me off the cliff."

They stared at each other.

"I thought it might be something like that."

"He thought I'd told Pete about the hunt with Rob. But I didn't." He broke off, staring across the room. Someone had brought him a poinsettia, bright scarlet. "Max must have assumed I'd die. Or left it to the gods, maybe."

"I don't think he did anything afterward. That says something, too."

"He could concoct some kind of story. But, yeah. I went to the lawyer right before Thanksgiving. She said the options were either an anonymous tip, or a statement that she'd work on with me. People need to be protected from him."

"Speaking of which, do you feel safe here? I'm paranoid he's going to come in and, I don't know, smother you with a pillow."

"There's that."

"I'm going to stay here with you. My finals aren't till next week. I can study here. I want you to stay alive."

"Okay." He patted her hand—about as far as he could go with physical affection without pain. She leaned and hugged him, avoiding his bad arm. Not long after, he managed to sleep.

The next morning, a nurse took his blood first thing—waking him to do it—and an hour or so later his doctor came to see him.

"We're going to need to keep you here another day, I'm afraid. You've got a raised white blood cell count, enough that we think you have an infection. It's best if we give you IV antibiotics till that clears out. Then you can be on your way."

Great. He'd called and calmed his mother's fears—no, she didn't have to come visit him, he was not at death's door. Now he felt as if he'd lied to her, though he'd had no way of knowing.

He sent Alyssa home. "Get a change of clothes at least. I promise not to get killed in the interim."

"I'm coming back tonight. Maybe it's weird, but I still feel like you're potentially in danger. I want to protect you. Is that wrong?"

A shiver went up his back.

"No. I appreciate it."

"I'll be back by seven."

She'd already brought him a couple of books and his

laptop, and he had television, but hooked to an IV he was still trapped in bed. After a while, he set aside his paperback and closed his eyes.

Then, with the sound of footsteps, a shadow crossed the half-open doorway. He wondered if the hospital was giving him a roommate—the room was set for two people, but the earlier patient had left.

"Here he is," said a nurse's voice.

Chapter 40

etal pounded on metal, sword on sword, thrust and counter-thrust. They danced around each other, clashing.

In a cleared field outside the village, between the two small armies, a space had been created, circled with a rope barrier.

High above, against an overcast, a hawk reeled. The cold air smelled of snow. They fought on dirt, still with a few clumps of grass, not quite dry but not muddy. Men in boiled leather armor or mail stood to either side of the roped space, watching closely.

The first day had been throwing spears. Maelan had a long slash on his leg, which periodically opened and bled. Daegal had a deep gouge on his shoulder that had begun to hamper his strength and reach. The blood rose and stained the fabric of his linen shirt.

He hefted his weapon. Sword clanged on sword; sword thudded on leather-covered wood.

At last, the red sun puddled on the horizon. A second short winter day ended. Lord Wihtred sent the boy who served as herald forward.

"We will stop the fight for today!"

Daegal let his sword drop, as did Maelan. They stood a few yards away from each other, across the scuffed dirt, watching each other.

The red-gold hair that strayed from the helmet had darkened; the muscles of arm and leg were more clearly defined. But he had the same height and broad shoulders, the same feints, the same speed.

He stepped forward, and Daegal came to meet him. They embraced.

In an undertone, Maelan said in his ear, "I did not know it was you. I knew they had a new fighter here. I wanted to fight their new champion."

"It was my lord's decision, and I had to agree. It is not how I would meet you again."

"Nor I."

Taking his face between his hands, Maelan kissed him deeply.

The scent of him, like spices from the East, mixed with sweat and blood.

His blood, Maelan's blood.

Daegal had a prayer to make, but he did not know who to ask. Woden? Frige?

He sent it anyway: *Let him not die by my hand, nor me by his.*

Puabi-Ekur returned to the field of single combat.

They couldn't go back in time and mend this.

For all they were a spirit, and could travel anywhere, they could only act in current linear time, Gus's time. Even there, their actions were limited. Easiest was suggestion, manipulation of emotion, perhaps a gust of wind.

This battle they could not change.

Full night had fallen after the second day of combat. Torch-light from outside lit the canvas tent, striped blue and red. Inside hung a candle lantern.

In this light, the healer from the village inspected Daegal's wounded shoulder as he sat on a camp chair. The healer cleaned the wound with water—"my gods that hurts!"—and put on a poultice of yarrow. As he completed his work, someone opened the tent flap and stepped out of the shadows: Louana.

"My lord, Lady Gunhild has asked that I attend you, since I am said to be a good nurse."

"There is not much to do, I think. Healer, what say you?"

"Keep the poultice on, and sleep, my lord. Let me know if the wound is disturbed, or the flesh around it becomes inflamed." With a nod in farewell, the healer pushed the tent flap open and went out, letting it fall closed behind him.

Louana stepped close enough he could hear her breathe, her blue eyes wide.

"You are so strong, my lord. It has been amazing watching you. They gave the lady a high seat, and I have been with her." More quietly, she added, "I saw you kiss the Brittonic champion."

Daegal inclined his head. "He was my foster-brother."

"Is it bad to fight him? It is, I see that! I am sorry!"

"It is the fate of men to do these things." He sighed. "I hope sunset tomorrow sees us both alive."

For single combat, Lord Wihtred's clan-group had the custom that if both warriors lasted three days, the fight would finish, even if no one was killed. The winner was whoever inflicted the most damage. The custom helped preserve fighters' lives, since hearth-guard warriors were few.

"I wish it for you."

The sun rose red on the third day of the fight and cast itself redly through the stripes on the tent canvas.

A ray crossed Daegal's eyelids. He blinked awake. His body felt beaten, every bit of it in pain, his shoulder worst of all.

He could use some mead to dull it. But not so much as to dull his edge. If that was possible.

He stood from his pallet, groaning, threw on his long undershirt, and poked his head out of the tent door.

Immediately a young boy who'd been watching the door ran up. "Lord Daegal! May I be of assistance?"

"Bring me some mead!"

Maybe that was foolish, but he needed something.

He looked around the tent, empty except for himself.

The mead appeared, with the young boy, the local healer, and Lord Wihtred. By then he'd thrown on his battle tunic and shoes and, sitting in the camp chair, was lacing up his legs with winingas, puttees that the Angles wore, which could help stop a blow.

The young boy danced forward, almost spilling the full goblet he carried. Daegal took it and drained half.

"Now, Lord Daegal, that cup had better be all," said Lord Wihtred. "You still have a full day of combat ahead of you."

"Yes, Lord Wihtred."

"Let me see your shoulder," said the healer. Daegal pulled his tunic over his head. The healer took off the bandages holding the poultice and peered at him. "It is healing well! I will clean and rebandage it." Daegal gritted his teeth and let him.

"Here is a loaf of bread too, Lord Daegal!" The boy handed it forward, and Daegal tore off a hunk. "And some roast pork!" Another chunk of bread served as a trencher; Daegal balanced it on his knee.

"Get some food in you," said Lord Wihtred. "The priest is sending you all his blessings."

The order of battle had been decided at the start. Throwing spears and darts had come first. Daegal was willing to let Maelan have swords the second day—he was surprised he'd survived it—to have fighting spears at the end. A spear was an Angle warrior's main weapon.

Part of his mind twisted, a rat in a trap.

There had to be some way to go at this—to fight almost his best, but not quite. To save both their lives.

He couldn't see how, and not to be killed by Maelan, who might not have gotten the message.

Finally he let it go. *Let the fight be with the gods.*

The horns blew; it was time.

He climbed back into the fighting space, between the hazel stakes at the four corners. The new sun cast his shadow on the dirt, which had seen both their blood already.

Across the combat space, Maelan's face was beautiful, unreadable, a cut on his cheek.

They began again, circling each other, watching for weakness.

Metal struck metal, then wood struck wood. A blow thudded, deflected by the flat of the shield. The next blow clanged, deflected by the boss of the shield. He punched his small shield forward, the spiked boss narrowly missing Maelan's ribs.

Both of them were tired, slower than the first two days.

They crouched behind their shields, always testing, thrusting with their spears.

"Daegal. You, with the sandy hair."

"Maelan."

"I see you still wear my deer-skull."

"I do."

"My feelings for you have not changed."

"Neither have mine."

Then Maelan thrust, almost outreaching his guard, except he turned at the last minute.

Then they didn't talk.

The horns blew again, cutting the fight in half.

The red haze cleared from his eyes, and he staggered out.

Midday. The sun stood at zenith, cold, small, pitiless, and far away.

In the tent, Louana was there—he didn't think to wonder at it—holding mead to his lips. He grabbed the goblet from her, tipped it back.

He'd been struck badly, a deep gouge across his thigh, bleeding. The spear had twisted in the wound.

He was lucky Maelan hadn't cut it through.

The healer came forward. "I can burn it." He meant cauterize the wound.

"Sir, the bleeding is stopping," the girl said. "May I just clean it?"

"I believe you are right, girl. Do."

Maelan was doing nearly as badly. His own leg wound had begun to bleed again, and a spear-butt to his face had broken his nose. But Daegal hadn't shoved the butt through his nose to his brain to kill him. He'd pulled the strike slightly, and Maelan had ducked away.

The healer and Louana between them tugged Daegal's

trousers off. A boy was sent for new ones, the leg of these nearly sliced off.

"Ow!" he shouted, allowing himself release as the girl dabbed at the deep leg gash with water. "Out, everyone! Everyone but the girl."

The remaining boy—he had such followers now—slunk out, the healer after him.

"Hand me the mead."

She looked sidelong, as if she disagreed, but handed it to him, with a trencher of roast pork and some bread.

He drank and ate what was there as she cleaned and bandaged the wound. The boy hovered at the door with his trousers, and Daegal called him in and sent him away.

"Is he gone?"

"Yes."

He tossed down the rest of the mead. Then, grabbing Louana by the hair, he pulled her to him and kissed her.

"For luck," he said, looking in the blue eyes, like bits of sky.

"For luck."

Their luck turned. It began to rain.

It had been overcast since midmorning, and now the sky released. The ground turned to mud.

The first time Daegal slid in it, he bellowed and righted himself. Someone laughed—Maelan?

Turning ponderously, he charged. Maelan backed sideways, to let him work off his rage by sliding to a stop.

But Maelan slipped and fell, flat on his back.

Daegal, spear pointed forward for the charge, tripped just before Maelan, in the same puddle, and fell too.

His spear went through Maelan's chest.

Daegal slid off, horrified.

Maelan's eyes went wide and fixed.

He was dead.

Daegal stood up, dripping with mud.

Maybe he was wrong. Maybe it wasn't so.

He slapped the cheeks of his opponent, leaving great muddy prints. "Healer! Help! Carry him off the field!"

The Briton line roiled as they saw what had happened. The healer rushed forward. Two Britons stepped forward as well.

"No desecration of the body!" They spoke the Angle tongue.

Daegal saw no one among the Britons knew him.

"There will be no desecration! He is my foster-brother!" He repeated it in Brittonic for good measure.

The healer knelt in the mud and checked the body.

"My lord, he is dead."

"No!"

He fell on Maelan's body, sobbing. "No, no, no, no!"

So quickly it had happened. Maelan was there, and then gone.

It felt like being ripped in two.

He wanted to set time back, but that was impossible.

The rain fell, a grey curtain.

The Britons, muttering among themselves, left him alone. After a while, Lord Wihtred stumped over to him.

"My dear boy, we see that you loved your foster-brother. But your cries will not bring him back. Let us give him to his people, so he can have a proper burial."

Maelan would want that. His father would want that. He owed it to both of them.

He stood, shakily. Lord Wihtred steadied him, looking around. Eadwine took his other side.

"You need rest and care and food," Eadwine said gently. "We all have had comrades die."

"I killed him! I did not want to kill him."

"I know. Come with me now."

"I want to see the scop! I want him commemorated in song!"

"Tomorrow. Now you must eat and sleep and have your wounds cared for."

They led him off the field.

Behind, in the puddles of mud and rain, his blood mingled with Maelan's, also his tears. The Britons carried the body away.

Chapter 41

Something about this last passage had made an opening. Now Puabi-Ekur could see the full fight between Daegal and Maelan, including Maelan's death.

They still held old anger for that.

But as a spirit, looking at it now, they saw different angles. Slips in muddy puddles, how Daegal had tried to pull his hits, how it was an accident. How Daegal cried over his body, inconsolable.

How Daegal mourned him the rest of his life.

Daegal stayed in bed nearly a month, because the healer made him. It rained the whole time.

They put him in a small cottage at the edge of the village, and Louana was there to tend him, which he didn't question.

His wound went bad, and for a while he had a fever.

During the fever, he kept seeing Maelan—Maelan as a spirit, angry with him.

"We finally found each other again," the spirit said. "And then you killed me."

"But I did not kill you. I swear," Daegal said. "You slipped. It was mud. It was ill-wishing, maybe."

He woke up at one point at night. He lay in a box bed built into the wall, Louana across the room on a pallet. A small fire burned, only a few low flames over coals banked in the central hearth. She must have just lain down.

He sat up on his elbows—to sit up fully was too painful for his leg. Something in him wanted to hurt someone. He didn't have the self-control he usually did.

"You ill-wished him, you witch. You knew I loved him, and you wanted him dead. You said, for luck, and the rain came, and it killed him."

She sat up from her pallet, hair frowsy, face drawn. She'd been working hard, tending him. "I did not understand. But I did not ill-wish him."

"You did. May the gods curse you."

Exhausted, he fell back on the bed and slept.

Puabi-Ekur saw it.

She also was tied into this nexus, orbiting it. Once again, she was trying to save him.

Alyssa.

Chapter 42

"Here he is," said a nurse's voice.

Max walked into Gus's hospital room as if materialized out of his fears.

His presence overfilled the room, vibrant against the pastel green walls, all muscles and shaved head, tattoos edging up from his collar. He wore a blue work shirt under a leather motorcycle jacket.

Desire flickered, but most of Gus's body froze in terror.

He should never have let Alyssa go. He looked around the room.

He was on an IV, but he could pull it out if he had to. Better rip up his arm than die.

"Hello, Gus."

Max stepped around the bed to sit in the guest chair, on the far side from the door. Closer to Gus, but it made Gus feel less cornered.

Gus let out a long, slow breath. Calm was important.

"How did you know I was here?"

"There was a news story about your rescue." Max gazed at him with surprising warmth. What was going on? "I'm here because I owe you an apology."

Gus's mouth dropped open in stupefaction. After a moment, he shut it.

"There are some pieces you don't know," Max said. "Jonathan met and talked to Bruni and me. He said you told Pete that Odin's Hunt killed Rob."

"Who's Jonathan?"

"One of the Antifa."

"I don't know this Jonathan, but he's talking out his ass. Ask Pete! I've got his phone number in my backpack."

Behind Max, out the window, one pale cloud floated on the indigo sky of early evening.

"I figured that out. I'm sorry I let my anger run away with me. I don't abjure violence, but I want to be just."

"The apology doesn't make it okay." It was more of a nonapology, anyway.

"I also wanted to give you this." Drawing up Gus's rolling table, he took a check out of his pocket, put it on the table, and pushed the table toward Gus. The check was for five thousand dollars.

Max threw around a lot of money for a tattooist and cross-trainer.

"That also doesn't make it okay. I don't want your blood money."

"Take it. You have student insurance, right? You'll end up owing money."

Max hunched forward on the narrow plastic hospital chair. He was too big for it.

"If I were you, I'd be tempted to press charges, and I'll tell you it won't work. I have an excellent lawyer, and it's your word against mine."

Gus tried to sit up and winced in pain. He lay back down, gritting his teeth.

"Fuck you, Max. I don't care how good your lawyer is. I'll take my chances."

"If you think you can go up against the Hunt, you're wrong. We have friends; we can set up a fundraising site. If you think you or your family can match that, think again. Money is what buys justice in this country. Besides, I'm going to be leaving."

Despite everything, a pang of sorrow crossed Gus's chest.

"Where to?"

Hearing the sorrow in Gus's voice, Max gave a crooked smile. "I have friends all over the world. It's time for me to do some traveling."

He stood up, gauging Gus's face.

"I'll miss you. I had a great time with you, the best I've had in a while." Pushing aside the table, he leaned over and kissed Gus, deeply, hand moving to Gus's crotch, cupping it a moment.

Despite himself, Gus gave in, closing his eyes.

Gods, if only—but no. He was still Max.

Standing, a smile playing on his lips, Max walked past the hospital bed and out the door.

Chapter 43

The fever passed. The wound closed with a scar that crimped Daegal's leg muscles. For the rest of his life, he walked with a slight limp.

It took a longer time than his wound's healing to mend things with Louana, after he'd cursed her.

Early in his convalescence, before he'd gotten out of bed, Lord Wihtred came to his cottage, on a rainy, muddy day before the snow began. Daegal was bored; he'd tried whittling, but it didn't come to much.

The lord leaned his head through the door.

"Is the girl here? No?"

"I think she stepped out, Lord Wihtred."

Wihtred came in and settled himself on a bench.

"She is yours now, Lord Daegal. She is a significant prize. I had not planned at this point to give you a slave. I was thinking land. But by honor I must give you something —you held off the Britons."

Daegal wouldn't call it holding them off. After losing their champion, the Britons had retreated back to their own lands.

A little pressing uncovered a further story. Lady Gunhild had discovered that Louana had become Daegal's concubine, and the lady wanted nothing more to do with her. The lady was convinced that Louana had wrecked her plans to get Daegal married.

"My lady expects an apology from you as well."

"Anything to keep the peace, Lord Wihtred."

"You understand."

Wihtred made a permanent gift of the cottage, so Daegal could spend some nights at his own hearth. He spent most at the hall. There, he sat by Lord Wihtred, not by Lady Gunhild. The lady considered him a friend no longer.

At home, Louana was the perfect servant. But she wouldn't meet his eyes, and she didn't come to his bed.

He apologized several times, over the long winter nights.

"Louana, you have to understand. I was angry and sad, and I took it out on you. I'm sorry."

"I know, my lord."

She heard him out with bowed head, and afterward returned to her pallet.

Over the winter, he had time to consider what to do next.

He could stay Wihtred's champion. Wihtred was impressed with him now. He could go home, too.

He also had time to consider what he'd lost.

"We finally found each other again. And then you killed me."

Some days, it seemed like the best thing to walk off a

cliff somewhere, go back to the gods. Or in the next heavy fighting, perform some exploit and die for his lord.

Some nights, as Louana slept across the fire from him, he still felt Maelan's ghost.

Puabi-Ekur could go back in time, though they could not make change there.

Some nights, they sat beside Louana and stared balefully at Daegal.

It was an old anger, and perhaps it didn't serve them. Perhaps they should let go of it.

Fate tugged them forward.

They needed to resist a while longer.

Chapter 44

On a winter morning, sky pink and icy, Gus crossed town on the bus for another eight a.m. appointment. Hashing out the police statement took several hours. He used most of the thousand-dollar retainer, which he put on his emergency credit card.

"I would expect threats once the police investigation starts," the lawyer told him. "Though if it's true Max Dwyer has left the country, you might be out of immediate danger."

"I doubt that."

"I'd go home for Christmas this year, if I were you. Consider taking a semester off."

Afterward, he felt emptied. But now the police could investigate.

He'd made a choice, the obvious, moral, right one. It made life easier. Part of him wondered why he'd waited so long.

Part of him missed Max like fire.

He knew this wasn't the end of it. There was no statute of limitations on a murder, and this thing was more complicated than one murder.

Next step was calling his mother. Getting a lawyer didn't exactly count as an emergency.

The coffee shop's espresso machine was decorated with a Happy Holidays banner; that and some white fairy lights were their nod to the season, besides eggnog lattes. Both Joanie and Alyssa had to work finals week, but today was mercifully slow, so they both got in some studying. The sunny day had a frozen stillness to the air, a low angle to the light.

Joanie let Alyssa take a long break, sharing her table a few minutes. Sunlight gleamed on the wood of their booth, striking shimmers from the purple-glass stone in Alyssa's necklace. Joanie warmed her fingers on her cup.

They hadn't had a shift together for a while. Alyssa filled her in.

"Max just took off?" Joanie said.

"Yeah. I suppose they can extradite him?"

"There's a ways to go before that. Why did Gus take so long to come forward? Homicide is the kind of thing cops are good at."

"I think he was afraid. And he loved Max." A movement from Alyssa sent a cascade of reflections across the table. "Please don't judge him harshly. He wanted to see if he could get Max to turn himself in. But that didn't work." She bit her lip and studied Joanie a moment. "Gus and I are thinking of getting engaged."

"That's dumb," Joanie said, before she could stop herself. "I mean, congratulations."

Alyssa cast her a blue-eyed look of death. "I heard you the first time. Why do you think it's a bad idea?"

Joanie had a million reasons. Legalized marriage itself was just a yoke for both people. It cost the couple more in taxes. It provided a certain security for children, but not more than they had anyway. And why would you have children in the world today? And this was Gus, the only-barely-former white nationalist, they were talking about.

"I guess it's an optimistic gesture. But I don't see how Gus could entertain the white supremacy thing even for a minute. These are the people who want my girlfriend to go back to Africa."

Alyssa tapped her fingernails on the heavily lacquered wood of the table.

"That was never the part he was interested in. He told you that himself. He's going to the law now. Please give him another chance."

"I didn't know you cared so much what I felt." Joanie blew on her cappuccino, making a hole in the foam, and sipped. "What do you see in him, anyway?"

Alyssa scratched her bottom lip.

"He's okay with the former-whore thing. You know not everyone is. He's understanding about my childhood abuse. He treats me well. He listens to me. He's kind to me." A curl of bright-blonde hair fell from behind her ear, and she pushed it back. "It took him a while to understand what

Odin's Hunt stood for. But now he has, and he's doing something about it. Please give him a break."

"I'll try."

"He still carries that Hekate stone from Samhain in his pocket. He feels like she helped him when he was on the mountain. I feel like he could be one of us, if we give him time."

The coffee shop door opened. Alyssa, looking over Joanie's shoulder, turned pink. "Oops. Here he is now."

"You invoked him," Joanie said. She stood and turned on her heel. "Hi, Gus! Alyssa was telling me about your ordeal."

He looked beaten up, with a bandaged head. He wore a neck brace and a sling, and walked carefully, toes healing.

"You could call it that."

"Can I give you a coffee on the house?"

She wanted to be kind. It was important to let people change. She'd made mistakes about people herself, like about her sugar daddy. Gus had loved his boyfriend.

"Sure." Gus slid in to take her place in the booth.

He probably thought Alyssa was off work. Well, she'd let him. She went to work on a triple Americano.

Alyssa leaped up. "Oh, Joanie, you should let me! My break is way over."

"No worries, I can do it."

"That's sweet of her," Gus said, watching her work.

"I asked her to give you another chance. Maybe she's doing that."

"Maybe." He turned around and took Alyssa's hands in his own.

"Your hands are cold!" Alyssa pulled them forward and blew on them to warm them.

"You remember Julia? When I took myself off the Odin's Hunt mailing list, I emailed her. She emailed back just now. She told me Josh got charged with assault and got a suspended sentence."

He kissed her fingertips.

"I was thinking about calling Pete. I want to know what the fuck Jonathan thought he was doing, making shit up about me. I like Pete, too."

"Are you going to become Antifa now?"

"I like that they protect people at marches. But the lawyer said I need to lie low." He stroked her knee under the table. "I'd be more interested in attending stuff with the coven, if that's a possibility."

Joanie appeared with the coffee and set it by Gus's sling.

"Happy holidays," she said, and smiled at him. "We have winter solstice in a week, if you want to come."

Gus had stepped up, even if it had taken a while. Joanie needed to give him a second chance.

You could consider it too, Puabi-Ekur. I hear you muttering up there.

It was time to close out the cash register for the shift.

From the counter, she peered out the window. The day had gone overcast, a streak of lemon-colored light at the horizon.

A week till solstice, the return of the sun. They'd muddle forward toward the light somehow.

There were precious few of them, witches and pagans and polytheists.

She needed to be kind to those she could.

Chapter 45

One winter evening, Lord Wihtred sent Daegal home with mead in a pottery jar, and when he got there he found Louana still awake. She was leaning elbows on knees staring at the hearth-fire, sitting on one of the inset benches. Hearing him open the door, she jumped up.

"Sit, please. Share some mead with me?"

"If you like, my lord." She didn't sit but went to a wicker box to get goblets. When she brought them back, he poured them both full.

"'Tis too much for me, my lord."

"I will drink what you do not. Please, sit."

He asked what she'd done that day. She'd spent the day weaving. She answered in the shortest possible sentences.

He sat back, sipping his mead.

A long time ago, she'd chosen him. Why not now?

Some people were so scarred, it was like trying to tame a

doe. You could work half a year, but one false step and the project was ruined.

So he would start over again.

As he thought it, she came over to the bench where he sat.

"At least I can sit by you, my lord. May I?"

"Of course."

She sat, gently kissing him on the cheek.

From the shadows, Maelan's ghost watched them—Puabi-Ekur.

If she could forgive him, if Joanie could forgive him, why couldn't Puabi-Ekur?

Their cord was still around Daegal's neck, with the deer-skull bead.

That love would never return, but perhaps they could make something new.

Puabi-Ekur stepped backward, further into the ether. They drew out the deer-skull bead that Hekate had given them, gazing at it, feeling the resonances. These rippled outward, past Gus and Joanie, to the entire loose-knit community around them.

In this web of karma, each thread was important, and so was the tapestry itself.

It was just like a goddess to try roping them not only into love for certain people, but also into love for community.

Good luck with that, Hekate!

Laughter echoed in the ether, but it wasn't Puabi-Ekur's.

As they watched, the deer-skull bead evaporated into mist.

Afterword

I'd hate for the reader to go away with the impression that all heathenry is aligned with white supremacy. Many heathen organizations actively stand against white-power politics.

One of these launched in September 2018, Forn Sidr of America. In their own words: "Our goal is to cultivate a Heathen identity that celebrates all forms of living Norse Paganism." Their intent is to represent and empower minorities through cultivating awareness and action and to create safe, supportive, and socially proactive heathen spaces. For more information, you can find Forn Sidr at https://fornsidramerica.org/.

Many other heathen groups also embrace a universalist, anti-racist faith.

–M.T.

Also by Mary Trepanier

Thank you for reading The Deer Stalker, second in the Tales of the End Times series. We hope you enjoyed it enough to consider leaving a review.

Did you read the first book in the series? If not, you can buy it by clicking: *Queen of Heaven's Daughter*

Mary Trepanier has also edited four collections of short vampire erotica stories. She has a tale in each volume that you won't want to miss!

Blood in the Rain: Seventeen Stories of Vampire Erotica

Blood in the Rain 2: Nineteen Stories of Vampire Erotica

Blood in the Rain 3: Nineteen Stories of Vampire Erotica

Blood in the Rain 4: Eighteen Stories of Vampire Erotica

Gillian Bainbridge and Damien Grey narrate the first collection —it can be found on Audible and iTunes.

Look for future releases by signing up for our newsletter at Cwtch Press.

About the Author

Mary Trepanier writes fantasy, horror, and erotica. You can find her short stories in the *Blood in the Rain* anthologies of vampire erotica, among others. For more of *Tales of the End Times*, check out *Queen of Heaven's Daughter*

Join my mailing list by clicking THIS LINK and be the first to learn about the second volume in the *Tales of the End Times* series.

Tumblr : https://marytrepanier.tumblr.com/

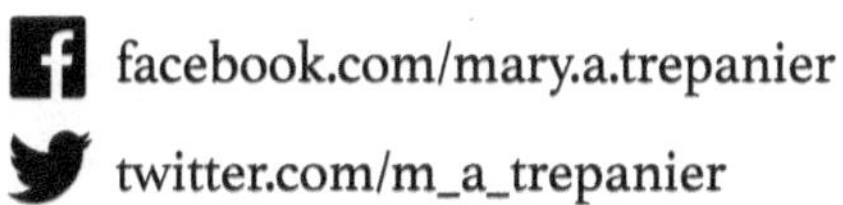

facebook.com/mary.a.trepanier

twitter.com/m_a_trepanier